The *Ganzfield* Series

Minder
Adversary (August 2010)
Legacy (2011)

MINDER

A GANZFIELD NOVEL BY

KATE

KAYNAK

To Elise,

Kate Kaynak

SPENCER HILL PRESS

Spencer Hill Press

Contact: Spencer Hill Press, PO Box 247, Contoocook, NH 03229

Please visit our website at spencerhillpress.com

First Edition June 2010

Kaynak, Kate, 1971—
Minder : a novel / by Kate Kaynak – 1st ed.
p. cm.

Summary:
Sixteen-year-old Maddie Dunn discovers her amazing abilities when she survives an attack that leaves several people dead. At a special training facility, she develops her new powers and meets the man of her dreams. But Ganzfield is a place where every social interaction carries the threat of mind control and a stray thought can burn a building to the ground. Maddie needs to figure out how to protect the people she cares about or she might lose them forever.

Cover design by K. Kaynak

ISBN 978-0-9845311-0-3 (paperback)
ISBN 978-0-9845311-1-0 (e-book)

Printed in the United States of America

To My Turkish Souvenir and Our Irish Triplets

CHAPTER 1

I felt the eyes on the back of my head, like a too-warm itch within my skull. Someone was watching me.

Hunting me.

Cold dread splashed through my chest and my pace quickened. I'd gotten flashes like this before—I knew to trust them. I needed to find other people. More than a block away, cars whooshed along the main road.

Hurry.

I pulled my bag in close and started to run, cutting across the suburban lawns in the fading late-afternoon light. Perhaps I could flag someone down or even step out into traffic and cause a scene.

I didn't make it.

I glanced back at the rumble of the approaching engine and a white van thunked over the curb behind me, screeching to a stop halfway on the sidewalk. The side door rolled back with a metallic scrape. Quick footsteps slapped the sidewalk and thudded in the grass behind me. Rough hands grabbed my arm and closed over my mouth, stifling my scream.

The driver pulled out so fast the tires squealed. Someone tried several times to close the side door of the lurching vehicle before the latch finally caught. The large hand of my attacker remained clamped over my mouth and my breath ripped through my nose.

Oh my God... oh my God... oh my God.

His weight crushed my chest and my hammering heart pounded against the pressure. The smells of stale cigarettes, cheap beer, and a slightly rancid locker room overwhelmed the small space. I nearly threw up.

The driver laughed. I knew that laugh—I'd heard it in the lunchroom and halls at school. Delbarton Evans was a junior—like me—although we weren't in any classes together. His friends called him Del, and I wasn't one of them. The other two in the van also looked familiar.

Mike. Carl.

Mike was the one holding me down. He joined Del in his laughter. Carl stared at me, paling to an even more sickly green when he realized I was staring back at him.

The van pulled into a garage and the door motor hummed overhead as the last of the daylight slid away.

Oh, no, no, no, No. No. NO. NO!

That closing door was my last chance. I shifted and bit down hard on Mike's hand. He yelped in pain, and then growled—actually growled—and punched me in the jaw. Pain speared through my head and I tasted blood. Del jumped from the driver's seat and grabbed the arm that Mike couldn't hold. The alcohol smell hit me again as his face came close to mine. He looked me straight in the eye. Then, with his free hand, he grabbed the front of my shirt and ripped it straight down to my waist.

Oh, God. No.

"Shut up and lie still," he said, as his eyes slid down my body. Mike laughed and grabbed at the button of my jeans. I tried to kick him away but he crushed my legs with his knees. Carl, still looking sick, hung back and silently watched.

How could this be happening? Panic threatened to overwhelm me again.

No!

I felt a surge of energy start low in my gut—growing taller and stronger—burning like an icy flame up into my mind. I squeezed my eyes shut. "No!" I shouted. It sounded as if I was in chorus with many other versions of myself as an unseen fire exploded from my forehead. The hands gripping me momentarily tightened, and then fell slack.

I opened my eyes. All three of my attackers had fallen to the floor. Del lay face down only inches from me. His eyes were open and empty without the colored ring of an iris.

What the hell?

I shoved myself out from under Mike. I felt as if an electrically charged spike had driven itself through my forehead. I was shaking so violently I could barely get to my knees. Mike was also shaking, but it looked like he was having a seizure. As I watched, he went still. He wasn't breathing. I glanced at Carl. He'd slumped against the side of the van and his face hung slack from his skull as though he'd started to melt. The only sound in the van was my own ragged breathing.

Dead—they were all dead.

And I knew—somehow—I had killed them.

I've got to get out of here. I stumbled from the van, tripping over Mike's sprawled leg. I couldn't make my mind work—

couldn't figure out how to open the garage door. I pulled on it, hearing my own desperate sobs echo in the cold space. The single bare bulb suddenly clicked out, plunging me into darkness. My scream came out as a whimper. *Oh, God. Help me. I'm trapped. I'm trapped in the dark and they're dead, dead, dead. Oh, God!*

My hands slid along the side of the van until I felt the handle. *Trapped in the dark.*

I finally opened the driver's door and the dome light flashed on. My fingers groped for the button on the driver's visor. I tried not to look in the back.

All dead.

Light worked its way across the garage as the outside world reappeared under the rolling door. I couldn't stop myself; I looked at my three dead attackers. *Oh, God. What happened—what did I do?*

WHAT AM I?

CHAPTER 2

By the time the world stopped tumbling around me, I found myself at home. I showered until I ran out of hot water and then dressed in sweats. Cold seeped through my body despite the fact that the day was warm for early October. The last of the afternoon light melted away as I sat on my bed in my darkening room. I'd stopped shaking, but my mind twisted and churned around the facts.

I'd been abducted and assaulted—punched in the face. They'd been planning to do terrible things to me. *After they ripped my clothes they would have—oh, God.* There was nothing I could've done to stop them but still… I'd stopped them.

What did I do?

Did I really kill three people with my thoughts? How was that possible?

Unnatural.

Was it because I'd gotten angry? I'd been angry at people before and they still had pulses.

Killer.

Was it because I'd been in danger? Had something changed when Mike punched me? The ugly bruise on my jaw hurt when I touched it or opened my mouth too wide. I experimentally opened and closed it, just to see when and how much it hurt. There wasn't much of a lump, which was good. I looked in the mirror as I applied concealer over the reddish-purple mark.

Freak.

The pale girl looking back seemed like a stranger, so I tried not to meet her eyes. How did I do it? Would it happen again? Could I stop it? If something like today triggered it again, would I want to stop myself from killing them?

Monster.

My mom came home in time for dinner. I avoided answering the unspoken questions in her green eyes. She looked young for her forty-seven years, although she needed to lose at least thirty pounds. My mom had put on weight after my father had died and, like her wedding ring, she'd never taken it off. She wore her grief like an extra layer of flesh.

"Do you want me to make cookies?"

I shook my head. She seemed hurt by my refusal, as though I'd dodged a hug.

I zombied through the remaining hours of the evening. I did my homework and threw a load of laundry into the machine. I'd shoved the ripped shirt I'd been wearing deep in the bathroom trash, hiding the evidence. A strange combination of numbness and hyper-awareness played tug-of-war with my senses. I heard noises in the neighborhood that I'd never noticed in the years we'd lived here; suddenly I was attuned to the auditory wallpaper of my life. A few late-arriving commuters pulled their cars into their driveways and the sound of one of their garage doors started me trembling again.

Flashback.

It was after midnight when I finally fell asleep, and nearly two in the morning when the first nightmare drenched me in a shaky sweat and shocked me awake. Across the hall, I heard my mother stirring, as though she'd also had a bad dream. I waited in the dark as she came to my door and pretended to be asleep when she silently checked on me. She stood there for a long time, watching me—worried. Finally, she closed my door. I heard her settle back in her own room, but I couldn't get back to sleep. Flipping on the light, I finished reading a book without registering the words on the pages, and then I started another.

Three students had been found dead and no one knew what had killed them. The school seemed electrically charged with rumor. Some people cried, but many discussed wild ideas with hushed voices and dancing eyes. Scenarios involving horror movie monsters and alien abductions bounced around the halls.

One girl stood alone just outside the main door with a look of grim satisfaction on her face. She held her books protectively against her chest. I didn't know her name, but I thought she was a year younger than me. I watched her for a few seconds and she glanced my way. As our eyes met, I had another of those flashes and I knew I wasn't the first person to be pulled into that van. I dropped my gaze and went inside.

I didn't have any close friends here—just a group of five other honors-track kids I hung out with sometimes. We ate lunch together and tried to separate ourselves from the other group of "smart kids," the ones who dressed up as wizards or hobbits or something on the weekends. My mom and I had moved to Chatham just over two years ago. This was supposedly one of the best public high schools in the state of New Jersey. That bar was apparently pretty low. Our little three-bedroom house was in the tiny strip of town that wasn't full of extravagant McMansions. More than half of the parents worked in the City, and their kids reaped the social-camouflage benefits from expensive clothing and cars.

I didn't blend in with the herd. My action plan had been to stay under-the-radar socially, get good grades, and get into a really good college. High school is full of games and I intended to win the one that mattered. But today, even getting into the Ivy League didn't seem important.

During third period, I heard the tinny sound of a police radio in the hallway outside my A.P. history class. Two uniformed figures threw silhouettes against the frosted glass of the classroom door. Something went tight in my chest. Mr. Storrs opened the door to their knock and spoke with them on the threshold. His eyes widened as he glanced in my direction. I felt empty and cold as I gathered up my books. The stares of the entire class followed my steps to the door and the urgent whispers started before it had a chance to close behind me.

So much for staying under the radar.

I wasn't in handcuffs, but I suspected my police escort from the building was going to hit the school rumor machine at a dead run as soon as history class ended. Normally, that would mortify me, but something told me I might not be coming back here anytime soon. Maybe I was in shock or something, but I just felt numb. I'd killed three people less than twenty-four hours ago, and now I was in police custody.

Monster.

I'd never been inside a police station before. We came in though the back entrance, passing an expensive, chauffeured, silver town car that looked out of place among the black and white police vehicles. The door closed behind us like the jaws of an immense steel trap. The officers escorted me to a small room with a frosted glass door, leaving me sitting alone at a table, staring at the empty chair across from me. I saw myself reflected in the one-way glass; I looked like my own ghost. My green eyes seemed glassy; my skin was wax; and my straight, brown hair fell lifelessly to my shoulders.

The sound of the door made me jump. A uniformed officer stood aside for a tall, African-American man who filled the room with his presence. "Madeline Dunn." An air of calm, competent power radiated off him.

I nodded, although it hadn't seemed like he was asking a question. The man looked about fifty. He seemed polished in his expensive-looking suit.

Formidable.

A bored-looking blonde girl in a trendy, black top trailed behind him. She sighed dramatically and then looked up at the cop and said, "You questioned Ms. Dunn for several minutes." Her voice had a strange, resonant quality to it. "You found she had no connection to the case. She is no longer a person of interest. You released her into Dr. Williamson's custody."

The officer nodded and left the room, closing the door behind him. I stood there with a furrowed brow and a few loose strings dangling from my thoughts.

What just happened?

The girl then looked at me. "Forget what I just said to the officers." Her voice still echoed with the resonance. Fog seeped through my mind and a gently-pushing thought—forget—floated across it. I could feel the memory slipping for a moment, but then I sharply inhaled and pushed back.

"No," I said. The memory came back as if it was being poured into my head, leaving a pressing ache behind my eyes.

The blonde girl gasped, as though I was being rude.

The tall man chuckled. "Thank you, Cecelia," he said to her. "That won't be necessary."

Cecelia gave me a narrow-eyed look of catty dislike. I hadn't made a new friend.

"We won't be long," he continued. "Would you prefer to wait in the car?"

Cecelia left the room with a long-suffering sigh.

The man turned to me with a pleasant smile and an extended hand. "Madeline, I'm Jon Williamson. It's a pleasure to meet you." I felt annoyed at being addressed by my full first name. *Maddie*, I thought, but didn't correct him. Instead, I clasped his hand hesitantly, meeting his eyes. My head spun with ideas. Had Cecelia just hypnotized the police officers? There had been a weird resonance in her voice when she'd spoken to them. She'd tried to do the same thing to me but it hadn't worked. Something strange had been in my voice yesterday as well, when the three of them—*oh, God.*

Dr. Williamson's smile disappeared and his eyes widened with concern.

What happened yesterday?

The thought floated across my mind, and suddenly I vividly recalled the scrape of the van door as it slid open, the smells, the fear, their hands on me, and then the rising anger and the intensity of the "No!" that had made them stop.

Made them die.

Dr. Williamson's hand tightened and I realized that mine was still in his grasp. I broke eye contact with him and pulled my hand away. I felt trapped in the too-small room. My heart pounded wildly, but it was from remembered fear. My instincts told me I could trust Dr. Williamson.

"Maddie," he said. He hadn't taken offense at my sudden pulling away. "I run a training program for young people with special abilities. I think you should join us."

"My mom—" I had no idea how I'd intended to finish that sentence. My mom needs me here? My mom won't want me to go away? My mom will freak out if I tell her I need to go somewhere she's never heard of with someone she's never met? I suddenly realized that I'd simply assumed I'd go with him. I wanted to go with him. It was as though I'd been waiting for the invitation. I had no idea what this program was or where it might be, but I knew two things: I needed to get the heck out of Chatham, and I needed to figure out what had happened to me in the garage. This "training program" sounded like it could do both.

Count me in.

Dr. Williamson waited until it was clear I wasn't going to finish my sentence, and then he smiled. "Don't worry about it. We'll talk to your mother."

I don't know what he and the blonde girl with the strange voice said to my mom when we stopped at her office. Dr. Williamson asked me to wait in the car. However, within two hours, I'd hugged my mom goodbye, packed my bags, and was sitting in the back of the town car.

Escaping.

On my left, Dr. Williamson worked on his laptop. Cecelia, who still seemed vaguely hostile, listened to her iPod on my right. My two suitcases filled the trunk. As we sped north on Route 287, I focused on the road and let my mind go blank.

CHAPTER 3

More than seven hours later, we pulled off the highway and wove through darkening pine forests. I'd seen the "Welcome to New Hampshire/Bienvenue au New Hampshire" sign more than two hours earlier and wondered why had they bothered to put it in French.

Occasional lights shone from porches and through windows—islands in a sea of darkness. These grew less frequent as we drove. Next to me, Dr. Williamson suddenly stiffened, as though someone had called his name. He scowled out the window into the night, his profile visible in the light from his computer screen. What had caught his attention? All I could see outside was the light from the town car's headlights cutting through the blackness. Then a sudden cold trickled down the back of my neck and I felt the same itch within my skull I'd felt just before Del and his friends—

My heart moved up into my throat and I suddenly couldn't get enough air. I gasped sharply as the headlights reflected off a car parked on the side of the road. I might have imagined a flash of movement in the vehicle—I couldn't be sure. Was someone watching me here, too? Had someone followed me from New Jersey? And why were we slowing down? The headlights fell across a forbidding metal gate. It sat in a new-looking brick wall that cut across the old-looking road.

Where are we?

The bronze sign near the security box read "Ganzfield." The driver tapped a code into the keypad and the metal gate slid sideways with surprisingly little noise. We rolled in through the blackness and the asphalt deteriorated into an unpaved, gravel drive that crunched under the tires. I turned to look out the back window. What was giving me this flash, this feeling that someone wanted to hurt me?

The gate clanged closed behind us and another thought shocked me. What the hell had I done? I'd gotten into a car with people I didn't know who had brought me to some kind of secure compound without any assurance they were who they said they were. To top it off, someone had been watching outside the gate. I felt—

Trapped.

What if they wouldn't let me leave? And if I tried, would the person I'd sensed outside the gate still be there, waiting? My breath got shaky and a little whimper escaped my throat. Then a thought went through my head.

Calm down. You are safe. Everything is okay.

Dr. Williamson. The idea made my eyes go wide and my heart seemed to stutter in my chest. My mom's a psychologist, so I knew believing that someone was inserting thoughts into my mind was textbook schizophrenia.

Dr. Williamson surprised me with a quick humph of laughter. I looked over at him; the light from his laptop screen washed his face pale. He smiled right up to his eyes. "Don't worry. You're not crazy."

My jaw dropped. A sharp ache came from my bruised face, pulling memories from the attack back into focus and splashing them cold across my heart. The smile left Dr. Williamson's face. "After dinner, I'd like to have one of our... um... doctors take a look at your jaw."

The mention of dinner made my stomach rumble, as if it, too, had been listening. That was just weird. We drove into a large, sweeping driveway. It circled an old crossroad edged by porch lights and the glow from curtained windows. The town car pulled up in front of an enormous, three-story, white farmhouse with a large, open porch. It made me think of an old lady dressed in finery for a family wedding.

We hadn't fully stopped before Cecelia opened her door. She stalked off toward another, slightly smaller white farmhouse, which wrapped an L-shaped extension around the driveway. It seemed to lean deferentially toward the main building and the old, red barn between them. This must be Ganzfield.

Whatever that is.

A breath of winter hit me as I slid out of the car. It was at least twenty degrees colder than New Jersey.

"Please don't take Cecelia's rudeness personally," said Dr. Williamson. "She's not used to dealing with people who are immune to her ability."

"Her ability? The thing she did in the police station?"

"Exactly. Come in. Let's get some dinner and I can explain things while we eat."

We faced each other across a thick, wooden table in a large, country kitchen. A heavyset, middle-aged woman who looked too stern to make tasty food grudgingly brought two plates. She muttered something about how people who missed dinnertime should go hungry, and then busied herself shutting clattering drawers and wiping spotless countertops in protest before stomping off down the winding back hall.

Once she'd gone, Dr. Williamson turned to me. "Maddie, The Ganzfield program is for people with special abilities."

I nodded and took an unenthusiastic bite of my food. Despite not eating for most of the day, I didn't really feel like chowing down. The trance of the road that had kept my mind blissfully blank on the trip was gone and traumatic memories of the attack filled my thoughts again. How could that have only been a day ago? Already it felt like it completely defined my life.

"Now that you are here," continued Dr. Williamson, "I'll be direct. I believe that you are a telepath—a mind reader—and a very strong one."

What?

I'd never read anyone's mind. A lump formed in my throat. I wasn't the special person they thought I was. They were going to send me back home to all of the problems waiting for me there. Perhaps the police would get involved again. How had they known to come for me?

As though I'd spoken aloud, Dr. Williamson replied, "Your fingerprints were found on the door of the van with the three dead boys. A set were already on file from an old background check. Apparently, you'd applied to be a camp counselor two years ago. We have someone in… well… a *sensitive* position. She watches for unusual cases like this. When she got the information, we immediately came down to New Jersey and to check it out."

I suddenly went cold with understanding.

Telepath.

"You… you read my mind… just now… and in the police station."

Dr. Williamson had seen the attack through my memories. *He'd seen me kill them.* I felt exposed and vulnerable and my whole body started to shake. Dr. Williamson's eyes widened. I suddenly knew he was afraid of what I could do when I got upset.

Everything is okay now. You're safe here. We're going to help you. The reassuring thoughts were inside my head, but I knew they had come from Dr. Williamson.

Dr. Williamson was speaking inside my head.

Holy crap.

Our eyes met as I acknowledged what he'd said… or thought. I felt my jaw set and I drew a ragged breath, willing myself calm. "Is that what you meant about me being a mind reader?" I forced myself to appear outwardly cool and blasé. A part of my mind sarcastically slow-clapped at my self-control.

Dr. Williamson sighed, and then smiled gently. *What you are experiencing is part of my gift. All telepaths can hear the thoughts of others, but I can project my thoughts to other people.*

I suddenly felt as though all of the energy had been drained from my body. I'd had a surreal couple of days and it all seemed to catch up to me in that kitchen—at that moment. I slumped down in the chair and for a second, I wondered if the energy drain was part of Dr. Williamson's "gift."

No, just the thoughts.

I looked back at him. "And you think I can do this, too? Because of the—" My voice broke and the jumbled torrent of horror from the past two days flooded out of me as if a dam had broken. "I couldn't control it! It just happened!"

And you're afraid it could happen again.

I nodded. Forcing the panic back down felt like swallowing a huge pill.

"Maddie," Dr. Williamson spoke aloud again and the sound made me jump. Weird—it'd seemed almost normal to have his thoughts directly in my mind. "A few of us—a very rare few— have a genetic abnormality that allows us to pick up on what other people are thinking. Everyone has moments when they just 'know' what someone else is thinking. We tend to have a bit more of this intuition."

I nodded. I'd had insights like that all my life.

Flashes.

I suddenly thought of my mother, who was so good at reading people. Dr. Williamson smiled.

"We call them 'G-positives,' those with this particular genetic sequence. I suspect your mother is one, as well, and she passed the code on to you. It's a recessive genetic trait, so your father was also a carrier if he wasn't a G-positive himself. Now, most G-positive people go through life fairly normally. However, the ability occasionally manifests more strongly, often in response to a massive rush of adrenaline.

"Several years ago," he continued, "I was involved in a government program called Project Star Gate. The goal was to develop extrasensory abilities for espionage—to make spies who could read the minds of their enemies or find the location of hidden weapons, that sort of thing. For years, the project had only mild success. Then, with the advent of gene mapping at NIH in the early 1990s, we found the G-positives and, shortly afterward, we developed a treatment that enhanced their abilities. The treatment is basically a synthetic neurotransmitter. Do you know what neurotransmitters are? The chemical messengers in the brain?"

I nodded.

"Well this one revs up a portion of the brain called the basal ganglia. G-positive people who receive this treatment develop certain abilities, like telepathy. They continue to get treatments about every four to six weeks to maintain these abilities."

Dr. Williamson looked at me intently. "Maddie, I believe that you are one of us—a G-positive. I also believe that, if we give you this treatment, you'll be able to control your abilities. Telepathy is a sensitivity to the electrical fields in others' brains. Our brains interpret those electrical fields in much the same way we process our own thoughts. I think your response to the attack was to overload the electrical circuits of their brains. I've seen that ability once before."

I fried them.

I was still processing what Dr. Williamson had just told me… still trying to believe it.

Basically, yes. You fried them. Not to take away from the seriousness of the situation, but I've seen your memories, Maddie. I personally think they had it coming.

I burst into tears. I'd been thinking the same thing about the three who had attacked me and I'd been feeling guilty about it. It was a relief to know I wasn't a monster.

Just a freak.

Dr. Williamson waited for me to regain control. He then spoke aloud again. "Maddie, I want to take you to our infirmary tonight. We can run some tests and take care of that jaw."

I touched my face and winced. Then I nodded.

The infirmary was on the ground floor of the house across the driveway in what had probably been the kitchen in the old farmhouse's previous life. An old wooden sign—shiny with amber varnish—hung over the front door. The name "Blake" was burned into it, surrounded by a curling, decorative design. As we entered, a woman looked up from a desk. She had dark brown skin, close-cropped hair, and large, kind eyes.

For nearly a minute, she and Dr. Williamson looked at each other without speaking. The woman momentarily cast a worried glance over at me and I realized Dr. Williamson had been silently sending his thoughts to her.

What was he saying about me?

I frowned; I didn't like being out-of-the-loop.

The woman smiled to put me at ease. "Hello, Maddie. I am Matilda Taylor." She spoke with a softly-accented voice; it sounded like she might be from Africa. She seemed to be in her mid-thirties, although she had an ageless quality to her that meant that my estimate might be way off. As Matilda stood to extend her hand, I saw that she was slightly built—even smaller than my five-foot-three. She sized me up and we smiled at each other in shortness solidarity. I liked her at once.

Dr. Williamson excused himself. "Maddie, please stay here tonight. There are beds in the other room. We'll talk in the morning and I can then introduce you to the program." He nodded at the woman. "Matilda."

She smiled back as he left, and then turned her attention back to me. "Maddie, I would like to take a sample of your blood tonight, and then see what I can do for the injury to your face."

At the mention of the bruise, I brought my hand up to touch it again and winced. *Ow.* Why did I keep doing that? I knew it was still there and touching it only made it hurt.

Matilda swabbed the inside of my left elbow with alcohol then drew the blood sample. I held a cotton ball on the injection site as she capped the vial of blood and placed the needle into a red plastic container. I expected she would put a band-aid over the cotton. Instead, she stripped off her latex gloves, and then gently gripped my arm with her thumbs on either side of the needle prick. An electrical current seemed to shoot through the wound.

Whoa.

It felt like intense pins and needles, like when my foot had fallen asleep—simultaneously hot, cold, and prickly-painful. I lifted the cotton from the puncture site to find the skin was smooth and healed. No scar—not even a mark—although the skin was still very pink and warm, as though it had been slapped.

"Wow." I said, although that didn't seem to cover it. Apparently, Matilda had some special abilities, too. What else could people here do? I'd assumed it was all telepathy and Jedi-mind-tricks, but here was something different.

Amazing.

Matilda flashed a quick, shy smile at me. She seemed both pleased and embarrassed. "Let's take a look at that bruise on your face." Her hands came toward me.

I flinched back before I realized what I was doing.

"Oh!" She seemed as startled as I was, and a belated wave of cold shocked through me. "I'm so sorry. I should have asked first."

"I'm sorry." My cheeks flamed and I dropped my gaze to the floor.

"No, I should know better." After what you've been through, I should've asked before I tried to touch you."

"Does everyone here know?" My heart thudded too loudly at the thought. *Are people here going to see me as a victim?*

A killer?

"I'm sorry. Dr. Williamson told me when you came in. I don't know any of the details. We don't have a psychiatrist on staff, but I'm here if you need to talk."

"My mom's a psychologist. I know I'm probably all posttraumatic stress right now. I just... I just don't want everyone to know that about me, you know? I don't want that to be what people think when they look at me."

Pathetic.

Matilda smiled kindly. "I understand."

I smiled back; she had a calming manner. She would've been a good doctor even if she didn't have that amazing ability.

"How do you do it?" I asked, changing the subject.

"The healing? Well, I just... well... visualize the damaged area. It is like I'm going in like a surgeon. I can *feel* the damaged places. Then I pull in the person's own healing mechanisms and... I suppose... I speed them up—give them extra energy. I focus them on the injury and the people heal themselves. It's hard to describe beyond that."

"Wow," I said again, impressed.

"We all do things with energy in our bodies. We receive it through our eyes and ears and sense of touch. We pulse it through our nerves to send messages and we send it out through the sound of our voices. What G-positives do is not so strange; we just have slightly different ways of processing energy. It's like sharks. Did you know they can sense the electrical fields of living things in the ocean? Even things hiding under the sand."

"We're like sharks?" I asked. Something about that was discomforting, like being predatory toward other people.

Monsters.

She flashed another shy smile. "Not very much like them, just in relation to having an extra sense. Now, is it alright if I take a look at your face?"

This time I didn't flinch. I also was ready for the pins-and-needles tingling that followed, which lasted longer and was more intense than in my arm. After she let go, I opened and closed my jaw experimentally, and then touched my fingers to the place where I'd been punched. The pain was gone.

"Thanks."

Matilda shrugged modestly. "It's what I do." She turned to the refrigerator in the corner and looked inside, pulling out a small vial.

I was suddenly curious. "How strong is your… ability? Could you… like… cure cancer?"

Matilda's eyes lit up at the idea. "Morris and I have been discussing how we could do just that. It's much harder since it involves tissue destruction. We're still working on how to tell the body to attack the tumor but not the healthy systems. Right now, we think it's safer for us to focus on injuries like cuts and burns and broken bones."

"Who's Morris?"

"My brother. He has the same healing ability I have. You'll meet him in the morning; I'm on-duty for the night shift." While she was talking, she prepared a syringe, drawing a dose of a clear liquid from the vial with a bright orange label.

Oh, crap. I suddenly realized that the injection was intended for me. A cold wave splashed through me. "What's the shot?" I asked, trying to keep my voice even.

Escape.

Could I make it out of the door ahead of her? She was even smaller than I was, so I didn't think she could force the injection on me—not if I was ready to fight.

Matilda read the anxiety behind my forced calm. "I'm sorry! I keep forgetting to explain myself. This is dodecamine; it's the synthetic neurotransmitter that enhances the abilities in G-positives."

"Don't you have to do the blood test to see if I *am* a G-positive?"

Don't touch me.

Matilda put down the syringe. "I would never give you an injection against your will. A dose of dodecamine is actually an effective test to see if someone has the genetic code. If you are a G-positive, then the effects of the neurotransmitter will start in a matter of days after you receive the injection. All neurotransmitters work like fitting a key into a lock; the key turns on the effects. If you aren't a G-positive, then you won't have the receptor sites in your brain and it will have no effect on you. A dodecamine injection is like a shot of saline water to G-negatives."

The same impulsiveness that had been driving my decisions all day took over. "Okay," I said as I held out my arm. Matilda gave me the injection, and then healed the needle prick with the same power she had used on my other injuries. She settled me on a surprisingly comfortable cot in the long annex room. It had a row of a half dozen beds lined up like a small hospital ward, although I was currently the only occupant. Matilda dimmed the lights and left. My racing mind could not win against my exhausted body and I fell into a dreamless sleep.

CHAPTER 4

I'm blue, da ba dee da ba die...

The music played quietly. If I hadn't been near waking, it might not've been enough to register. It had a bouncy techno quality— good dance music. I slid my feet to the floor and pushed around with my toes until they located my shoes. In the main infirmary next door, a man whom I guessed was Matilda's brother, Morris, sat at the desk with his feet up and hummed quietly along with the music.

Except there isn't any music playing.

I gasped and the music abruptly ceased, along with Morris's humming. I felt concern coming from him like a warm wave. *This must be Maddie. Is the dodecamine having any effect on her?*

"Yes, it is," I said, before he could ask aloud… then I collapsed onto the floor. I didn't faint; my legs simply gave out. *Such a loser.* Who fell down like that when something freaked her out? Morris picked me up and carried me lightly back to the cot. I felt like an idiot. After all, I'd been warned the drug would allow me to hear thoughts. But wasn't it supposed to take a few days?

Morris picked up a handset from the wall, hit some numbers, and then said, "Dr. Williamson, I think you need to come to the infirmary immediately." He hung up without waiting for a reply. His family resemblance to Matilda was strong and he had the same West African accent with warm vowels.

"Maddie," he said, looking at me with wide, serious eyes. It struck me as strange to be so concerned with the well-being of a stranger, but I could feel the worry coming off him. Why did he actually care?

Did she hit her head when she fell?

"No," I said.

"No, what?" Morris asked.

"No, I didn't hit my head."

This is the fastest reaction to dodecamine I have ever seen. This shouldn't happen for another day or two.

"Is having a fast reaction bad?"

I have no idea. "I don't think it's a problem."

I frowned at the lie. It was almost as if his spoken voice had interrupted his thoughts, yet I'd heard both clearly. I would've asked more questions, but I was suddenly distracted.

"Dr. Williamson's coming," I said. I could actually *hear* him outside, as though he were talking to himself. His mental voice grew louder as he got closer. I could hear him wonder what the problem was. *Holy*—My eyebrows shot up. I could sense his thoughts; that made it more real, somehow, than hearing Morris's.

Dr. Williamson was dressed more casually today, but he was still impeccable. He radiated power and authority, like an idealized father figure. I could barely remember my own father, but took comfort in the impression that a competent, caring person was going to make everything okay.

What's wrong? I heard it as clearly as if Williamson had spoken aloud. In fact, his mental voice was louder and stronger than Morris's, as though it was amplified through a high-end sound system.

Maddie is already responding to the dodecamine. She can hear my thoughts.

But the blood test won't be back for —

Matilda gave her the first injection last night.

What? How much?

Morris's eyes flicked to the chart on the desk. *2 ccs.*

But Maddie is still recovering from trauma! She is still having flashbacks and nightmares. The high residual cortisol and epinephrine levels would magnify the initial effects.

I felt cold blossom in my chest. *That doesn't sound good.* Dr. Williamson's head whipped around even before I spoke aloud. "Is that bad?" I asked.

He wasn't kidding. How much did she hear? "Did you hear what we were discussing?"

"I think ... I think I heard everything."

This isn't the way I would have introduced you to this. I thought you would do better with a gradual approach. I suppose Matilda thought this might help you adjust faster. His voice was in my head so I tried to frame my thoughts to answer him.

Am I going to be okay?

Physically, you should be fine.

He was concerned about my emotional stability. I hated being considered emotionally weak. I paused for a moment and concentrated on how I was feeling. This morning I felt okay. I wasn't nearly as freaked out about hearing other people's thoughts as I probably should've been. It seemed almost normal. *How weird is that?* They were all babbling around me now; I could hear the two men in the room very clearly, especially Dr. Williamson. The other people in the building were there as background noise, like strangers talking down the hall at school.

A sudden, burning pain made me gasp and my concentration broke. I looked at Dr. Williamson, mentally demanding an explanation.

One of the sparks. He paused for a moment, as though listening. He seemed to be feeling the same pain; his brow furrowed and his jaw clenched. *Drew, I think.* "Morris, Drew McFee is on his way."

Stupid sparks. Morris pulled some medical stuff out of a cabinet.

"What's a spark?" I asked. It came out in a gasp. I trembled from the pain, which grew stronger with every passing second. It hurt like a fresh injury, yet I could feel that the pain wasn't coming from my own body.

Beyond weird.

"Sparks is our name for people with pyrokinesis," Dr. Williamson said. "They have the ability to control fire—make it move where they want it to go or make it die down." He squeezed his eyes tightly shut for a moment and exhaled strongly. "Most of them can start fires, as well."

Drew crashed through the infirmary door. It hit the wall hard enough to raise plaster dust from the new indention made by the doorknob. Drew was tall and built like a linebacker—strong and wide—with red hair and blotchy brown freckles. Black marks singed his t-shirt and burns blistered his hands and torso. He carried another person over his shoulder. I realized with sudden dread that I couldn't hear any thoughts from this person. *Is he dead?* Drew practically flung the other boy onto the exam table.

"It's Harrison," Drew said, breathing heavily. "He torched his own bed in his sleep… again."

I watched as Morris moved into action, smoothly and without panic. He touched his hands to Harrison's chest, and then gave an involuntary, inhaled hiss through his teeth as he assessed the extent of Harrison's burns. *It's bad.* I watched through his mind as he felt out the burns and injuries. It was a strange sensation—I could tell his thoughts were not my own, yet I was able to see how his mind worked with clarity, as if I was watching a movie from inside his head. His first priority was the heart and lungs. He checked to "feel" Harrison's heart, and then mentally spider-walked through the delicate lung tissues, repairing burnt bits as he drew some kind of energy through the damaged portions. I had no idea how he was doing it.

Harrison regained consciousness just as Morris finished repairing his lungs. A scream filled his thoughts and the sudden awareness of his pain lashed through me. It was much worse than what I'd felt from Drew's burns. I crumpled and bent over with a moan.

Drew moved quickly to my side. "Hey, are you okay?" I could feel his genuine concern though the pain. *She's pretty, but too short.* It was such a guy thing—to be noticing what a girl looked like when he was in the middle of a trauma. "What's wrong?"

I worked my way to the nearest cot and sat down heavily. I forced myself to refocus, trying to calm my racing heart and wild breathing. Morris applied first aid spray to Harrison's burns before channeling energy through them. It must be a painkiller; the sprayed areas stopped hurting as intensely. I could think again and could finally feel things beyond the boy's agony. Why would a guy with super healing powers use first-aid spray? Oh… antibacterial. There'd be no pockets of infection later.

Dr. Williamson had gone through the same experience I had—Harrison's pain had also hit him strongly, although he seemed better prepared for it. As he clutched the doorframe to keep himself standing, he met my glance and I suddenly knew this was normal for people like us.

You're handling this well.

Thanks. I smiled weakly. I felt clammy and sweaty. If this was taking it well, then a bad reaction must be horrible.

Next to me, Drew thought I was about to faint. From his point of view, I was not handling this well. He reached out to steady me and I flinched away from his hand, causing him to pull it back.

The minds of the other people in the room faded slightly into the background as I concentrated on Drew.

Oh, good. She's not going to pass out. She'd be better looking if she were taller and had a bigger rack. She's probably another charm… like we need another stuck-up bitch around here. Maybe if I'm nice to her before she gets the shot, she won't force me to do crap later on.

"What's a charm?" I asked him.

His face reflected the tumbling emotions of his thoughts. All of his concerns for my well-being were forgotten as he jerked back from me. *Crap! Not a charm. Minder! Did I have any sex thoughts about her? Don't have any now!*

"Just that I needed a bigger rack."

He laughed good-naturedly, embarrassed.

Decent guy.

Drew's almost stereotypical head of Irish-red hair was sooty and disheveled, and his face was open and friendly. It matched his personality, as far as I could tell. I realized I was going to be able to tell a lot more about people from now on.

"So, what's a charm?" I asked again.

Drew glanced at the others in the room before leaning in and telling me quietly, "Charms are what we call those who can 'push' people into doing what they say. It's like hypnosis."

"That Jedi-mind-trick stuff? 'Forget I was ever here?' That sort of thing?" I remembered Cecelia in the police station and the pull of her voice, telling me to forget.

Drew smiled at the *Star Wars* reference. "That's it. Nearly half of the people here are charms. You're only the fourth minder."

Don't think about sex!

"Minder?"

"It's what some people here call telepaths," Drew replied, lowering his voice and glancing at Dr. Williamson.

I could've mentioned that Dr. Williamson could hear his thoughts so lowering his voice probably wasn't doing anything useful, but I decided not to interrupt.

"It's short for mind-reader, I think, but also it's because they're always in charge."

I was going to be in charge?

His eyes met mine as he earnestly added, "Stay clear of the charms. They're…"

Psychotic. Vicious.

"…they like to… um… use their abilities on the rest of us." Drew's fear and embarrassment twisted through me. I blushed in response.

Harrison sat up, rubbing his arm. The familiar pins and needles echoed to me from his newly-healed injuries. He looked around the room, trying to figure out where he was and how he'd gotten here. His eyes landed on Drew. I felt a wave of hot guilt radiate from him as he took in Drew's burns.

"Sorry, bro," he said, chagrined.

Drew popped up next to him and clasped a hand onto his shoulder. "No harm done." *Except to the bed. The fire is probably still going.*

Morris took the opportunity to heal the burns on Drew's hands and torso. Drew paid little attention to the process. His focus was on comforting Harrison, who seemed to view starting fires in his sleep as the pyrokinetic equivalent of bed-wetting. *Pathetic and embarrassing.* Their thoughts gave color commentary as they talked.

Apparently, Harrison accidentally set fires in his sleep a lot, so no one but Drew would room with him. Drew's fierce, bearish protectiveness toward his younger brother extended to the other sparks and felt almost tribal. Pyrokinetics weren't treated well by the other G-positives here at Ganzfield, at least in Drew's opinion.

It was odd—I didn't feel guilty reading other people's minds, at least at first. Then I remembered how invasive Dr. Williamson's intrusions into my thoughts had seemed yesterday. I guessed others might feel the same way about me. But what could I do? There was no way to cover my mental ears. If I drew my attention away from the thoughts of one person, someone else's immediately filled the void.

In the room directly above me, a girl named Rachel thought, *I wish Sean would ask me out,* and daydreamed about kissing him.

The damn sparks are going to burn this whole place to ashes someday. Morris's thoughts were sour as he stowed some medical equipment.

Someone had a song stuck in their head, much to our mutual annoyance, since now I kept hearing, *It's raining men! Hallelujah, it's raining men! Amen!*

I tried to shut out their minds, their thoughts, their feelings, but it wasn't like closing my eyes to block what I could see or covering my ears to block what I could hear. There was no way to block out the incoming thoughts.

This could be a problem.

Dr. Williamson looked at me. *I'll show you a few things that will help.* He'd recovered from Harrison and Drew's pain. I was still a bit shaky.

Harrison stood up, fully healed. Drew looked at me, his friendly smile wide across his face. "See you at breakfast?"

Dr. Williamson answered him before I could. "Maddie needs a few more tests before she starts training."

Her name's Maddie. Drew made a mental note.

"Oh, okay. See ya, Maddie." He grabbed Harrison in a brotherly headlock as they left the building.

Dr. Williamson turned back to me. *Are you hungry?*

No.

Then let's get started.

The tests were laughably easy. They began with Zener cards—Morris looked at a plus sign, a circle, or some wavy lines, and I had to say aloud what he saw. We started face-to-face, then a room apart, and finally Morris was outside. I found that as Morris got farther from me, his mental voice faded, as well. Most of his thoughts centered on the fact that he was missing breakfast. I might not be hungry, but Morris was and his annoyance and hunger increased as the testing progressed. I felt a bit guilty about that, but Dr. Williamson seemed to think that Morris was a bit of a complainer.

After nearly two hours, Dr. Williamson released Morris to seek out the remnants of breakfast. We sat across from each other at the infirmary desk and Dr. Williamson bounced thoughts off of my mind. I didn't need to answer aloud—he could hear what I was experiencing. It was exhilarating. Communication was so fast—so efficient—with almost no misunderstanding. I revved up to the challenge. It felt like taking a test that I knew I was going to ace. *No problem.* This was cool. Freakish, but cool. After several minutes, Dr. Williamson sat back with a sigh.

Wow.

How did I do? I waited for his response but I already knew. He'd never seen anyone become such a clear telepath so quickly. I felt a slight smugness at that; I love to be the best.

Welcome to Ganzfield.

I smiled. *Thanks.* If everything stayed this easy, this was going to be a great experience.

Of course thoughts like that only jinx the person thinking them.

CHAPTER 5

Once Dr. Williamson finished testing me, he called Rachel—
the girl who had a crush on Sean—to be my guide for the day.
I said nothing about the crush, of course, even though I didn't
know anything else about her. I had a feeling I was going to be in
on lots of secrets from now on. I might not be able to keep out of
other people's heads, but at least I could be discreet about what I
saw there.

Rachel Fontaine had at least six inches on me, but she held
herself hesitantly so she didn't seem as tall. Pretty and blonde,
she shared Drew's concern that I might be a charm. *What is it
with the charms?* I was getting an ominous feeling about them. My
memories of Cecelia, bored and disdainful in the police station,
didn't help. Were they all like her? Why was everyone so wimpy
about standing up to them? It didn't seem that hard to resist their
ability.

Our first stop was the dorm room directly above the infirmary.
It was her room, and now it was also mine. There was another

bed as well, so we probably had a third roommate. I grabbed a quick shower before dressing in jeans and a navy sweatshirt.

Looking in through the glass-paned French doors of the three rooms on the ground floor, I saw small classes of other teenagers. I suddenly realized this was a school. *Duh.* I felt stupid for not realizing it earlier.

One class discussed international relations. Yikes. Way more advanced than my AP history class. Some students concentrated and tried to keep up. The others drifted in their own sex fantasies, frenemy-dramas, or fears of charms. Many had the same intimidated feelings that Rachel and Drew had. What was wrong with this place? Why was Dr. Williamson allowing this bullying to continue?

The next class worked on memorizing different types of tanks and ordnance. The minds of the eight students in the class felt stupored by the material. I hoped I wouldn't be taking this class with them.

The third class worked on some kind of advanced physics. We heard some of the lecture: thermodynamics. *Ugh.* I recognized Drew and Harrison among the other students. Drew saw me in the doorway and gave me a smile. More than half of the class looked like they must be Drew and Harrison's close relatives. They all had the same red hair, bear-like build, and blotchy freckles. Another half dozen of the students were African-American—all similarly slender with prominent cheekbones.

Only one student looked different from the two main types—a tall, lanky guy with straight, dark-brown hair hanging too long over his eyes. As I looked through the door, the girl in front of him dropped her pencil. The guy with the dark-brown hair reached out, picked up the pencil, and put it back on the girl's desk.

But my eyes were on him and he hadn't actually moved.

Huh?

The hairs on the back of my neck stood up as I did a mental double-take. What had just happened? My eyes had been drawn to him; I'd been watching him the whole time. His body had remained behind the too-small desk in the relaxed sprawl of a guy who has recently finished a growth spurt. But I'd felt his thoughts. He'd seen the pencil fall and he'd reached out and picked it up. The pencil had moved up to the desk.

Who was this guy? How had he done that?

This place was getting weirder and weirder. Rachel led me past the infirmary and out of the building. The leaves glowed brilliant shades of red and orange in the crisp, cool air. I took in my surroundings, smiling as the babble of minds became less noticeable the further we got from the building.

In the daylight, the big, red barn between the two white farmhouses looked faded and run down. Its wide doors sagged on their hinges. Behind the barn, a huge, sloping field ended at a picturesque lake right out of a New Hampshire vacation brochure. Several squat, grey buildings clustered near the water's edge, lessening the postcard view. Power lines radiated among them from a central post, like the spindly legs of an enormous spider. The field and lake formed the bottom of a shallow valley. Low hills rose in a bowl around them, their dark trees already beginning to turn vivid orange in places. Several wind turbines topped the hill behind the lake. The distant mountain peaks blued with the haze of distance; the tallest of them already had snow.

A quick movement at the barn door caught my eye. A brindled, brown cat wiggled through one of the gaps and trotted into the field. I had a subtle, quiet image of mice hiding in the grass and a small pang of hunger. Hey! Could I read the minds of cats, too?

Next to me, Rachel daydreamed about Sean again. I noticed an invisible, shining line connecting her back to the building we had just left. I opened and closed my eyes a few times, wondering how I was seeing something that was invisible. *Weird.* Rachel had a clear picture in her head of the physics class, particularly of one of the red-haired guys who seemed to be enveloped in a pale glow. *That must be Sean.* The shimmering line she traced from him shifted and followed her as we walked. I figured the line must have something to do with her ability, whatever that was.

Rachel seemed to have little interest in conversation with me. No, it was more—*fear.* She was wary of me, trying not to draw attention to herself.

We stepped onto the large porch of the main building where Rachel continued her silent tour. Talking was largely unnecessary. Even if I hadn't been able to read her mind, I could figure out that the room on the second floor with all the books was the library and what the row of laundry machines in the basement was for. Rachel avoided the third floor; apparently that was off-limits to students.

We ended the silent tour in a large dining room. Ten narrow tables lined the walls; each looked to seat about eight. That probably meant that there were no more than eighty students, give or take. As people started filtering in, I followed Rachel's lead as she picked up a tray, chose a sandwich and soda, and then sat down at the table in the farthest corner. There was no cashier; I guessed we didn't have to pay.

I started to get a sense of the same high school hierarchy that I loathed at home. As my mind filled with dozens of people's thoughts, I began to pick out common threads. Sex was on the brain of a large chunk of them, and everyone who wasn't a charm seemed to be trying to avoid their notice.

A group of sparks came in together. Their laughter faded as several charms looked their way. The golden thread from Rachel's mind changed position, ending in a shimmer around the beloved Sean. A quick glance into Sean's mind showed he wasn't aware of Rachel's adoration. He was thinking about something called Fireball.

Fireball? That sounded interesting.

How rude was it for me to be looking into everyone's private thoughts? It was like I couldn't stop bumping into people in a crowded room, although no one noticed that I was doing it.

As students picked up their food and sat down, I felt the seating pattern become apparent. The tables along the wall with the windows were for the charms. The fear and the "be invisible" thoughts came from the side where Rachel had led me, which was now filling up as people sat with their friends. It was directional, like listening to their voices. The combination of the verbal and mental babble made the room seem doubly-full.

For a moment, I became lost in my new ability, pushing out with it and trying to zero in on the minds of specific individuals, figuring out which voices came from which people. I could easily keep more than one train of thought straight at a time. It was easier, at least, than trying to listen to two different people talk over each other. However, the constant, prattling input was beginning to wear at me. I couldn't shut out the thoughts pressing into my head.

A few people noticed me. It felt like catching sight of my own reflection in an unexpected place or hearing someone call my name—I couldn't ignore it. A few of the charms saw me, as well. The table across the center aisle from ours was now filled with them. Three girls discussed my appearance with catty superiority—apparently my sweatshirt wasn't fashionable enough for them. I rolled my eyes. I was used to being persona non grata with the fashion police.

Two of the guys at the same table began to have fairly obscene thoughts about me. I felt myself blush as one mentally undressed me. The other one pictured me doing something perverted and humiliating. Anger washed over me in a wave of steel-grey energy. I could actually "see" it building around my skin. Cold clenched at my gut—twisting it—replacing the sickly pink heat of embarrassment. I put down my sandwich as I glared at the boys. Rachel saw my attention shift and she seemed to shrink into her chair.

The boys noticed my gaze as well. The tall, black-haired one might have been good-looking without the cruel smugness that seemed permanently etched into his features. "Hey, new girl."

The people around me had gone quiet. Most of the thoughts around me were of the *uh, oh* and *oh, crap. Michael* variety. I gathered this was Michael and he was feared. Rachel had an intense, sickened feeling at the sight of him—like she wanted to cry. As I focused on his mind, I suddenly saw why. In a second or two, he was planning to use his charm ability to force me to feed him his lunch like a Roman slave girl. Later, he imagined getting me away from the group for a lap dance and other things—things that were much worse. Cold fury boiled within me, churning my gut into a lump of rock. I felt my jaw tighten.

"Come over here," Michael said, his voice heavy with the resonance I'd heard once before in the police station—when Cecelia had told me to forget. I noticed Cecelia sitting at the next table, watching this exchange with cool interest and casual disapproval. I felt a small pull of obedience to Michael's voice, but it wasn't very strong. I brushed it away easily.

I met Michael's gaze. "Go to hell." I was amazed at how hard my voice had become; there wasn't even a quiver of fear. This wasn't like in the van. I was no longer powerless.

There were audible gasps from the people around us. The rest of the conversations in the dining room died down. People stared at me in shock. Some seemed amazed that I would dare be so rude in my refusal. A few others had grasped that I hadn't moved. Apparently, when Michael used his ability, people obeyed.

Michael's face and mind both flushed red. "I said, COME HERE!" He truly planned to humiliate me now; his status among the charms was at stake.

I could feel the power flowing through me, fueled by my steel-cold anger. I hadn't even been at Ganzfield a full day and I could see the inequality, cruelty, and just plain wrongness of how things were here. I was *not* going to be treated that way!

"I SAID NO!" Energy shot from me with each word.

Michael fell backward off of the bench, clutching his temples. I wasn't sure what I was doing or how I was doing it, but I could feel the power blasting into Michael like a taser to his brain.

What the hell am I doing?

As soon as I gained control I stopped, as surprised at myself as everyone else was. The echo of Michael's agony hit me as well and I winced, although it wasn't as painful as Harrison's burns had been. Was that because I was the source of his pain?

Except for Michael writhing on the floor, everyone in the room was staring, silent, and slack-jawed.

Staring at me.

On the floor, Michael's thrashing slowed and then stopped. *Oh, God—did I kill him, too?* Was this like the boys in the van? No, I could still feel emotions coming from him. Michael was terrified;

he was in pain; he felt weak and humiliated; he hated me. I guess that meant he was going to live. That was probably a good thing.

Probably.

This didn't feel like the attack in the van. I'd overloaded Michael's mind with my mental voice. "I SAID NO," reverberated through his head—slowly fading. He'd had no way to block the excruciating blast.

I felt slightly guilty I didn't feel more upset about hurting him, but I'd been justified. Would there be fallout from this? At the very least I'd made an enemy and, from what I could see, he was the kind who held a grudge.

Well, no one had promised me a fun-filled camping experience where I'd make best friends for life. And so far, it still beat being in New Jersey.

Only a few seconds had passed, although it felt as if time had slowed. From somewhere above me—I guessed the third floor—I heard the now-familiar mental voice of Dr. Williamson. *What is going on down there?* In the continuing silence of the dining hall, his rapid footfalls on the wooden staircase sounded ominously loud.

Okay, there was a distinct chance I was in trouble. My first thought was to run out, but I quickly threw that one aside. I really didn't know where I was or where I might go. Besides, I *had* been justified. I simply stood up straighter and turned toward the door. As Dr. Williamson entered the room, a sudden, cold realization hit me: he might be able to do to me what I'd done to Michael.

Dr. Williamson took in the scene quickly. I suspected he was already up-to-speed from hearing our thoughts. Still, several of the charms from Michael's table started thinking *she attacked him for no reason* at him.

The four of them all had facial expressions of wide-eyed innocence and shock. I looked in their minds and saw that they'd done this before. It was standard operating procedure to cover up the charms' worst behavior. Clearly, they didn't know how well telepaths could read their deceit. It showed plainly, as if they were holding up written signs that said, "We're lying."

Dr. Williamson ignored them and looked at me. *What happened?*

I showed him my thoughts by simply replaying my memory in my head, including what I'd seen in Michael's mind. I finished up and asked indignantly, *You allow this sort of thing here?*

No, if he'd actually done what he intended, he'd have been expelled from the program.

So what? You would have turned him loose out in the world? Let him hurt women that way? Do you know what kind of pain… what kind of damage that would cause? My eyes filled, blurring my vision. I told myself the tears were from anger and I wiped them away.

No. He'd have been confined until his most recent dose of dodecamine left his system before he'd be allowed to leave the compound.

It was only as I received this reassurance I realized that the entire dining hall was still silent. Everyone sat watching Dr. Williamson and me staring at each other. It didn't seem silent, though, as their thoughts filled my mind.

New minder on the loose!

She's more dangerous than the sparks!

Ooh, she's a telepath like Dr. Williamson.

What's her name?

I don't care if she's dangerous. I'd still do her.

Where are they going to put her? She can't stay with us!

I hope she fried Michael. Maybe they'll finally cut him off and kick him out.

I held Dr. Williamson's gaze. *Check his mind—he's been hurting the other students. It seems like everyone here is scared of the charms.*

Dr. Williamson looked at me sadly. *Unfortunately, the charms need to practice their abilities. If they cross the line, they get kicked out.*

If that's not over the line, then the line needs to be redrawn. I glared back, a little shocked at my forwardness. Wait, was I allowed to talk to him like this?

Dr. Williamson smiled. *Part of your training here is learning how to use your ability to redraw the lines. Go for it.*

Okay, I hadn't expected that. What was this place? Had I just been made sheriff of some supernatural, Lord-of-the-Flies high school? What the hell?

He heard that train of thought and chuckled aloud. *Here are the rules. You cannot kill. You cannot maim or cause other permanent damage. You cannot compel someone to have sex. You cannot use your abilities on instructors. If you break the rules, you'll stop receiving dodecamine and you'll revert to a regular person with occasional flashes of insight. Then you will leave and never return.*

I swallowed hard. Dr. Williamson wasn't as nice as he looked.

Ganzfield is a training facility for people with extraordinary abilities. Normal rules are unenforceable, at least in normal ways. And we have enemies—enemies in the real world who don't play by the rules. We need to toughen up the people in this program… to prepare them for what they'll face when they leave here.

That threw me.

Enemies? It sounded as if we were being trained as soldiers in a secret war.

It's not quite that bad anymore, but it could come to that again. The Sons of Adam know about this place now. Maddie, when the dodecamine reaches full effectiveness in you, you'll probably be very powerful. I hope you'll use your ability to do great things. We have very few telepaths, and most of us can't stand to be around other people very much. There was a pang in Dr. Williamson's thoughts as he said this—a sense of loss that I couldn't quite pinpoint.

I can see why. It's exhausting hearing everyone's thoughts all the time. How do you shut them out?

Dr. Williamson shook his head. *You can't. You can only get used to them… or get away from them. When I return, I'll arrange for a cabin for you away from the other buildings so you'll have a place to escape.*

When you return? You're leaving? I felt a flutter of panic. I was being thrown to the wolves of a sociopathic high school— sociopathic, adolescent wolves. Yikes!

If you need anything, Seth will be in charge. With that, Dr. Williamson turned and left. My jaw hung open as I stared at where his back had been. I had no idea who Seth was or what he'd be in charge of if there were no rules to enforce. At least I wasn't going to be punished for incapacitating Michael, who'd managed to sit up and now regarded me with sullen, wary hatred as he rubbed the back of his neck.

The phrase *hell of a way to run a railroad* passed through my mind and I wondered if it had originated in my own head or someone else's. I couldn't place the source. With Dr. Williamson's departure, the conversations around me restarted, although they were hushed.

I avoided looking at anyone as I sat back down and deliberately finished my sandwich. I took small bites so the lump in my throat wouldn't choke me when I forced myself to swallow. As I chewed, I sampled the thoughts around me.

No wonder I couldn't charm her; she's defective. That came from Cecelia.

I rolled my eyes and shook my head slightly. *Nice.*

Pretty much everyone seemed afraid of me. At least that had a silver lining; the charms weren't going to bother me for a while. No… wait. Two of the guys at Cecelia's table quietly considered getting a group to work together. Would their combined abilities be enough to force me to do something?

"An ambush, with overwhelming force."

"She won't be able to retaliate against everyone."

I pulled their names out of each other's minds. Alex. Josh. I'd need to know my adversaries.

What the hell have I gotten myself into?

Two tables away, I felt someone think, *She's brave, but I bet she was really scared.* It seemed somehow… warmer… more pleasant than the other mental contacts I'd experienced so far. I searched out the source and my eyes met those of the lanky, dark-haired guy who'd picked up the pencil without moving. After a second he smiled—a grin that lifted into his brown eyes. *Hi, telepath. If you can hear me, welcome to Ganzfield. I have a feeling you're going to make things very interesting around here.*

I felt myself smiling back and I dropped my gaze as I flushed pink. Wow. I couldn't believe I was reacting like some gooey, crush-struck teenager—not with all of the other things I had to deal with right now. But there was something that drew me to this guy. He was different somehow.

Special.

People gradually relaxed and returned to their normal lunch routines. Rachel stood up to leave, and I followed her back to the other building, listening to her unspoken freak-out as we went. *What did she do to Michael? Is she dangerous? Should I be afraid of her?*

We sat down in one of the empty classrooms. I gathered that one of the afternoon classes would start here soon and that

Rachel and I were supposed to be in it. Several people came to the door, saw me, and then kept walking. *I know I'm supposed to show her around today, but is there a way I can leave without pissing her off? I don't want to be rude to the dangerous telepath.*

Finally, I turned to her with an exasperated sigh and said, "You know what he was going to make me do, right?"

Rachel startled as if I'd snarled at her. I rolled my eyes, annoyed at this timidity. "Geez, I'm not out to get you or anything. What's wrong with this place?"

Rachel looked at me, her thoughts a confused jumble. *Should I tell her what it's really like here? How the charms run the place like they're the Varsity Hypnotizing Team, treating everyone else like A.V. club nerds?*

I took a risk and let her see what I could do. "Varsity Hypnotizing Team?"

Rachel went very pale. She moved her mouth silently for a few seconds, trying to make something coherent come out.

I smiled in what I hoped was a reassuring manner. I wanted to make friends here—or at least allies. "Yeah, I guess I'm a mind reader."

The smile helped. Rachel smiled back, warming to me. *The charms avoid her, so maybe she's the lesser of two evils.* It was faint praise, but I could work with that.

"So, what's the deal with this place?"

"Ganzfield?"

"Yeah. How did it start?"

"My Uncle Charlie was one of the founders back in the late 1990s."

Cool. She was an expert.

"He and Dr. Williamson were part of a government project that tried to use extrasensory perception to spy on the Russians."

"The Star Gate Program?" Dr. Williamson had mentioned something about it.

"Yeah. It's declassified now. You can Google it. Uncle Charlie's an RV, like me."

"RV?"

"Remote Viewer. For, like, twenty years, Project Star Gate tried to enhance people's ability to locate people or objects wherever they were. It was like, 'the missiles are hidden in this valley in Hungary,' or, 'there's a battalion of tanks stationed at this Soviet base.' That sort of thing."

The golden thread to Sean I'd seen in her mind must be part of this RV ability. I didn't want to embarrass her by bringing it up, though. There was something brittle and fragile about her that didn't want to get too close to others.

"So…" Rachel continued. "Then the Cold War ended and the U.S. government didn't need to keep up with Russia's psychic spy program. Around the same time, the genetic sequence common to all G-positives was discovered. That led to dodecamine—a drug that activated the genes the same way growth hormones cause a growth spurt.

"Dr. Williamson and Uncle Charlie were some of the first people to get the treatment. It worked better in them than it did in most subjects. Uncle Charlie said that Dr. Williamson and one of the first charms convinced several senators and congressmen to kill and discredit the program. The G-positives were then able to start again in the private sector. Dr. Williamson handled the funding." Rachel didn't say, …*by going down to Wall Street and reading the minds of investment bankers for inside information*, but the thought bounced through her mind with the savory tang of a secret.

"Where's your Uncle Charlie now? Does he live here, too?"

Rachel shook her head, unfocused her eyes, and concentrated. In her mind, I saw golden threads shoot out in all directions from her, like a tiny sun. Several of them faded after a few seconds, then more and more, until only one direction remained. She seemed to travel along that line as though flying—the world blurring around her—until an image filled her head. In her mind, I could see a gorgeous beach with a pudgy, sunburned man in a lounge chair in the center of the mental picture. After a moment, she smiled. "Looks like he's back in Cancun."

"Cancun?"

"Yeah. He's on the beach. It's sunny. He's wearing a bathing suit and his favorite fishing hat is down over his face. I think he's taking a nap."

I didn't mention that I could see it, too. I gathered that Uncle Charlie was somehow retired from all of this.

"That's a neat trick."

Rachel pinked with pleasure at the compliment.

"Why do you think you can do that and I can read minds? Why do we have different abilities?"

"Uncle Charlie said we all work with energy… that we all basically do the same thing in different ways. Like… if you and I both catch a cold, I might have a stuffy nose and a sore throat. You might notice the sore throat more and maybe have a cough. Or like that mental illness where people have to wash their hands fifty times a day, or count the cracks in the sidewalk, or check that their stove is off every two minutes?"

"Obsessive-Compulsive Disorder?"

"Yeah. The symptoms show up in different ways, but the underlying cause is the same."

"I saw a guy. He was tall and had dark brown hair. He picked up a pencil… sort of without touching it."

Rachel smiled. "That must've been Trevor Laurence. He's really nice. Trevor's the only telekinetic here."

"Telekinetic? He moves things with his mind? How is that possible?" Despite having seen it, I was still confused. From his thoughts, it felt as though he'd simply picked it up with his hand. I was still trying to process the sensory disconnect between what my eyes and my mind had experienced. It was like looking at that picture of a vase that suddenly became two faces in profile.

And he smiled at me in the dining hall…

"No clue how it works. They run a lot of tests on him. Trevor's friends mostly with the sparks." I noticed her thoughts turn back to Sean as she mentioned the sparks. Rachel was about to say more, but a bell rang, and reluctant students trickled into the classroom followed by an instructor who noticed me only as the "new girl."

We sat through traditional high school classes for two hours: English composition and Calculus. The Ganzfield program had classes for sophomores, juniors, and seniors, although the upper grade classes were larger since most G-positives came here for about two years. These courses were simply to keep us at the right grade level while we learned how to use our abilities.

After calculus we had a short break. Most people hurried over to the dining hall to grab a soda or a snack. As she packed up her books, the calculus instructor—a middle-aged woman whose name I forgot within a few seconds of hearing it—said I should, "Go find Seth for your practical," and gave me curt directions to a cabin halfway around the lake.

Before I could ask her who Seth was or what a "practical" was, she bustled out of the classroom and left the building. A quick glance into her mind showed she was already thinking about what she would make for dinner and whether the cat needed to go to the vet. There was nothing about this Seth person.

I considered getting a snack or something to drink, but the idea of going back to the dining hall made my appetite vanish. Perhaps I'd discovered a new form of weight loss: the humiliation-avoidance diet. As I went outside, I heard the distant strains of singing coming from the main building. It sounded like a small choir or singing group practice—except I could hear the charm resonance in their voices.

Siren song. Great, just great.

I headed toward the lake, trying to remember the directions to find Seth. Was this the same Seth who Dr. Williamson said would be in charge? Was he a minder, too?

Several people gathered in a cleared area near the water's edge. A huge, whooshing burst of flame jumped up from the center of the group, mushrooming into a ball of fire about three feet wide and hovering about twenty feet in the air above them.

Whoa.

I stopped stock-still, watching with my mouth hanging open. The flaming ball seemed to quiver in place, and then move in jerking bursts back and forth several times until it broke free and soared, still airborne, away from the group. Three people ran with it—two guys and a girl—their hands upraised toward the ball of flame, pushing at the air and jostling one another. Several others fanned out to take positions on what I realized was a playing field. I remembered Sean's thoughts about something called Fireball. This must be it.

The group headed toward the goalie, a dark-skinned girl with high cheekbones and many braids that she wore tied back from her face. She protected a large, oblong watering trough, the kind used for farm animals. As the ball of fire approached, the goalie lifted her hands and braced herself, as though physically pressing against the incoming ball of flame. I saw flickers of light reflected in the beads of sweat on the players' faces and arms. They seemed to push the ball back and forth; it wavered in the air in front of the trough several times. Suddenly, the goalie called out, "Mel!" and the fireball flew directly at a red-haired girl near the sidelines. Mel raised her hands to a point where they nearly touched the flames. It slowed slightly then shot upward and over her like a comet, launching toward the trough at the other end of the playing field.

As I moved cautiously closer, I could pick out thoughts of strategy and gameplay from the players' minds. It seemed pretty simple: ignite a light framework of wire and cloth then try to dunk the fireball into the opposing team's water trough. I found that most of their thoughts focused on the game, and it was clearer and less chaotic than hearing thoughts on many different themes simultaneously. Their exhilaration—their joy at playing, using their abilities, and being part of a team—filled me. I found myself getting caught up in the game. The sparks' awareness of the fire seemed to hum through their bodies and sing in their blood. They could actually feel it—like it was an extension of themselves. There was no fear of fire in any of them; on the contrary, they loved it.

Another of the red-headed boys played goalie for the other team. He attempted to block the incoming fireball, but it came in too fast. He flinched out of the way as it singed his hair and plunged into the water trough behind him with a hiss of sizzling steam.

A high-pitched cheer went up from several of the players, and a chorus of female voices shouted, "Goodness Gracious, Great

Balls Of Fire!" I suddenly realized they were playing girls versus guys. The scorer jogged back to the center of the field; two of her teammates patted her on the back.

The red-headed goalie for the boys' team made a running jump into the lake to cool the burns on his face and arms. As he slogged back out of the water, dripping and smoke-streaked, Matilda, the healer from the infirmary, stood up from a metal bench along the sidelines. While another player headed out from the bench to cover the goal, Matilda's healing pins-and-needles spun through the goalie's face and arm. *Gah—I can't believe I let her score! I should've—ow—should've been able to block that one. I'm better than that.* The goalie barely noticed the pain of his blistered skin. In his experience, burns were more common than letting goals in.

I watched for several more minutes, although no one scored again. It was a lot like soccer, although this soccer ball was three feet wide, flying, and on fire. Finally, I forced myself away to find this Seth person.

I saw the cabin under a stand of trees about halfway around the lake. It took me nearly twenty minutes to walk the meandering trail that loosely followed the water's edge.

Too loud! The single thought filled my head. I stopped where I was. *New minder?*

I understood what he meant. Distantly, I could feel my thoughts in his mind, bouncing in like the bass from an unwelcome car stereo. It wasn't so distant to him—it was loud and brash and he felt annoyed. No, it was stronger than that. He felt—assaulted by my presence, even though I was still out of his sight. I guessed that two telepaths could converse by reading each other's minds, even without purposefully sending out thoughts. I had a brief flash of confusion. While I could hear his mind more strongly than other people's, Dr. Williamson hadn't had this response to my thoughts. I also hadn't had this reaction with other minders.

Well, good for you. Seth's thoughts dripped sarcasm. I tried to quiet my mind, but I wasn't really sure how to do that.

It won't help. Just go away.

I tried not to be offended.

Please go.

That made it a little better.

I turned around and made my way back along the path. I hadn't gotten within fifty feet of Seth, but I'd made his acquaintance. Apparently, I was not going to get a "practical," which I now assumed must be a lesson in using our special abilities.

At least not today.

Too bad. I had a lot of questions about how telepathy worked. Why could some of us project thoughts and others only hear them? Why was I too loud to Seth but he wasn't too loud to me? And what had happened in the van? How had I killed those boys? Could anyone else do that—kill people by overloading their minds? Should I be worried? Well… more worried?

I considered going back to see the rest of the Fireball game, but then I noticed thoughts softly bombarding me from the surrounding trees. I stopped, closed my eyes, and focused. The mental flutter came from birds, squirrels, and a few other creatures. They were mostly thinking about food. It was all images, smells, and a few sounds—there were no words. I opened my mind wide, attending to as much as I could, suddenly deciding I would make my own practical lesson. A bird took flight from a tree branch above me and I flowed into its mind, feeling the sensation of beating against the air with wings, of moving swiftly with the land falling away beneath me.

Flying!

A lightness filled me, as though I was also in the air. The feeling grew fainter and then died out as the bird flew out of my range. I took a long, slow breath, feeling the cool autumn air fill my lungs. I was away from people out here. I took another breath, cleansing my soul with the quietness, the smell of fallen leaves, and the dampness of live trees and earth. The only thoughts were from the animals; they were gentle, like a pattern on wallpaper. If I concentrated on them, I could notice the details. Otherwise, they just faded into the background like the sound of crickets on a summer night.

A second trail broke away from the one I'd been on. I followed it away from the lake, noting the direction so I could find my way back. A couple of anxious deer sheltered under the orange canopy of leaves, wordlessly wanting me to go away. I walked on, hearing the quiet thoughts of animals, the rustle of an occasional breeze through the trees, the crunching thuds of my footfalls on leaves, twigs, and dirt. After a few minutes, another building caught my eye. It seemed to glow faintly in the golden afternoon light. The path opened into a clearing where a white, steeple-topped church overshadowed an old graveyard. Granite stones tilted in their rows like crooked teeth. I went closer—graveyards had never bothered me. The cemetery at home was the only place I'd been able to visit with my father. I used to go and sit by his grave. When I was younger, I'd even had conversations with him, although I'd been the one doing all the talking. I frowned. I hadn't done that in a long time.

This cemetery dated from the early 1800s. The most recent stones I could find were those of a husband and wife who'd died within a few months of each other in the 1970s. I did some quick math on the dates; they had both been in their nineties. Most of the names on the stones had Eaton or Blake as a surname or middle name. A few had both in combination. They were probably all related; generations who had lived and died here until that last couple. I wondered about them. Had they been the last of their line? Or had their children moved away and made new lives for themselves, away from their old family home?

I smiled. The minds of the dead didn't intrude on my thoughts. *Peaceful.*

The church was a little run down and it looked unused. The black door wore so many layers of paint that the details carved into the wood were now merely lumps—like ancient, eroded foothills. Another path led away from this side of the clearing, back into the woods. If my internal map was correct, it went toward the main building.

The door was unlocked, so I pushed it open. I didn't hear anyone's thoughts—no one was here. The small room just inside the door was dark and my eyes took a few moments to adjust. The low ceiling ran the front width of the building, and the windowless space was just wide enough to buffer the inner areas from the cold of a New Hampshire winter. Empty bars hung at eye level along each of the side walls. Had they once been coat racks? I pushed through the inner doors and into a single, large, high-ceilinged room. It was plain white and the old wooden floor had central paths worn into it from generations of pious feet. Shutters covered most of the tall, narrow windows and slivers of light entered between the slats. A single, missing shutter allowed a rectangle of golden afternoon light to fall toward the front of the space, illuminating the raised dais and its short railing. There were no pews, but the remains of an ancient coal stove squatted in one corner. Half a dozen cots had been pushed against the back wall, along with a pile of blankets, pillows, and other bedding. This must be for housing overflow if they ran out of space in the dorm buildings, or perhaps these were extra beds. I remembered Drew thinking that Harrison's bedding had been set on fire. Maybe he'd take one of these back to wherever he slept.

I stood silently for minute, feeling reverent, although I wasn't a very religious person. I thought about these special abilities we all had. Were they part of a divine plan? In earlier centuries, we might've been thought of as witches. Were our abilities inherently good or evil—part of something greater than this program? Were they natural? Supernatural?

I liked this place. I felt a sense of peace here that I couldn't find around other people. I walked slowly back, taking the path from the front door. I was right; it led back to the main building. I noted the entrance into the woods as I stepped back into the world. I could come back to this church when Ganzfield got too intense.

I thought again about Seth and how I'd been "too loud" for him. I wasn't at my full abilities at this point, but would other people become too loud to me as well? Would I find it necessary to live away from them—alone and isolated?

Why had Dr. Williamson left him in charge? I suddenly realized I probably knew the answer. Minders must be immune to the charms. We could tell when they were using their abilities. Other G-positives—even other charms—might not be able to do that. I'd have to ask Dr. Williamson when he returned.

I grabbed some food from the dining hall and ate outside on an old granite bench. The sunset over the lake was pretty enough, but the cold stone seeped up painfully through my jeans. I returned to my new dorm room. Blake House was blissfully empty of other minds, although the mental babble from the dining hall echoed faintly in my head.

A stack of books and a course schedule rested on the end of my bed, so I changed into a t-shirt and PJ pants and settled down to read. If I was going to take part in this program, I was going to master it.

An Introduction to Psychology. That made sense; I was going to be spending a lot of time in other people's heads. What else? More books on neurology and psychology... and a manual on FBI interrogation techniques. What the hell did they want me to do with that? I had another queasy twist in my gut. What kind of program was this? I put the manual face down under the bed then picked up *Introduction to Psychology* and skimmed the first few chapters.

The thoughts of other students returning to the building after dinner hit my mind before their voices hit my ears. They buzzed with a jumble of intense emotions, concerns, dramas, fears, and joys as their footfalls creaked up the wooden stairs. I was getting better at locating each mind. Most of the charms climbed up to the attic. The entire top floor was a large common room with couches and a large television.

Some of the charms felt intimidated by the others. Huh. I hadn't noticed that earlier. But now, I was able to flit from mind to mind with my own personal window into the drama that filled everyone's heads.

—*glad I wasn't the one Victor had licking the bottoms of his shoes*—

—*want to be alone with him. But if we go back to my room and start kissing and stuff, can I charm him to stop before he can charm me to take off my*—

—*pathetic loser can't even keep from being*—

—*if she looks this way, I'll charm her to leave me alone before she can*—

—*still called "brown nose" after being charmed to kiss his a*—

—hate him, hate him, hate him, hate him, want him dead—

—three days since she told me to shut up and no one's taken it off. I may never talk again and no one cares—

Yikes. Charms could charm each other. No wonder they were scared. For them, every social interaction carried the threat of mind control. And I'd thought high school in New Jersey had been full of games. Wow…

A sudden flash of icy fear grabbed my attention. Rachel and another girl stood in the doorway. The girl stared at me, wide-eyed. Her memory of Michael, the charm, falling to the floor of the dining hall hit me like a brick to the head.

Rachel's eyes darted between us. "Uh… Hannah… this is Maddie. She's new." *What's wrong? Am I missing something? Something dangerous?*

"Hi," I said, sitting up.

Hannah was a fair-skinned African-American girl—tiny and bird-delicate. A small, gold cross hung around her neck. Her horror flavored my mind with sour tension. *Now there's one in my room? I don't want to stay here anymore. I just want to go home where people are nice.*

Crap.

What was I supposed to do about this? My new roommate found the dog-eat-dog environment of Ganzfield overwhelming, and she looked at me as though I was the newest pit bull in the kennel.

I shrugged and tried to go back to my book, but it was hard to concentrate with Hannah's incoming thoughts. The other mental voices filling the building didn't help, either. They were louder now—much louder than they'd been this morning. How bad were they going to get?

Rachel looked from me to Hannah, trying to figure out what was going on. She waited until Hannah went down the hall to the bathroom before asking me about it.

"She saw what happened in the dining hall today and she doesn't want to have anything to do with me. In fact, she just wants to go home," I explained.

Rachel silently processed this for a few seconds. She knew what Michael was capable of, and she was sure I must've been defending myself. Apparently, Hannah didn't have the same experience.

"Why don't the charms pick on Hannah?"

Rachel's surprise only lasted a second. *Oh, that's right—minder.* "Hannah's a healer."

"And the charms don't pick on healers?"

"They might need them. They don't have much respect for the RVs or the sparks, though. They know the RVs can't hurt them and the sparks will be expelled if they light up in a building or attack another student. Also, we're not the ones being trained for the most valuable positions. Charms are placed in the most important government and diplomatic jobs."

"Why? What's the plan?" I'd wondered what the big picture was.

"Well, we need to have G-positive people in positions of power and influence. There are groups out there who think people like us should be removed from society. Isolated. Sterilized."

Killed.

I grew cold and my gut clenched as images of concentration camps and witch burnings filled my head. "What groups?"

"One calls themselves the Sons of Adam. They started when the Star Gate Program went public. They think we're dangerous mutants. They keep a pretty low profile. Most people think they're nuts." *And there was the man who wanted to kill us all, just like he killed Aunt Lucy.*

"Aunt Lucy?"

The color drained out of Rachel's face and she shook her head. Flashes crossed her memory from when she must have been about seven years old, listening behind a closed door as adults discussed what had happened to Lucy. *Torture. Vivisection.*

I covered my mouth with my hands. I felt like I might throw up.

Oh, God.

"I'm so sorry," I said.

Hannah stood in the doorway. "What's going on?" She looked at me accusingly. *What is she doing to Rachel?*

I felt the now-familiar heat of anger wash through me. "I'm not doing anything to her! We were just talking." The rage pushed me on. "And another thing... you're a healer, so you don't know all of the crap that the charms put the RVs and the sparks through here. Michael has been... a bully." I would've said he was torturing people, but the images of actual torture conjured by Rachel's memories gave me a little perspective. "If you paid a little more attention to what everyone else was going through here instead of just being homesick and wallowing in self-pity, you'd understand why I did what I did in the dining hall today."

I then put my nose back into my book and pointedly ignored Hannah. I forced myself not to smile as she considered what I'd just said. I'd hit the right nerves—now hot, sickly-sweet guilt flavored her thoughts. She stared at her laptop screen without seeing it.

Hannah was no longer afraid of me. Now she twisted with shame. *I've been so selfish... so un-Christian.* I didn't leave her suffering her own self-recriminations for long.

The sound of my voice made her jump. "Look, let's start over. I'm Maddie." I gave my best apology face.

Score!

Maybe I didn't need this psychology book I was reading. Hannah sighed and gave me a tentative smile. "Hannah."

"Where're you from?"

"California... near Los Angeles."

"You miss it."

She tightened her lips and looked out the window for a moment, as though she could see all the way home. She nodded.

"How'd you end up here?"

"Dr. Williamson knew my grandmother from Project Star Gate. He tracked us down last year and did DNA cheek swabs on us. My little brothers are both twelve. We're all G-positives." *And in a couple of years, they'll have to come to this place, too.*

"The worst part is not being able to tell my friends why I had to leave." I saw two girls vividly in her thoughts; the three of them had been best friends since kindergarten. Hannah felt cast adrift without them.

"Why didn't your parents come here with you? Aren't they G-positives, too? Isn't that where you got it?"

"Some of the parents are; some are just carriers. It's a recessive genetic trait. But we're here because the dodecamine treatment works best on immature brains."

Rachel gave a quick, hesitant laugh. "We're immature?"

"Yeah. We've been discussing it in anatomy class. The dodecamine causes the basal nuclei in the brain to go into overdrive, building connections throughout the brain. Fully adult brains are less adaptable. The changes have to take effect while we're still undergoing a lot of myelination, and the last big burst is during adolescence. Most G-positives who get dodecamine for the first time as adults don't get very strong abilities."

I'd been wondering why there wasn't a wider age range here, and I could see why they wouldn't give such abilities to younger children. A six-year-old with the power to force people to do his will? Yikes.

We shut off our reading lights when a thunder of footfalls came from the attic stairs. The boys were all leaving the building and going to their dorm—wherever that was. Apparently, we all went to sleep by 11 p.m. here at Ganzfield. Once Hannah closed her laptop, the darkness in our room was complete.

I thought about my mom. I hadn't emailed her or anything. Ah hell. Now I felt deflated by my own insensitivity. My laptop was still in my bag—I'd seen it when I'd grabbed my nightclothes. I couldn't call—the surrounding mountains cut off cell phone reception. My phone's battery was probably dead anyway—it never held a charge for very long. I still needed to finish unpacking to see if I even had my charger. I made a silent promise to email my mom in the morning.

All around me, the minds of my roommates and the girls in the surrounding rooms settled, and then drifted into silence. *Sleep!* I couldn't hear people when they were asleep! I might be able to get some rest here, after all.

Oh, it's you. The girl who's too loud. The thought came from outside the building.

Seth?

This is bed check. Go to sleep. You're too loud. I can't hear the others clearly.

Sorry. Okay… going to sleep—now.

I could actually feel him rolling his eyes. Listening to his mind didn't seem to distract him the way my own thoughts did, though, so I followed Seth's check as he counted us. Thirty-one charms, twenty sparks, eleven RVs, four healers, three—no, four—minders, and one telekinetic. Of these, eighteen girls were assigned to this building.

Seth seemed to be a stronger telepath than me. He could hear and identify minds, even when they were asleep. Once he identified we were all female and accounted for, Seth silently faded out of my range.

CHAPTER 6

Mike grabbed me and pulled me into the van. He punched me in the jaw. Del held me by the arm then ripped my shirt down the front.

Help!

I bolted upright, jerked awake by the sound of screaming. The light from the moon cast a blue-grey glow on one side of Rachel's face. She sat up as well, wide-eyed and breathing fast, clutching the front of her nightshirt to her. In Rachel's mind, I saw Del's drunken face as it had loomed over her.

No!

In the moonlight, Hannah absentmindedly rubbed her jaw. She still felt the phantom sting of the punch to the face.

Oh my God.

I could feel thoughts from other rooms in the house—four other girls in Blake House were suddenly awake, shaken by the same nightmare.

My nightmare.

I watched as Rachel and Hannah both settled back to sleep. *Just a bad dream.* They hadn't noticed each other's reactions. My heart raced and I felt my hands trembling, although I couldn't see them. I hugged my arms tightly around myself, pressing my chin to my chest and squeezing hard to make the shaking stop.

I'd sent them my dream. I must be able to send thoughts as well as receive them, like Dr. Williamson did. That would be a cool thing if I could control which thoughts I sent. The horror of having my every private thought broadcast to the world filled me with dread. No wonder Seth lived alone in a cabin in the middle of nowhere.

I needed my own cabin, and I needed it soon.

Now.

The sudden thought of the empty church had me on my feet and looking for my shoes. There were even beds there; it'd be perfect. No one would have to share my nightmares if I slept there. It was getting colder and I was just wearing a t-shirt and PJ pants, so I wrapped the blue and green quilt from my bed around my shoulders. Stepping lightly on the stairs, I tried not to make any noise as I left the building.

I remembered where to find the path and the moon was bright enough for me to see where I was going. The white church glowed faintly to my dark-adjusted eyes. I pushed open the inner doors to the sanctuary.

My sanctuary.

It was darker inside, but the glimmer of moonlight that fell through the broken shutter was enough for me to see the outlines of the empty beds against the wall next to me. I grabbed a sleeping bag from the pile and unrolled it on the nearest cot. The pillow had a musty, camping smell, but I could live with it. The silence enveloped me and I felt the tension drain out of my body. With the gentle touch of a few nocturnal animals fluttering against my consciousness, I fell asleep.

Mike forced me down on the floor of the van. He punched me in the face. Del grabbed my shirt and yanked. Mike reached for the front of my jeans.

The van door squealed open. Mike suddenly flew backward through the air, slamming hard against the far wall of the garage. Shovels and rakes clattered to the cement floor. Del flipped end-over-end, tumbling against the closed garage door. The impact of his shoulder cracked the wooden panel. Carl, still huddled in the corner, emitted a painful "oof" sound as something unseen pinned him back.

Trevor stood in the doorway of the van, looking at Carl.

Trevor?

What was Trevor doing here? His normally kind, brown eyes glared at my attackers. They softened with concern as they focused on me. "Are you alright?"

A wave of conflicting thoughts filled me as my worlds collided in strange, surreal ways. I no longer felt the terror of the attack.

A dream.

Oh, this was just a dream. Trevor was here and I was safe. I didn't like the idea of being a damsel in distress, but having a white knight come to my rescue kinda worked for me right now.

Trevor tried to gauge my reaction. I exhaled a shaky breath and nodded. He extended his hand to me. I held my torn shirt closed with my other hand as I stood.

Behind him in the garage, Del got to his feet. He grabbed one of the fallen shovels from the floor and rushed Trevor.

"Look out!" I cried.

Mike stopped mid-stride—like he'd hit an invisible wall. After a quick moment, he flew backward and slammed against the garage wall with a sickening thud.

A splintering clatter pulled me out of my subconscious. I had only a second to look into Trevor's eyes as the dream-world disintegrated, leaving me breathing hard in a swirl of fading images.

Something in the church rolled through the blackness with a hollow, wooden sound, and the dream—*my* dream—floated half-remembered in someone else's mind.

Trevor.

Someone's in here. I could feel the tingle of trepidation flow through him.

"I am," I said aloud, hearing my voice echo slightly. "I'm here."

"Maddie?" The threads of the dream revived slightly in his head as he tried to figure out what was real. For my part, I had a sudden rush of warmth as I realized that Trevor knew my name, but it died as soon as I realized now he also knew my nightmare.

A flashlight clicked on in the middle of the large room. The beam swung over to hit me in the face and I flinched at the sudden brightness.

"Maddie?" Trevor asked again, sliding the light down so I was no longer blinded. "What are you doing here?"

I felt my cheeks flush. I seemed to be blushing a lot around Trevor. At least it probably wasn't obvious in the dim light. "Sorry. I didn't mean to wake you. I didn't know anyone else was here."

"You didn't wake me. I had a… dream." He was suddenly embarrassed; the warm, sick feeling flowed off him in waves. "You shouldn't be in here. It's dangerous." *I'm dangerous.*

I felt a sudden, strong desire to comfort him. "How are you dangerous? That was *my* dream!"

Confusion. "What?"

I stood up, wrapping the quilt around my shoulders again and checking that the front of my shirt was still intact. I walked over to where Trevor sat up on a solitary mattress on the floor in the center of the room. "I came out here because…" it spilled out of me in a confessional rush. "Apparently, I'm the kind of telepath who can broadcast thoughts as well as hear them and I woke everyone up in the dorm with my nightmare tonight." I felt like crying.

Trevor might not be a telepath, but he picked up on my distress easily enough. "Hey, it's okay." He set the flashlight next to him on the floor so that it pointed straight up, creating a small fountain of light. It dimly reflected off the white ceiling and revealed a constellation of dust motes that swirled in the air above us. Still in his sleeping bag, Trevor pulled his legs to the side and gestured for me to have a seat on the mattress.

I hesitated for a second—I'd never been on a guy's bed before. No, it was okay. Trevor was… nice. There was a warmth to his thoughts, like hot chocolate after a day out in the snow. A gentle strength pulled me in and made me feel safe. If only everyone's thoughts felt this good. I tucked my legs under me and pulled the quilt tighter as I sat.

"That was *your* dream? Are you okay?"

I smiled at him. "I am now. You kind of came to my rescue. Thanks." *Man of my dreams* flitted through my thoughts and I rolled my eyes at myself. What kind of sappy fantasy was I weaving about Trevor? *Yeesh.* I wasn't that kind of person. "You were very brave." I meant it, but I winced as soon as it left my mouth.

I sounded so stupid!

I had no right to start crushing on Trevor. Someone so kind and decent wouldn't want to be with someone like me. I was dangerous.

A killer.

I'm not brave. "You're the brave one. You stood up to Michael today." *Fearless... Vibrant... Beautiful.*

I dodged the spoken and unspoken compliments and jumped at his first thought. "Why don't you think you're brave? You just took on those three guys in my dream." Inside, I felt my gut do an electric flip-flop. *He thinks I'm beautiful?* Asking about that one would have to wait—it was too much to process right now.

Trevor again flushed warm with embarrassment. "That was just a dream. It wasn't real. People are getting hurt here. The charms have taken things too far and we haven't stood up to them. You got here, and on your first day you took down one of the worst."

"It's just... I think I'm immune to them. Maybe it's because I can hear their thoughts. It cancels out their ability or something." A rush of cold flashed through me as I realized what would happen if Trevor took on the charms. I could see the plan start to form in his mind. "No! Don't try it. You can't expect to save a drowning person if you can't swim, right?"

Trevor nodded, guiltily relieved by my logic. "Yeah, I think that's why Dr. Williamson always puts another minder in charge when he leaves. You guys are the only ones who wouldn't be... forced to do things. But what did you do to Michael? How did you, um, hurt him?"

I felt my heart plunge. If I told Trevor what I was capable of, he'd stop liking me. I could avoid answering, or I could lie, but I felt... protective of him. He should know the truth. He shouldn't be duped into being with someone like me. He was amazing and kind and I—

I'm a monster who can kill with my thoughts.

That's not what someone like him looked for in a girl. I felt the silence draw out. I was still trying to put into words what I wanted to say. The dim light revealed the planes of Trevor's face in pale greys and shadows. His hair fell slightly askew over one side of his face. I smothered the impulse to brush it back from his forehead. The reflected light from the flashlight danced in his warm, brown eyes. I'd had passing crushes before, but I was already beyond that feeling with Trevor. How crazy was that?

Maybe dodecamine was an aphrodisiac.

He waited for me to speak, and so, with a sigh, I ripped off the band-aid. "I kind of… blasted his brain—like yelling into a stethoscope or something. I overloaded him. I'm not even sure how I did it. This is all really new, you know?" I gave him a quick smile, but I was deflating inside.

Maddie, the dangerous freak.

I felt my eyes welling up with sudden tears and I started to scowl at myself for being so weak. Then I felt Trevor's touch—but he was still at the other end of the mattress.

"Hey. It's okay." The gathering embrace was a strange sensation. Gentle. Unlike when people touched me unexpectedly, this connection didn't startle me. I was simply surrounded by his presence. It was comforting.

Safe.

He searched my face then slid over and put one of his arms around my back, squeezing my shoulder gently. He was warm, even through the quilt on my shoulders. I leaned against him tentatively. He smelled woodsy—a masculine scent.

Trevor actually wanted to be closer to me? I tried to force the tremor out of my voice. "You're not freaked out by me?" It came out higher pitched and more pathetic than I'd hoped.

He laughed, which was a great sound. *Note to self: make Trevor laugh more.* His laugh was a rumble, low and gentle in his chest. It rolled off him in warm ripples. "I'm actually amazed that *you* aren't freaked out by *me*."

"Are you kidding?" I felt my energy return as a giddy rush of amber light. I turned and met his eyes. "You're so nice!"

Nice. That's the kiss of death. Girls don't want nice guys.

My jaw actually dropped. "I'm a mind-reader, remember? I'll take nice thoughts anytime. Your mind is so incredibly… well… nice is a high compliment from a minder."

Trevor suddenly wanted to kiss me. We were facing each other in the dim light, only inches apart. I wanted to kiss him, too, but a sudden, scary flashback of the attack in the van made me pull away.

Too soon.

"Nice," he said with less distaste than he'd felt in his earlier thoughts. "I'm not nice. I'm out here, alone, every night because… because I hurt people." He lowered his eyes as shame twisted in his gut. He felt unworthy. Lonely. Unwanted.

"No." I couldn't believe it, although the pain of his admission pressed at me from his mind. "You wouldn't."

"Not on purpose. Do you know what sleep paralysis is?"

"I read about it in my psych book. It's when you're dreaming, right? The connection from your brain to your body shuts off so you don't act out your dream? But sometimes it doesn't work completely… like the little paw kicks a dog makes when it's sleeping."

Trevor smiled sadly. "Yeah, that's right. My problem is that I move stuff with my mind—"

"—and that doesn't get shut off by sleep paralysis." I suddenly got it. "So that crash that woke us…"

Trevor swung the flashlight around the church. Part of the front railing lay askew across the choir bench. Several of the upright dowels had been pulled loose, leaving the remaining ones angled off to the side.

Whoa.

I looked back at Trevor, now nearly hidden in the dark. "How strong are you?"

Trevor's voice sounded small. "I lifted a set at four-eighty-two yesterday."

"Four hundred eighty two *pounds*?" I asked, incredulous.

"Yeah. That's my one of my practicals. I go to the gym and move the machines or free weights. They also have me practice the small stuff like typing and lock-picking." He flashed the light from the splintered wood along the length of the floor to his mattress. "I thought that railing was out of range." Moving the light along the walls, I could hear him guesstimating the size of the building. *I might end up homeless this winter.*

"Homeless?"

He smiled. It didn't bother him that I picked up his thoughts. He kind of liked that I understood him so easily.

"Yeah. This room is the largest open space on Ganzfield. I need a clear area so I don't throw things around." *Or break down walls… Or cave in the ceiling.* I suddenly saw a boy lying unconscious, crumpled on the floor. Guilt colored the image in his memory.

"You threw that boy in your sleep?"

"Yeah. I had a dream that someone was attacking me. I fought back. Reed was my roommate."

"What happened to him? Is he okay?"

"He's okay now, but…"

"It's not your fault."

"I know." I could sense his remorse and pain.

"Trevor, it's not like you killed anyone." Something in my tone let him know it wasn't an idle comment.

"Did you?" His voice was nearly a whisper.

"You met them tonight," I said with more calm than I felt. A flashback of Del ripping my shirt hit me like a punch to the gut. I caught my breath; it sounded almost like a sob.

His moment of confusion turned to horror. "That was a *memory*?" he asked, appalled. "That wasn't just a bad dream?"

I couldn't speak for a moment. I could feel turbulence within him, writhing in his mind. Was he disgusted by me? Afraid of me? Trevor's jaw shook, the quivering outline clear against the lighter wall behind him.

Maybe I should just go.

Suddenly, his thoughts crystallized. He wanted to hurt them… badly. He wanted to hurt the people who'd hurt me. He wanted to hurt them more than he'd ever wanted to hurt anyone. His own intensity shocked him.

I didn't know what to say. A few minutes around me and this gentle person, who'd been filled with kindness, wanted to hurt people.

I really am a monster.

"I'm sorry," I said, nearly crying at what I'd brought into his life.

That shook him. "You're sorry?"

I nodded. "I should never have put this on you. I don't know how I'm doing it. I don't know how you ended up in my dream rather than just seeing the images. That's even worse." I choked up. "I'm so sorry." It was inadequate for the pain I'd caused him. I felt as though I'd rather burn alive than cause him pain.

A second later, I was gathered in his invisible embrace again. "It's okay. They can't hurt you now."

I felt so selfish that I had put this on him. "You're not... disgusted by me?"

He turned me so I faced him and looked me in the eyes. His mind, so close, drew me in. He wanted to help me—to make it all better.

"After what they did to you, it's understandable."

"Before."

"What?"

"Before. They didn't..." I paused, trying to swallow the lump in my throat. "In the dream, just about the time you saved me. If you hadn't, then..." I was rambling, making very little sense. "I just... felt this burst of energy flow out of me, and... then... they were dead. All of them. That's why I'm here at Ganzfield now."

Trevor looked deeper into my eyes, which intensified my ability to read his thoughts. Part of him was relieved that I hadn't experienced that horror. Another part was astonished. "You did that before you'd ever had dodecamine?"

I nodded.

"Wow."

"So please understand that, when you say you're dangerous, I kind of... well... I don't really see it that way," I finished lamely.

We still faced each other, looking into each other's eyes. My heart beat faster and Trevor's giddy relief mixed with my own. Together.

Safe.

My lips parted slightly as I took rapid little breaths and drank in his eyes. This was the strongest telepathic connection I'd ever experienced. Trevor's every thought poured into me as words, pictures, and feelings.

I hope she doesn't have a boyfriend. Her eyes are beautiful. There are flecks of gold in the green. I hope she meant it when she said she wasn't freaked out by me. She's even braver than I thought. I want to know her better. I want to keep her safe. I want to kiss her. I want to do more than kiss her.

He dropped my gaze and pinked up. *And you just heard all of that, didn't you?* In the light from the flashlight, I saw the blush creep all the way up to his hairline. We both looked away and tried to calm the matching, rabbit-fast beats of our hearts.

"No, I don't have a boyfriend," I said when I trusted myself to speak.

Trevor grinned. *Want one?*

I grinned back. *I might. Are you offering?* I froze at the expression of shock on Trevor's face. It took me a second to realize what had shocked him. "Oh! I've never done that with a non-telepath before," I said when I realized I'd just thought my answer into his head rather than speaking. "I didn't know I could. Sorry."

"That was wild." His voice was a little unsteady. "I've never heard someone in my head before." *Can you do it again?*

Can you hear this? It was easy—as natural to me as speaking aloud.

He grinned and nodded. His eyes stayed locked with mine and I felt my pulse quicken again. Trevor was the most amazing guy. I didn't think there were many people out there who could take this sort of thing in stride.

So, tell me about yourself. He leaned back onto his elbows with affected nonchalance.

Can you guess where I'm from? I tried to imagine the nastiest stretch of the Jersey Turnpike at him, the part near Newark airport where the factory smokestacks spewed foul-smelling plumes, some of which were on fire.

He grimaced. *Where is that? Hell?*

I snorted. *Close—New Jersey. Can you see it?*

I think I can even smell it. He wrinkled his nose.

Sorry! Let me try to show you something nicer. Home? I showed him my mom in the kitchen. She was at her happiest when she was cooking. After a moment, I added the scent of her incredibly addictive chocolate cookies baking in the oven. I could send him images, words, and smells simultaneously.

Cool.

What else could I show him? *Have you ever felt what it's like to fly?* I sent him the memory of the bird in flight.

His face lit up. "You like to fly?" he asked aloud, slithering out of his sleeping bag and jumping up. I let out a little shriek of delight as the mattress I sat on rose into the air, moving in a large circle around the perimeter of the church. It was like a flying carpet out of Arabian Nights. Trevor pivoted as he guided me, slowly and deliberately, though the dark, making two rotations around the open space then setting me down in the same place in the center. The surprise on my face sent happy little tendrils of green energy through him.

I laughed out loud and couldn't stop smiling.

What are you thinking? he asked.

How lucky I am to have met you.

He grinned because he was thinking the same thing about me. We sat there, gazing into each other's eyes, just digging on each other. Threads of desire wove between us, pulling us closer. It felt like… magic. After drifting timelessly for a while, we reluctantly shook ourselves out of it. We'd need to get some sleep at some point.

I returned to my cot, slightly aquiver with the anxiety each of us felt for the other. I worried I might send him another traumatic dream. He worried he would drop something heavy on me. I honestly felt it was a toss-up as to which was worse.

Trevor pointed the flashlight at the broken railing. When he used his ability, it was as though he grasped the pieces of wood with a second set of hands, although they seemed to change in size and shape to suit his purpose. I could see them now—hints of golden energy extending from him. I wondered about that; did I actually see the energy, or did my brain interpret an echo from his mind? Either way, the little shimmers were strangely beautiful.

Trevor pulled the railing straight, gathering the individual dowels from their scattered locations on the floor and fitting them back into position. He slid his mattress further from me before he resettled. I felt him gauge the distance between us.

Keeping me safe.

I drifted to sleep wrapped in the warmth of Trevor's thoughts.

CHAPTER 7

Morning light fell on my face, turning the inside of my eyelids red. I shifted position, hearing the creak of the cot beneath me. Air fell on my now-exposed arm. Cold. I pulled that arm back in and reached out with my mind. I couldn't hear Trevor; he was either gone or still asleep. I craned my neck up. A guy-shaped lump filled his sleeping bag. My heart flipped within my chest. Last night had been real.

Outside, the birds brightly called to each other in the morning light, softly pecking at my thoughts with their own. I sat up and scanned the floor for my shoes. Wrapping the quilt around myself, I opened the door gently to avoid waking Trevor.

The outer door creaked loudly anyway, but a quick check for Trevor's mind showed he was still deeply asleep. Actually, I didn't hear any snoring or even the sound of breathing. He could have left a pile of pillows to imitate a sleeping person; I wouldn't be able to tell the difference. I frowned at that. Why couldn't I hear sleeping people the way Seth could?

Matilda was awake in the infirmary by the front door. I felt her concentrate on a half-wilted plant as it greened up and bloomed at her touch. I went around to the back since I didn't want to have to explain to anyone why I'd been out all night. The inevitable round of awkward questions and assumptions didn't appeal to me.

No one else was awake. I tried to keep the old floors from squeaking as I went directly to the bathroom. A steaming hot shower removed the chill of the New Hampshire morning. It was only early October, but it must be near freezing outside.

I thought about Trevor. Was he going to sleep in that cold church all winter? Why didn't he have a heater? I answered my own question as soon as I asked it; he might throw it in his sleep and set the place on fire. I shuddered at the mental image of the explosive damage he could do with a propane tank.

It wasn't right. At that moment, I resolved to find a way to get him a better place. Maybe I could get the money the same way Dr. Williamson had—by picking the brains of the financial experts on Wall Street.

Whoa.

Was I planning to buy a *building* for a guy I met *yesterday*? I searched through my feelings.

Yup.

Deep down, I truly believed it was a really good idea. I could ask Dr. Williamson to give me some practical lessons on investing so I'd know what to listen for.

Wait… reality check. Wasn't I getting a little over the top here? I could chalk it up to the intensity of my recent experiences; or the environment of Ganzfield; or the effects of the dodecamine; or to an adolescent crush.

No.

In my gut—in my heart—I knew it was more than that. Trevor was so much more than that.

Trevor.

Giddy energy danced across my skin when I thought of him. Wow. The remembered warmth of his mind made me feel... *more alive.* Like there was magic in the world. Real magic. I'd only known him one day and one night, though. It took time to develop intense feelings for someone. Everyone knew that.

But not everyone could read minds. Thanks to my new ability, I already knew Trevor better than I knew just about anyone else.

Amazing. Wonderful.

He was the best person I'd ever met. Just thinking about him made a goofy smile spread across my face. Trevor was kind and good... and he deserved better than to freeze in an old church all winter. And yes, I wanted to give him a building—a really, really nice building. I rubbed my hands across my face.

Oh, man. I've got it bad.

I got out of the shower, used the hair dryer quickly, and then padded back to my dorm room wrapped in my blue and green quilt. Once I'd replaced it on the bed, all evidence of my overnight disappearance was gone. Maybe I wouldn't need to explain anything after all.

I dressed in a dark crimson sweater that made my skin look a nice peachy color. I spent a little more time on my hair. I even put on a little make-up and the gold earrings my mom had given me for my birthday last January. Primping. I was giddy with the idea of seeing Trevor again. Was he awake yet? I was much too far from the church to hear his thoughts. In Blake House, I felt a few people move around the dorm, their minds still cobwebby with sleep.

I logged onto the Blake House wi-fi and sent my mom a quick "I'm fine" email. I should've done it earlier; she might be worried. Although, if Cecelia had charmed her into letting me come here, maybe she wouldn't be worried after all.

I then grabbed my course schedule and the books for my morning classes. The schedule listed a full day of lessons for me, even though today was Saturday. I'd never taken school classes on the weekend before, and I could feel the resistance of my internal calendar—a sense of wrongness—telling me I really shouldn't have to get up and do anything academic today.

Rachel stirred. I waved a silent "good morning" to her across the room, keeping quiet so I wouldn't wake Hannah. I felt like skipping as I crossed to the main building. And I was hungry. Despite my less-than-regular eating habits of recent days, truly feeling hungry was new. It was like recovering from a bad bout of the flu. I felt alive again.

The dining hall was nearly empty. A few people sat alone or in small groups over bagels, cereal, eggs, or coffee. Trevor wasn't here. I deflated as uncertainty crept over me. Was I really getting this worked up over a guy I'd just met? How would he feel about me this morning? Had I just imagined the incredible connection we'd shared?

Trevor!

He was coming from one of the smaller houses that served as a boy's dorm. *Is Maddie in the dining hall? I hope I can find her again. Did last night really happen? I want to be with her... to talk with her again. She's the most amazing person I've ever met.*

A zing of joy spiked through me while part of my mind did a little happy dance. All of my doubts puddled away. I left the dining hall and flew out to meet him at the outer door. I felt the double explosion of excitement and joy—his and my own. We both lit up like Vegas and smiled like fools.

Hi.

Hi.

We stood there, just looking at each other.

Beautiful. Trevor admired how the sunlight shone on my hair. He liked the point of my chin. My green eyes sparkled for him.

I'd never felt adored before. *Wow.*

My heart quickened. Trevor's eyes glowed with chocolate-brown warmth. Comb marks in his still-wet hair caught the sunlight. I drank in the planes of his cheeks, his straight nose, his strong jaw, the ridge of his forehead, his dark eyebrows. He seemed taller in daylight—definitely over six feet. I wanted to throw my arms around him. Instead, I just blushed.

Trevor noticed and he thought the color in my cheeks made me even prettier. He wanted to be closer to me. I reached out impulsively and took his hand, giddy at the little thrill that echoed from his mind.

Are you hungry?

I nodded. Then sudden concern chilled my gut and the smile fell off my face. *Are you sure you want to be seen with me in there?*

He knew what I meant—he'd be associated with one of the charms' least favorite people.

Yup. He didn't even hesitate. He gripped my hand more tightly as we walked back inside together.

How can he think he isn't brave?

The people in the dining room registered our connection with a few bursts of subdued curiosity. We both picked up bagels, cream cheese, and coffee from the breakfast spread in the kitchen. I followed him to his usual table.

Trevor's emotions brightly colored the energy that fluttered around him. The intensity of his own feelings scared him. *I'm going to come off all stalkerish if I don't hold back. I want to be with her. I can't be too clingy. I just met her. I'll drive her away if I take things too fast.* He dreaded being unwanted—rejected.

He'd forgotten, it seemed, that I'd hear this internal struggle. Or perhaps he just wasn't able to control it.

The lump in my throat made it hard to swallow, let alone talk. I had to remember to breathe. Wanting to buy a building for this guy suddenly didn't seem so excessive. His emotions were as overwhelming as mine. Could I make the first move? Should I tell him how I felt? What should I say?

We sat down across from one another and both occupied ourselves with spreading cream cheese on our bagels. If I showed him my own little nest of weirdness, clinginess, and vulnerability, would he still like me? What if I freaked him out? I took a bite of my bagel to buy time. It tasted like cardboard spread with cream cheese. I wasn't sure if that was because of my emotional state, or because most bagels outside of New York City's sphere of influence were pretty crappy. I took another bite, which still didn't answer the question.

Okay, enough procrastination. Trevor's emotional insecurity twisted him painfully. I could fix this. I could make him feel better. I took a deep breath. No guts, no glory.

You know I feel the same way, right?

The wave of emotions coming from Trevor hit me like a tsunami, making my heart thud in my ears. *You do?*

I nodded.

Really?

I suddenly realized what an unfair advantage I had in this situation. Trevor had no idea what I was actually thinking and feeling. Well, I could fix that, too. I looked into his eyes and sent him a burst of all of the tumultuous feelings from my own mind: the giddy tendrils of white energy that snaked through my gut; the joyful light that seemed to make everything brighter when he was around; and the warm, peaceful touch of his thoughts in my mind.

He inhaled sharply, his eyes wide. I pulled my emotions back, breathing fast as I clung to the warm brown of his eyes. Was that too much? Had I just come on too strong? Geez—we'd just met *yesterday*. That may have been *way* too strong.

I want to kiss her. I want to kiss her right now.

I'm not the swooning type, but right then I felt like swooning—big-time. I could see the silver-white energy crackling across our skins. We were all lit up with one another. Reaching across the table, Trevor took both of my hands in his. The energy danced across the connection between us, growing stronger. I felt the pricks of curiosity from several minds around us. The dining hall had filled up over the past few minutes. I hadn't noticed.

From a few feet behind me, Drew McFee's mind registered that his friend, Trevor, was holding hands with the new girl. He changed directions midstride and sat at a different table.

I didn't take my eyes from Trevor's. His arms were long enough that we could hold hands across the table without having to stretch. His fingers curled around mine and my heart somersaulted in my chest. I seemed to have forgotten to breathe.

Perhaps I should do that.

It felt anticlimactic to resume eating. I just wanted to stay in suspended animation with Trevor. *Trevor.* The name became an endearment. *Trevor.* I thought it at him again and watched his eyes dance.

Maddie. Beautiful Maddie.

I got another flip-flop in my gut. Wow. *I could get used to this.*

Me, too.

But then we'd starve to death.

His smile widened. *Maybe not.*

My half-eaten bagel lifted off my plate and hovered just to the side of my mouth, within reach of an easy bite. Trevor's did the same. With a gleeful, darting motion, he took a quick bite. His eyes never left mine.

I laughed aloud, delighted. Several people at surrounding tables startled at the sound. They looked at the two of us, hands clasped, silently communicating, with bagels hovering next to our faces. We looked ridiculous. I laughed again and shared the image with Trevor. He chuckled. Who cared what they thought? I tuned them out.

Tell me everything about you. I took what I hoped was a delicate bite from the bagel anchored in midair next to me.

There's not much to tell. What do you want to know?

Where are you from? How did you end up here? What do you like to do? I didn't add, *and how did you become this incredible person I can't stop thinking about?*

We found that the pauses that occur because people need to stop talking when they chew and swallow no longer slowed us down. We could eat, hold hands, and converse all at once.

I grew up in Michigan. Barton Hills. It's a little town just outside of Ann Arbor. He released my hands to hold up one of his own like a mitten and point to a spot near the bottom joint of his thumb. Oh, the hand was like a map. *Brothers and sisters?*

Trevor dropped his eyes and bit his lip. His mind had suddenly flushed with a grey, nebulous anxiety.

Did I just ask the wrong thing?

No. His eyes flashed up to mine again, filled with trepidation. *It's not you. I... I...* He stumbled over an emotional hurdle. It felt prickly-painful in his mind. *My grandparents raised me. Laurie— my... mother—had me when she was sixteen.* Trevor tried not to think about it, but his grandparents—

Oh. He felt like they hadn't wanted him. He felt ashamed for existing. In his mind, he was the result of the worst thing that had ever happened to his family. He had tried so hard to please them—to be good enough to belong—but he'd never felt worthy.

My fingers tightened on his. What could I say? How could I tell this guy I'd just met that he was probably the most wonderful person on the planet and his family were idiots if they made him feel unwanted?

Trevor watched my eyes closely, trying to gauge my reaction to the teen-mom thing. I wondered why he thought it would make a difference in how I felt. *I'm not going anywhere.* Was that reassuring enough?

Trevor closed his eyes and took a slow breath. The tight feeling in his chest eased. *So, yeah, I have two half-sisters. They're eight and six, but Laurie is more like a sister than a mother to me. Does that make sense?*

I nodded.

I've got another half-sister and brother on my father's side, but I've never met them. Something seemed to squeeze his heart. *I only met my father once—about four years ago. It was... awkward... and the weird stuff that happened didn't help.*

Weird stuff?

Trevor's lips twisted as he recalled the scene. *Yeah, things kept falling. It really freaked Jared out. He couldn't wait for me to get out of his office. He kept making comments about poltergeists.*

I saw the scene in Trevor's mind—felt the painful clumsiness of his gangly, thirteen-year-old self, out of place in an expensive Chicago office while his father, the stranger, considered his existence with disapproval. He cringed at the remembered crash of the painting falling off the wall and at the shatter of the glass award that had seemed to leap from the desktop.

Was that from your ability?

His smile didn't match his inner turbulence. *Yeah. When I was a kid, things always seemed to get knocked over around me, especially when I was nervous. I didn't know I was... I couldn't control it.*

That doesn't happen anymore, though.

Just in my sleep.

So you stay in the church at night.

For more than a year now. I felt his stomach give another guilty lurch at the memory of throwing his roommate. He regarded sleeping in the church as a form of penance.

But it gets so cold.

I just pile on a couple of extra sleeping bags. It's not so bad.

Yes it was. Trevor deserved so much better.

He reluctantly let go of my right hand and picked up his coffee.

Afraid you'll spill? I playfully tried to lighten his mood.

I ran out of hands.

You have two—

—mental hands, yes, he finished.

How does that work? Your ability, I mean.

Well, they've run a lot of tests—PET scans and stuff like that. I'm the only telekinetic here, so they are trying to figure me out. Trevor felt a little uncomfortable with this special status. He was being modest. I wanted to hug him—to curl up in his arms and never let go.

It looks like I use the same parts of my brain to control my ability that I use to control my regular hands.

The motor cortex?

How'd you know? Psych book? He'd shaken off the strain from revealing his past.

I nodded and grinned even more broadly. I felt a bit proud of knowing about the motor cortex—the part of the brain that controlled the movement of the muscles of the body. In fact, I felt ready to be a *Jeopardy!* contestant. Did Alex Trebek have the answers in front of him when he read the questions? I'd be unstoppable. I could pay for a new home for Trevor after only a day or two on the show.

I can… feel the things that I touch with my ability. He pictured two large, glowing, golden arms of light coming from his sides, his multi-limbed silhouette making him resemble one of the Hindu gods. *No hot, no cold, no pain, just… pressure—like I'm holding something in my hand. It works through walls, too, since it's an energy field. Solid matter doesn't block it, but it makes it harder. It's better if I can see what I'm doing.*

Neither of us noticed the bell ring, although suddenly everyone else in the dining hall was standing and gathering books. I reluctantly dragged my focus away from Trevor to dip into a few other minds and figure out what was happening. He glanced at his watch, surprised to see it was time for class.

Trevor's presence was like a cardio workout for my pounding heart. My cheeks hurt from smiling so much. He bussed our trays with telekinesis, trying to impress me. He didn't realize that my affinity for him had nothing to do with his ability. His inner self— his soul—drew me to him. Wrapping myself in his thoughts immersed me in joy.

I felt all sparkly inside as he took my hand again.

CHAPTER 8

Trevor was in my first class. Yay! Something inside me did a little happy dance. Trevor and I could continue our conversation during the lesson. Wait… did I actually just think that? Such counter-academic tendencies wouldn't have entered my mind in my old life. About twenty students filled the crowded, old living room of Blake House. Trevor and I took seats together in the back.

Crap.

My good mood deflated as I recognized charm after charm around me. Michael gave me a dark look and his mind spat steel-grey hatred at me.

They're all charms? I asked as the instructor began to lecture. A quick glance into the instructor's mind confirmed the material came directly from the book. Okay, this was going to be easy. I'd read this chapter last night. I kept facing forward with the outward appearance of paying attention to the class. If the teacher asked me a question, I figured I could just pull the answer out of his head. Was that cheating?

I think you'll have a lot of your classes with the charms. Trevor gave my hand a sympathetic squeeze. *Seth did when he was still taking courses. The stuff you'll need to learn as a minder is similar to what the charms learn. They just tossed me in here because they didn't know what else to teach me.*

Seth took classes?

Until last year.

That surprised me. I'd imagined him as older, in his late twenties or something. His mind had seemed world-weary, bossy, and cynical. *Why did he stop?*

He couldn't take the telepathic overload anymore. Just like Ann. Worry suddenly splashed sticky and yellow within him. Would I have the same problem? He tightened his grip on my hand.

Would I overload, too? I didn't feel like it would happen anytime soon. Trevor's mind buffered the rest of them. I didn't really notice other people's thoughts as much when he was next to me. Right now, a classroom of hostile charms surrounded me, but the harshness didn't grate on me as it had yesterday.

Trevor, even if I get to a point when I can't stand to be around the rest of this bunch, I indicated the charms with a dismissive glance, *I'll still want to be around you.*

Are you sure?

I gave him another mental pulse of the giddy-happy-wow thing I had for him. Out of the corner of my eye, I watched him blush. I gave his hand another squeeze while I pretended to take notes with the other. I still couldn't stop smiling.

My other morning class was a language elective: French, Spanish, or Mandarin. Trevor had thermodynamics, the physics class in which I'd first seen him. Separating from Trevor felt wrong—like taking off a couple of limbs and leaving them at the door. Was that normal? Probably not. I reluctantly headed back to the main building, following the herd.

The language courses met in four upstairs rooms and were filled with charms. Were the language lessons for cross-cultural mind control? Ugh. No surprise that Rachel had avoided this place on yesterday's tour.

Which class should I join? I'd taken two years of French and three of Spanish already, so I leaned toward one of those two. The hall emptied as the other students entered the different classrooms. I'd have to make a choice soon.

In the first room, Michael and some of his friends thought in what sounded like German. Yikes. For some reason, mind-control in German seemed even scarier to me than in English. *Ve haf veys of mekking you tok.*

Spanish seemed okay until one of the charms—whose name I remembered vaguely as Alex—caught sight of me in the doorway. He nudged his friend, Josh, next to him. They smiled maliciously at me as their minds both filled with the same pornographic image. Apparently, they'd worked out this particular torture last night, finding the most offensive picture on a dirty website and then imagining my face on it. I took a step back, feeling dark heat flower across my face. Alex and Josh laughed when they saw my reaction. Wrong move. My eyes narrowed as anger flowed blood-red through me.

Cut it out. Now! I reached out into their minds. Hey, I could focus my thoughts into two minds at once! Cool. *Or I'll mess with the parts of your brain that control your sex drives and make you fall in love with each other.*

The blanched looks of horror on their faces were priceless. I wished I had a camera. I'd even guessed right about their homophobia. Ha! Jerks. I didn't believe for a moment I could make good on my threat, but they didn't know that. Terror filled them both as the repulsive porn image fled their minds. They avoided looking at each other.

This could be fun.

Spanish it was. I took one of the empty seats with a smile.

Señora Lopez had obviously-dyed, red-gold hair and looked about sixty. She started in on the imperative case, listing verbs on the board. My head whipped around as one of the other students answered her first question with charm resonance in his voice. "¡Vaya!"

What was he doing? Charming the instructor? Ah, hell. He'd just sent Señora Lopez out of the room.

"¡Venga!" said the charm as the class dissolved into laughter.

As soon as she got back in the door, another charm called out "¡Vaya!"

There she went again.

"¡Venga!" called two others at the same time. Back she came.

Wait. No nasty intentions here. Señora Lopez had actually expected it. She'd been doing this for years. Apparently, she found that her charm students learned the imperative case best this way. It was more memorable for them.

I silently chuckled. Yes, this was how charms should be training! No one was being hurt here. Not all of the charms were sociopaths. They just needed more instructors like Señora Lopez and lessons like this that channeled their abilities constructively.

And maybe they just need someone to give them a good scare if they get out of line.

The charms got Señora Lopez to write, dance, sing, and eat. I wondered what she would've eaten if she hadn't had mints in her purse. After a few moments of compliance, someone would say "¡Pare!" to get her to stop. This happened especially quickly when she sang a few cringe-inducing bars of "Guantanamera." Music definitely wasn't one of her talents.

We weren't supposed to use our abilities on the instructors. Dr. Williamson had made that clear. But if the instructor was all right with it, there couldn't be too much harm, right? Besides, I'd pulled the correct answers out her mind when she'd called on me, so I wasn't completely innocent, either.

I rubbed my temples. Focusing was harder here; the minds of the other students jostled my thoughts more strongly now. But the Spanish class was actually kind of fun. I found I could tune out the people in the surrounding classes, at least when they were thinking in other languages.

Background noise.

By the end of Spanish, I felt better about most of the charms, and better about Ganzfield overall. I brightened further when I felt Trevor coming to the main building. Another flip-flop from the vicinity of my heart rocked through me. I took the stairs at a run and met him at the front door again. Was I eager? Oh, yeah.

We grabbed sandwiches and sat at the same table we'd occupied at breakfast. I looked into his warm brown eyes until I felt like I might fall in.

How was your class? He'd really taken to this telepathic communication thing well.

It was actually pretty good. I chose Spanish. How was thermodynamics?

Unnecessary. I can't do anything with fire.

As if summoned by his mention of burning objects, a smoldering ball of paper flew over Trevor's head and landed on his sandwich. Did the sparks have something like telekinesis over fire? The paper stopped smoking and opened flat in front of Trevor. It took me a second to realize he had opened it with his ability. The motion looked like it might be coming from the ball itself. After the strange things I'd seen in the past few days, I didn't rule out anything. Trevor read the message inside, grinned, and then asked me aloud, "Do you have a pen I could borrow?"

He turned the paper over and wrote a quick note. *A leftie.* The paper re-crumpled, lifted into the air, and gracefully landed two tables over. After reading the note, Drew McFee smiled up at us, waved, and yelled, "Sure, Maddie can come! Hi Maddie!" across the dining hall.

Trevor looked at me. *How much of that did you catch?*

Fireball? A cookout?

"Would you like to come with me?" Sudden tension sparked grey within him. Even though Trevor knew how much I liked him, asking me on our first date still gave him jitters of insecurity. A slow flush crept up toward his hairline.

Absolutely. I glowed inside. Trevor held out his right hand and I put my left in it. That would work; he was a leftie. We could both finish eating one-handed. I could manage half a sandwich that way.

It's so easy to be with you.

It just feels right. He grinned.

We'd pretty much skipped the uncertain little dance of emotions, the back-and-forth tango of "I think I like you—do you like me?" that two people did as they got to know each other. Trevor and I shared an instant connection. Okay, this part of telepathy—*awesome.*

Maddie… um… are you coming back to the church tonight?

Do you want me to?

A fervent *Yes!* conflicted with a worried *but I might hurt her* that flashed through his head. Another set of feelings—a deeper issue—also flickered within his thoughts. He was attracted to me. A crackly, scarlet energy hummed across his skin as the feeling grew. My heart pounded and something twisted within my core as a matching red energy flitted across me.

I leaned in closer to him but then stopped cold. Why did Trevor have a problem with being attracted to me? My chest tightened and the smile melted from my face. Was he holding back because of my nightmare? I didn't want him thinking about me as emotionally traumatized. *Just because I… after what happened in the van… I'm not… damaged.*

His eyes widened. "No!" *I don't see you that way. That's not… I mean… I'm the one with the issues here.*

Oh. He stressed about the romantic stuff because of his parents. Their impulsive behavior had resulted in his birth. He worried that he'd screw up his life the way he felt they'd screwed up theirs.

I thought for a moment. It's not like I wanted to rush into anything physical. I just… I wanted to be around Trevor—all the time. It wasn't about sex. Although the thought of kissing him—of Trevor touching me—made red energy sizzle through me, melting something deep and low within me. Wow. I should take a breath.

Calm down. Focus.

Think about something else. The church. Solve the problem with the church. *Do you think we could fix up that coatroom for me? Would that be okay? Then I'd be out of range of your ability.* And we wouldn't be sleeping together or anything…

He brightened. *Absolutely. You're brilliant!*

I smiled back at him for a moment, but then another thought hit me. *Oh, that won't work. My nightmares. I'll be out of your range, but you might not be out of mine.*

I don't mind.

I don't want to do that to you. The idea of causing Trevor pain made my appetite dissolve. I put down my sandwich.

"If you need me, I'll be there," he said aloud. "I want to be."

Even in my dreams? I could feel my smile creeping back.

Even in your dreams.

I started blissing at that, and a shiny feeling welled up within my chest.

Then a tall, slender blonde girl appeared next to Trevor.

"You don't like her anymore." Her voice carried a charm's resonance along with her Southern accent.

My heart fell into my gut. In Trevor's mind, I could feel his emotions deflate. He dropped my hand as the light left his eyes.

Something inside of me curled up and started wailing in agony. The girl, whose name was Gretchen, gave me the meanest smile I'd ever seen.

My soul turned stony and cold. In a flash, I was around the table and grabbing her arm, hard.

"Let go of me," she said in her charm voice. She wasn't worried—because she didn't know how much I was holding back to keep from killing her. I gripped her arm harder. Gretchen's bangs quivered around her face with the violent trembling coming through my hand. The dining hall had gone silent, watching us.

I really should stop eating lunch here.

I grabbed Gretchen's other arm and forced her face-to-face with me. *Don't kill her.* I forced myself to stay in control. *Don't kill her.* I really wanted to fry her, but I didn't want to be a monster. *Don't kill her.* My own nightmares and the thing in Spanish class with Alex and Josh had given me another idea.

Looking deep into Gretchen's mind was easy. She was so close and I had physical contact with her. Her eyes widened with the growing realization I hadn't obeyed her charm voice.

Boy, is she stupid.

I slammed open a door into her thoughts. *What's your worst memory?* She had no way to block the images that percolated up. When Gretchen was nine, she and her mother had come home early to find her father naked on the couch with a woman who lived down the street. *Devastation. Divorce. Pain.* Her family had been the subject of malicious gossip in their small Atlanta suburb for months.

Take back what you did to Trevor or I broadcast that to everyone here. Right now. I let that sink in for a moment until I was sure she understood the threat. Okay, she had it. I released one of her arms so she could face him.

"You like her again." Gretchen's weak voice didn't carry the full charm resonance.

Louder. I gave her arm a little shake. She was taller than I was, but she had the upper body weakness that comes with waif-like thinness. Both muscle tone and rage were on my side.

"You like her again."

I felt Trevor's emotions surge back—filling him and washing over to me.

I kept my voice low and controlled. "Apologize to him." To reinforce it, I flashed her a sharp little image of dad and the neighbor lady.

She choked back tears. "I'm sorry."

"You will *never* use your charm ability on Trevor Laurence again." My voice was still low, barely above a whisper. "Do you understand?" Gretchen nodded and I released her arm. I might have left a bruise. I kind of I hoped I had.

The other charms watched, wide-eyed and slack-jawed. I could see myself though their eyes, red-faced and enraged.

Psycho!

Okay, don't mess with Trevor Laurence when she's around.

What a bitch.

Trevor touched my arm. "Do you want to get out of here?" he asked gently.

I nodded. The part inside of me that'd been wailing in agony curled up in a fetal position and quietly whimpered.

Outside, we walked behind the main building. Not touching. Not speaking. The tall grass brushed against our legs with a swishing sound with each step, and the wind coming off the lake traced cool fingers against my hot face. My hands still clenched in tight fists. I felt like I might throw up.

Trevor was less shocked than he probably should've been. I'd really gone over the edge just now, and he'd seen the whole thing up close. But in his mind, my actions in the dining hall were like his own in our shared dream—protective, not psycho. *I don't like it. I know she's immune to charms, but… No. She shouldn't have to do my fighting for me. I want to take care of her, not the other way around.* He thought I'd been brave.

But I hadn't felt brave. I'd been furious.

I began to shake uncontrollably and my legs threatened to let me fall. Trevor put his arms around me and pulled me close. I buried my face against his chest and unsuccessfully tried to will myself calm. Trevor's embrace felt warm against the autumn air. I closed my eyes and wrapped my arms around his waist.

We stood there, holding each other, breathing in and out. Eventually, my racing heart slowed and I stopped trembling. I gave him a squeeze as I stepped back and met his eyes. I searched his mind and his face simultaneously. Did he still feel the same way about me as he had before the thing with Gretchen? Had her command changed what we shared? Had my actions messed everything up?

Trevor wasn't a telepath, but something in my face let him know I needed reassurance. He slid his hands up to my cheeks and gazed into my eyes. He wanted to comfort me, to take my pain away. *Oh, my.* Tingling energy flowed across my skin, leaving a trail of goosebumps that had nothing to do with the cool air.

I felt another strong impulse to kiss him as I drifted into the chocolate warmth of those beautiful eyes. The world around us seemed to dim and fall away. I forgot how to breathe.

"There you guys are! That was awesome!" Drew McFee—with none of the tact he'd shown at breakfast—hurried toward us. The intensity that had flared up between Trevor and me dialed back to a simmer. We broke eye contact and I took a ragged breath. *Wow.* I felt dizzy.

Trevor also felt dazed. *What was that?*

Drew was nearly glowing. "Damn, Maddie! You're not even here two days and you've smacked down two of the nastiest charms in Ganzfield! You... Are... The... Queen!" Between my new connection to his best friend and my "smack-down" of two of the most dreaded charms, my stock was pretty high with Drew.

I didn't feel particularly royal at the moment, although Drew's high spirits did make me feel a little better. If I'd done something like that in most high schools, it would've been social suicide. Apparently, at Ganzfield, my loss of temper had actually improved my social standing. Man, this place was so messed up.

Drew continued on past us, heading toward the ugly little cinderblock buildings by the lake. His thoughts centered on a missing textbook. *Maybe it's the charred, black thing on the floor under my bed.*

"Glad you're coming to Fireball later. See ya!" he called, jogging backward for a few paces so he could wave at us.

We saw the exodus from the dining hall and suddenly recalled that, yes, there were still classes, and yes, we were still expected to attend them. As we started walking back in that direction, Trevor tentatively put his arm around my shoulders. I leaned in and wrapped one of mine around his waist. It was a natural fit. Comfortable.

Perfect.

Throughout my afternoon English and calculus classes, I kept touching Trevor's mind telepathically. I needed the reassurance of our connection. I still felt grey and nauseous when I recalled Trevor's reaction to Gretchen's charm-voice—how his mind had gone emotionally blank. Even two rooms away, his thoughts stood out for me—like hearing a distinctive voice in a crowd.

I tried, but I couldn't direct a specific thought to him. I just couldn't focus well enough. I could read his thoughts, though. Trevor was still upset. I kept getting remembered flashes from him of the way Gretchen had manipulated him. Her words had made him feel numb and apathetic—dead inside. It scared him how easily she could take his feelings away.

It scares me, too.

I felt like a telepathic stalker, peeping into his brain like this. I no longer had any issue with Rachel's golden thread to Sean. I understood her now.

Rachel sat next to me in class. *Maddie took down another charm! I'm so glad we're roommates. Is she going to protect all of us from them?*

I considered it for a moment. Yeah, I could do that. Fine with me. Okay, I guess there's a new sheriff in town. Maybe next time I wouldn't get so crazy-intense. I'd gone off the charts when Trevor was targeted. Would I have done that with someone else?

Doubtful.

Maybe I can get Maddie to invite me to the Fireball cookout. Sean will be there. I shook my head slightly. Nope—tough luck. I wasn't going to bring her along on my first date with Trevor.

Rachel's ulterior motives got me thinking: was there a basis of self-interest to most relationships? Was there one between Trevor and me? I remembered hearing that love develops out of how the other person makes us feel. I looked into my own soul. Was I just being selfish in my desire to be with Trevor? He was so kind, generous, and amazing. Being with him made something shimmer and glow within me. I bit my lip and sighed. He deserved someone better than me.

The pressing thoughts of the other people around me seemed to confirm the direction my own musings. There was a lot of daydreaming and fantasizing going on. The huge amount of sex-on-the-brain wasn't too surprising in a building full of horny adolescents. Some were romantic; others were impersonal or even downright nasty. But it was all about what *they* wanted. Was anyone thinking about someone else's best interest? Of helping the person they cared about? Of making another person happy? Were most people fundamentally selfish? I started a survey of the minds I could touch, tallying the results in the corner of my notebook. The final results showed nineteen people thinking about the course material. Fortunately, that included the three instructors. *Good thing I hadn't peeping-tommed sex fantasies from them. Ick.* Thirteen people—mostly girls—filled their minds with romance. More than one wanted a prince-charming-type to sweep them up in his arms and take them away from this dead-boring calculus class.

Okay, I really couldn't blame them for that.

The remaining twenty-one filled their fantasies their own selfish gratification—usually sexual—although two people were hungry and their daydreams centered around food. Maybe I should put them in another category.

I couldn't shut any of their thoughts out. My little poll had made things worse. Now I felt all judgmental and cynical. I'd plummeted into a full-fledged funk by the end of class. I scowled down at my desk as the people around me gathered up their books and headed out.

Maddie? Trevor silently called me.

In here. I flashed him an image to show where "here" was.

Trevor looked me over for a moment and sized up my mood. *What can I do to cheer her up?*

Just feeling his thoughts and emotions so close again was like a shot of morphine to my bad mood. The clatter of all of those other people was no longer between us. Light seemed to pour back into the world—Trevor was here. I exhaled, feeling the crinkly, itchy, mustard-yellow anxiety flowing out of me.

Sorry. I was feeling a bit grumpy. I think I'm better now. I wanted to be closer to him. I wanted to kiss him. The impulse took my breath away.

"Can I carry your books for you?" They floated unsupported about a foot off my desk, bobbing slightly as though they were doing a little dance. I smiled.

Trevor wanted to cheer me up and I decided to let that happen. Since our hands were free, I took one of his in mine, feeling the mental connection strengthen between us as I did. *Warm. Right. Wonderful.* Upstairs, he parked the books on my bed. I grabbed my heavy coat; it was going to get cold after the sun went down. Excitement coursed through me. *A date with Trevor!* I was too eager to be nervous.

We wandered down to the lakeside together. Bright fall colors dappled the tree-covered hills surrounding the valley. Sunlight bounced off the lake, which rippled in the slight breeze. Trevor's strong fingers twined with mine. The habitual way he moved—slightly self-conscious and shy, like he didn't want to impose his nearness on others—made me want to pull him close and fill him with my adoration until he was comfortable in his own skin. I settled for chafing my thumb across the back of his hand.

We were a bit early; they were still setting up. Drew's bright mental burst of recognition made me turn a second before he called, "Trevor! Maddie!" in greeting. "Cheerful" seemed to be his default setting and his energy was infectious. Trevor and I changed course to join him in front of a huge pile of wood, one of several in the area. Despite the chill, Drew wore a vintage t-shirt that featured a bear in a hat that read, "Only YOU Can Prevent Forest Fires." He and Trevor were about the same height—both a bit over six feet, I guessed. However, Trevor was long and lean compared to Drew's bulk.

"I'm setting up the fire now," he said. Drew focused on logs in front of him. I felt the electric tingle in his mind as a tentacle of invisible flame caught the edges of several logs. The impact came through the soles of my feet as the huge pieces of wood crashed down from the top of the pile and began rolling toward the beach. Drew shepherded them from the side, his hand twitching as he used his ability to grab the burning portions and adjust their direction.

When flaming logs start rolling toward them, people clear out of the way fast. At the beach, Drew stacked the logs into a cone in the firepit. The wood smoked as he fiddled with the structure.

Two girls joined us as Drew put the finishing touches on his project. One was red-haired with freckles—big-boned and friendly-faced. She looked enough like Drew to be his sister. The other girl was African-American—tall and rail-thin with prominent, angular cheekbones. Trevor introduced me to them. They were Ellen McFee, Drew's cousin, and Katie Underwood. Both were sparks.

"How's it look?" Drew asked his assembled audience.

"You call that a fire?" teased Ellen.

"Hey, things burn when I tell 'em to burn," Drew grinned.

Trevor's quiet concern floated through me. *How's Maddie taking this? I hope she likes my friends. Do they like her? Are they comfortable hanging out with a minder?*

I caught his eye and smiled. *They're as nice as you think they are.*

Trevor had again forgotten that his thoughts were open to me. His quick startle was a little chagrinned; then he smiled back. *Good.* He gave my hand a squeeze.

Metal benches and folding chairs formed a circle around the firepit. Drew fussed with the logs—flaring up the flames in one place, tamping them down in another. For sparks, bonfires were works of art. While Drew muttered to himself and manipulated the flames, Trevor went in search of sodas for us.

"You're Drew's cousin, right?" I asked Ellen. "Are most of the sparks related?"

Ellen laughed and Katie gave a strained, closed-mouth smile.

"There are two families of sparks," she explained, "and you're looking at us." She gestured to herself and Katie. "The McFees and the Underwoods. The McFees are all first or second cousins. The lot of us are descended from old Sean McFee. Four generations of Irish firefighters," she said. I liked talking to Ellen. Her thoughts felt like they bounced: friendly and energetic.

"Before we started dodecamine," she continued, "we were just good at knowing fire—what it was going to do and how to stop it. Now…" she snapped her fingers. A bright yellow flame suddenly popped up, and then wisped into smoke. "We can start it, stop it, move it, whatever. If it burns, it's ours."

Ellen gestured to her friend. "Katie's great-great-grandfather was the famous William Underwood, the first known pyrokinetic. Most people think he was a fake." She guffawed at this. "But we know better." She gave Katie a one-armed hug, bringing their heads together. "Can't you see the family resemblance?" She laughed again.

The two could not have been more different. Coloring, body type, and other physical differences aside, the two just "felt" completely different. Katie's mind felt cool and reserved. A cool fire-starter. How ironic.

Oh. A lump formed in my gut. Katie wasn't usually this cold and shy with most people. Being near a minder made her uncomfortable. She worried that she was going to think something embarrassing, private, or rude. She thought the words *nothing, blank, empty, nothing* over and over, keeping other stuff from percolating up in her mind. Katie took the first opportunity to move across the circle to talk with someone else.

"She's a little freaked out by me," I said quietly in response to Ellen's unspoken *where is she going?* Indignation flashed sharply through her. Ellen believed that people who could start fires with a glance should be a little more tolerant of other people's differences. I stopped her before she confronted Katie and her prejudices.

"It wouldn't help right now," I said. Katie would resent it. "Give her a little while." To distract Ellen from her sudden zeal for minder-equality, I asked, "Can you give me a tour?"

The sparks' cinderblock buildings were even uglier up close. The sparks seemed separate from the rest of Ganzfield since they didn't sleep in the wood-framed dorms, for obvious safety reasons. Each squat little house contained one main room with two windows, twin beds, and a fireplace. All of the fixtures were metal: the door to the tiny bathroom; the roof; the light fixtures suspended from the ceiling; the window and bed frames. Only the bedding and mattresses were fabric.

"All cotton," explained Ellen. "If they catch fire, they burn instead of melting like synthetics. Synthetics melt into the skin. The burn is much worse." Lockers held their clothing, books, and other combustibles away from the buildings.

"Sparks start fires accidentally all the time. If we're awake, it's no problem; we just think them out. Most of the time, they flare less than the average match. Often, they're just a warm spot before we feel them and kill them. When we're sleeping, though, things can get out of hand."

I remembered Harrison's burns and suppressed a shudder. I could still feel the echo of his pain in my mind. I nodded.

"We use the fireplaces for heat," Ellen said. "It's easier for us to think the flames higher when it gets cold than to adjust a thermostat. It's good practice, too." Now the large supply of wood made sense.

I felt Trevor's mind as a warm, mental caress. My eyes closed for a moment and I smiled. "Trevor's coming back." The happy skip in my heart must have come through in my voice. Ellen gave me a long, appraising look. She wondered whether I would be good for Trevor, whom she thought of as a brother and an honorary spark.

"I'm going to try to be good enough for him," I said, startling her. Why did people keep forgetting that I knew what they were thinking? Maybe it was because the other minders didn't socialize.

"I really don't know what he sees in me," I said, wondering why I was confiding in a person I'd just met.

Ellen smiled. "I think I do." I blushed. Ellen also saw me as brave. She didn't know all the bad stuff I could do.

We returned to the firepit just as Trevor arrived. A washtub full of ice and sodas floated in front of him. When he'd gone to get us sodas, I'd expected him to return with a can in each hand. Instead, he had hauled several dozen drinks all the way across the field. I felt a primal thrill at his strength then smirked at myself. Geez! Why didn't I just put my hair in a ponytail so he'd have a convenient handle to drag me back to his cave?

"Does it tire you out?" I asked him, once he'd set the tub down. Just being next to him filled me with a fluttery excitement, and a little red tingle darted across my skin. Trevor grinned and reached for my hand.

"I'm not feeling tired," he said. We got stuck staring into each other's eyes again. Trevor's soul seemed to pull at me and I felt the world around us dimming.

At that moment, Drew's fire sent up a mushroom cloud of flame, drawing "oohs" of appreciation from the assembled onlookers. It also startled us back to reality. As I tried to remember how to breathe, I noticed that the crowd had grown to about thirty people.

The sun sets early at this time of year in New Hampshire, but it takes a good long while to actually do it; the sky still held a wide swath of pale blue over the mountains. The faces around the fire glowed with the warm, yellow-gold colors of the flames, contrasting with the surrounding purple-tinged gloom.

Most of the people I saw in the firelight now looked somewhat familiar, although that may have been partly due to family resemblance. More than a dozen McFees clustered in happy conversations, including three new arrivals who seemed older than the rest of us. They stood out in the strange way that college kids at a high school party do as they hung back and spoke with Matilda and Morris Taylor, the other grown-ups.

By popular acclaim, two of the Underwoods clearly cooked the best burgers, which they did by setting raw meat patties in frying pans and thinking flames at them. Several other sparks watched them do this with the intensity of avid sports fans.

A hesitant new arrival at the end of dinner caused a wave of startled thoughts. People greeted Ann like someone returning from a battle with cancer—with sympathy and things left unsaid.

—couldn't stand being a minder anymore—

—only family Williamson has left. He raised her after his brother was killed—

—overloaded all the time—

—alone in her cabin for months—

Ann's bronze complexion was much fairer than Dr. Williamson's, suggesting mixed-race parentage. At least half a foot taller than me, she was strikingly pretty—like a model—with high cheekbones and hazel eyes.

Why is everyone walking on eggshells around her? I asked Trevor.

Trevor didn't want to tell me. *She's leaving.*

She's a minder?

She was, but she's not active anymore. Ann refused her last shot of dodecamine. She's been waiting for the effects to wear off. This is the first time she's been around other people in months. He told me this reluctantly, worried that a similar life of unhappy isolation might be in my future.

Ann's face and thoughts lit up as she caught sight of Trevor. She waved and began to make her way around the circle toward us. What the hell was this model-pretty girl doing waving at

Trevor like that? A growling feeling started low in my gut. It made me want to grab Ann by the shoulders and shove her into the lake.

Whoa. Where had that come from? I needed to chill.

I focused on Ann's mind. How interested was she in Trevor? Was my reaction *completely* inappropriate or just *way* too strong? Ann wasn't picking up many thoughts from other people. The ones she sensed were the faint, indistinct rattling of echoes in a distant hallway. Tonight had been a test—she could no longer hear other people's minds. Ann's relief flowed through her like clear water. Her eagerness to leave Ganzfield grew brighter as she reveled in the silence in her head.

I decided to play nice. I greeted her with a bright mental *hi* when she worked her way around the circle to us. Ann paled, horrified she was picking up other people's thoughts again.

Bad Maddie. Mean. No biscuit. "Sorry," I said. I really meant it, too. At least, I meant it once I realized she didn't have romantic notions toward Trevor—platonic affection only.

Urge to kill: fading.

I felt the need to make up for my earlier negative thoughts about her. A sad gentleness filled Ann, as though her mind was delicate porcelain. Hearing the harsh things other people thought all the time must've been hard for someone like her. Despite my unanswered questions about telepathy, I really didn't have much to ask her. She was leaving. The amazing potential of our ability wasn't enough to keep her here. She couldn't show me how to use it better. What she knew wasn't good enough.

The crowd moved away from Drew's fire as the players set up for the game. Trevor found us seats on the metal benches that lined the Fireball field. I started shivering after only a minute on the cold metal. Invisible arms wrapped around me, shielding me from the cool evening air. I leaned closer to Trevor, thrilled at the silent joy that my nearness gave him. Warmth grew between us, flushing us both pink.

Fireball at night cast a spell of beauty and drama over the field. Tonight, the families played as teams—Underwoods versus McFees. Nearly all of the sparks played at some point, with four players for each team on the field at a time. The ball lit up the immediate area around it, casting the players into sharp, golden relief against their long, dancing shadows. Beads of sweat caught the light like jewels. The ball of flame jumped in the air, changing direction as though bouncing off of invisible walls. Sometimes it held, quivering in place. Other times it soared like a comet. Dark afterimages filled my eyes.

This part of Ganzfield was great. Could this feeling of community be expanded and shared with the rest? It would probably be easy enough to bring in the RVs, and Hannah was one of only two student healers. Matilda and Morris were already here, enjoying the game and healing the burns. Spanish classes with the charms had gotten me thinking about their role here. Some of them—no, most of them—might find this an improvement. Perhaps the people here had learned to endure a situation that could be better. Maybe I could do something to change it.

After the game, the party started breaking up. At a glimpse of Ann hugging Matilda goodbye, a sudden thought flashed through me. I was halfway to Seth's home already. Could he hear me? *Seth? Seth!* I focused hard, sending my thoughts out into the night in the direction of his cabin across the lake. I had no idea if I was close enough.

What?

His dim mental voice still conveyed his customary annoyance, but I was far enough away that I wasn't causing him any pain.

Don't raise a search party or anything. I won't be at bedcheck tonight.

Yeah, you will.

No, I won't.

Why not?

I decided to go with the original reason; it was true enough. *Nightmares.*

Nightmares?

I had a nightmare last night and gave it to half the other girls in the dorm.

You're projecting nightmares?

Yeah.

That sucks. He actually seemed sympathetic. Maybe he could relate. *You got a place to go?*

Yeah.

I guess it's okay, then.

G'night. I was ready to end the conversation before he asked anything more. I wasn't certain, given the "regular rules don't apply" aspect of Ganzfield, but I suspected underage couples sharing a room might not meet with approval.

G'night. He seemed almost civil. I barely recognized his thoughts.

Trevor's anxiety tingled against my mind. I realized I had my eyes scrunched shut in concentration and the hand he wasn't holding had tensed into a half-raised fist.

"Huh?" It seemed he'd spoken.

"I said, are you okay?" He was worried that I was overloading like Ann and Seth. Was it only a matter of time?

I'm fine. Don't worry. I'm not overloading. It was true. The thoughts of the surrounding people had been like crowd noise. It was there and it was annoying, but I could still think of other things. I'd been able to tune it out, to a degree. I felt his skepticism. *Really. I'm okay. Better than okay. I'm with you.*

His joy shot through me, little fizzing zaps of spring green. Sensing Technicolor emotion like this was kinda trippy—in a good way, though.

Ready to go? he asked.

Ready.

He pulled a small, pen-sized flashlight out of his jacket pocket and lit the path along the shoreline for us. We turned onto the same trail I'd taken when I'd felt the bird fly. The sky still held a narrow band of pale blue in the west, and light from the newly-risen moon turned the trunks of the trees silver. The leaves overhead glowed with washed-out moonlight, outlining the veins within them.

My hand was still in Trevor's, his fingers strong and sure as he guided me through the darkness. As we moved away from the sparks, the noise in my head faded and was replaced by an increased awareness of Trevor. His thoughts and feelings twined with mine.

Joy.

An exuberant happiness glowed pale green within him. *Maddie's really here right now. What does she see in me? She's so beautiful and vibrant and amazing. It's like there are new colors in the world when she's around.*

Oh, my.

Distracted, I tripped on a tree root and started to fall. Invisible hands caught me instantly. Trevor held me suspended for a second, and then gently set me upright. I couldn't see him—just the cone of light from the flashlight—but I could feel him close to me in the dark, an electric awareness. His face was very close to mine.

"Are you all right?" His voice was a near whisper. My free hand was on his chest; I could feel his heart beating wildly under my palm. My breath quickened, and suddenly his lips were touching mine. My soul expanded with explosive intensity. My hands went around his neck, pulling him in. His arms tightened around me. My lips parted and his moved against them— tentatively, and then stronger.

Wonderful. Wonderful. Wonderful.

I wasn't sure who was thinking it, probably because we both were.

I woke up in the pitch-dark. It took me a moment to remember that I was in the coatroom of the old church. Trevor and I had lain awake for a while last night, mentally conversing across the chasm between the two rooms.

I melted as I recalled how his lips had felt on mine—those incredible kisses in the woods. *Wow.* Red energy crackled over my skin in a delicious shiver. Okay, the separate rooms thing was probably a good idea. After all, we'd just met, what… a couple of days ago? It didn't feel like it. We already knew each other so well.

Trevor's thoughts came into focus as he started to dream. While I couldn't hear deep sleep, REM sleep must be close enough to normal consciousness to be readable for me. Trevor's dream combined a surreal mishmash of old and new memories. A gawky, pre-teen Trevor overheard Laurie, his mother, tell a friend she should have had an abortion. A deep, sad ache hit him in the chest like the thrust of a sword. *Unwanted.* A much younger Trevor watched the embarrassment in his grandfather's face as he explained that Trevor was Laurie's son. Trevor lay alone in the church the first night after he'd injured his roommate, sick with guilt, not knowing if Reed would recover. Trevor kissed me again in the dark, but something pulled me away and I vanished into the night, lost to him.

I tried to push into his dream—to become a part of it the way he had been in mine. I couldn't do it. Why couldn't I just jump into his dream? Stupid limitations.

I slid out of the sleeping bag in an instant. My hands moved along the unseen wall until I found one of the inner doors and I pushed into the sanctuary. The old wooden floor felt icy beneath my sock-clad feet, although I still had on the rest of my warm clothing.

A few steps in and I yelped in surprise as invisible hands lifted me, pulling me toward Trevor. I suddenly found myself sprawled face-to-chest across his sleeping bag as most of the air whooshed from me in a graceless "oof." I wasn't hurt, but it took a few seconds to get my lungs to work again.

Trevor floated in that confused state between dreaming and waking. I felt his arms tighten around me as his mind registered that I was real. The anxiety of his dream faded as he pulled me close. I relaxed into his embrace and tried to catch my breath.

"What are you doing in here?" he asked, pressing his cheek against my hair as he pulled me even closer.

Your dream.

He tensed with embarrassment.

I pulled myself closer to him. *You needed to find me. I came.*

His arms tightened around me. Knowing I'd seen his dreams made him feel extremely vulnerable. Fear trilled through him, cold and grey. I was privy to his innermost insecurities. Exposed—his mind was naked to me.

My heart thudded against my ribs. Could I make this okay? I sent him a long, slow pulse of emotion—my adoration for him—warm, tingly, and filled with longing. I didn't hold back. After all, I'd seen his bare emotions. He deserved the same from me. He deserved to feel cherished, too.

Trevor's breathing turned harsh and ragged. Silver light flowed over us both. The physical closeness began to register on another level as well, and the energy shaded red and tingly.

Oh, wow.

At the same moment, we both thought about kissing the other… then we both had concerns about morning breath.

Maybe we should keep some mints around here.

He chuckled aloud at my thought, gave me a squeeze, and rolled us both up to sit.

We opened the church's outer door to leave. Ugh. A cold, grey rain fell outside, sucking the warmth from everything.

Do you have an umbrella?

Never use one. He grinned wide. I barely had a moment to register his intentions before he swung me up in his arms—Rhett Butler-style—and strode out the door, pulling it shut behind him with his foot. Above our heads, the rain rolled to either side, leaving us untouched. Trevor's invisible arms pressed wide to cover us and the rain sheeted off in tiny rivers. I tightened my arms around Trevor's neck and snuggled my head into his shoulder.

The *Gone with the Wind* theme played through my head. I shared it with Trevor and I felt the low, gentle rumble of his laugh all the way to my toes.

Trevor deposited me on the covered porch of Blake House. No one had seen us arrive; the grey weather and lack of scheduled classes on Sunday morning kept most people sleeping in.

Brunch? We were very close on the porch, leaning into each other, reluctant to break apart.

I nodded.

Do you have plans for the day?

I hoped I could spend it with you.

His mind gave a little leap of joy that bounced back into me. His smile grew even wider, making little crinkles around his eyes.

Okay, I knew what I needed to do. I was going to make Trevor feel cherished. If I could do that, if I could drive away those feelings of being unwanted, maybe I'd almost be worthy of him. There would be no coyness or holding back with him—no playing hard-to-get.

Do you have a laptop?

I nodded.

Could you bring it, and maybe some of your books? We could have a study date.

It wasn't what I'd been expecting, although I really didn't know what I thought we would do. Were we even allowed to leave Ganzfield? I hadn't thought to ask, but I'd gotten the impression that it wasn't considered safe. A study-date was actually a practical idea, since I needed to read up for my classes. Trevor was also trying put something else about our study date into words.

What's "lyric dreaming?"

His forehead furrowed in frustration. *It's not lyric dreaming, but it's something like that. "Lyric dreaming?" "Locus dreaming?"* He shook his head, trying to focus. *Whatever it's called, it's something I wanted to research, if you're up for it.*

Sure! We were going to spend the day together. I'd conjugate Spanish verbs and fill out calculus problem sets all day if it meant spending time with Trevor. I met his eyes and the dancing light within them took my breath away. Yeah, something told me today would be less "study," more "date."

CHAPTER 9

Apparently, Ganzfield's Sunday brunch was a big deal. The kitchen staff had prepared a fancy spread with trays of eggs, sausages, pancakes, and waffles. The salad bar overflowed with fresh fruit. There was even apple pie with cheddar cheese on it… for breakfast… ugh. Must be a New Hampshire thing. It seemed wrong on so many levels.

I parked myself by the window in the front room of the main building to wait. A large bag held my laptop and two textbooks. My umbrella dripped lightly where I'd left it, leaning with a few others out on the porch. Now that I knew about the alternative, umbrellas seemed *so* obsolete.

I felt more presentable since I'd showered, changed, and brushed my teeth. My hair was a disappointment, though. It hung limp in the humidity.

Awareness of Trevor's mind sparkled within me as he approached. I jumped up to meet him. He didn't seem to think there was anything wrong with my hair. He lit up both inside and out when he caught sight of me in the doorway. His forest green wool sweater looked great with his eyes. Maybe I was biased, but pretty much everything seemed to look great with his eyes.

In the dining hall, I loaded up my plate with fruit, feeling healthy and righteous. Trevor grabbed a large helping of pancakes, which he smothered with butter and maple syrup. He burned off a ton of calories with the energy field he created. No wonder he was so lean; he needed more calories each day than most professional athletes.

We sat and ate at what I now considered "our" table. Looking into Trevor's eyes, I kept forgetting we were in public. Other people's thoughts faded away when Trevor was around. I only flicked back to awareness when someone thought one of our names.

—like the new minder's hypnotizing Trevor, or they're—

—creepy the way they just stare at each other then suddenly laugh or smile, like they're—

—making me lose my appetite. What does he see in that bi—

Right now, I didn't care what anyone else thought.

The meal passed without any problems. Apparently, brunch was different enough from lunch that I could eat in the dining hall without having to fend off charm attacks. After we finished, Trevor led me upstairs to the library. Over-full bookcases lined the walls, spilling their contents onto the windowsills and tabletops. A beige couch and three matching armchairs formed a conversation circle in the center of the room.

Almost no one ever actually comes here. Trevor felt the pleasure of sharing a secret with me.

But you do.

I spent a lot of time in here last winter when the church got too cold. A pang of his former loneliness touched him.

Nope. That wasn't allowed anymore. I wanted to kiss it away, so I did.

The doubly-electric jolt from my mind mixed with his intoxicated me. Red energy crackled around us and my heart fluttered as though it'd grown wings. My fingers twined in his hair. I inhaled the clean scent of him around me. Trevor's lips held the phantom sweetness of maple syrup. Invisible arms encircled my waist and lifted me gently, pulling me closer. I floated several inches off the floor in his double embrace.

"Oh!" A mousy little RV ducked into the library, her thoughts showing an interest in finding a good historical romance. Our timeless little bubble popped and we were back in the world again. We'd been so wrapped in each other that I hadn't heard her approach, but now her embarrassment pressed into me.

We broke apart and Trevor set me back on my feet.

Wow.

My knees were weak. I staggered and nearly fell, but invisible hands caught me, guiding me onto the couch. My breath came in ragged gulps. Trevor sat at the other end of the couch and his face held the same expression of stunned giddiness that I'm sure mine did. He tried to calm his body down. I flushed pink when I recognized the physical effect I'd had on him.

The little RV grabbed blindly at the first book on the shelf and quickly scuttled out.

Have you ever felt anything like this before?

Trevor shook his head, giving me a shaky grin. *Not even close.*

I marveled at our connection. *It's like a runaway train. No unclear intentions or misunderstandings to slow us down.*

Yup. Full throttle.

I made a halfhearted effort to pull myself together. I felt delightfully mussed. *So... I wanted to give us both a chance to regain control of ourselves. What's this "L" dreaming you mentioned?*

"Lucid dreaming!" he said aloud with happy relief as the right term finally came to him. I handed him my laptop and he did a web search.

"I was thinking..." he said, typing. "If we're going to share dreams..." More typing. "...maybe we could do something more fun than revisiting our childhood traumas."

I pulled in closer to him and read over his shoulder that, "lucid dreaming is a state in which a person knows he or she is dreaming and therefore has control over the content of the dream."

I loved this idea.

The technique involved "reality testing" in the dream. Basically, we should just keep checking if things are real. If they weren't, then we were dreaming and we could just wish things to happen, and they would. I laughed out loud.

Okay. Reality. I'm reading your mind and you're moving things without touching them. Yeah, reality. That'll clear things right up. He chuckled, which sent silvery shivers of delight through me. Oh, I loved that sound. I wished I could bottle it.

Trevor's hands flashed across the keyboard. Like many lefties, he was a fast typer. *What do you think? Aruba? Paris? Safari in Kenya?* He rapidly brought up several websites for exotic, expensive resorts. Hey, if it was imaginary, I supposed we could pull out all the stops.

I leaned against his shoulder as I looked at the screen. *I've always wanted to go to the Caribbean. Somewhere sunny and warm.*

We scanned pictures from a five-star resort: empty, sugar-white beaches and impossibly blue water.

Perfect, he thought. *Okay, next time we share a dream, let's see if we can just open a door into this place.*

Brilliant. I love you.

Oh my God—did I just think that at him?

Trevor had gone still, his hands frozen halfway above the keyboard. The computer slid off to the side, guided without a physical touch to the floor. Trevor's entire body vibrated with tension and he avoided my eyes.

Oh, crap. Those were *not* idle words to him.

Stupid, stupid, stupid!

Had I just messed everything up? Why had I put *those words* out there? I looked within myself. Oh my God. I hadn't just said it—I'd *meant* it. I had absolutely meant it. I knew him. Anyone who could see what I could of Trevor's soul couldn't help but fall in love with him.

I love him.

Trevor had forgotten to breathe. When he suddenly remembered, his breath caught roughly. *Why would she say that? Did she mean it? Why would she love someone like me?* His eyes flicked back up and caught mine. The intensity of his thoughts roiled like magma inside his head. The energy within Trevor flared with shifting colors. Bright green joy. *She's so amazing. She's wonderful.* Grey fear and unworthiness. *She can't mean it. She just said that the way people say they love a song or something.* Something began to glow silver-white. *But I think I'm falling in love with her.* He shook his head. *No, I've already fallen in love with her…*

He felt it, too?

Oh, thank heavens.

Suddenly I could breathe again, although I hadn't realized I'd stopped. I moved closer, placed my hand on Trevor's chest, and looked deeper into his eyes. I could do this. It was easier for me to put myself out there because now I knew how he felt.

"Trevor, I love you," I said aloud.

Pale silver energy flared over his entire frame. Trevor opened and closed his mouth twice. Finally, the power of speech returned to him. "I love you, too," he whispered hoarsely. His lips found mine as energy flowed strongly between us.

He pulled back to look at me—to read this new development in my face. His hand caressed my cheek reverently. He floated in a dreamlike confusion. *Can this really be happening?*

I grinned. *Do you want to do some reality testing?*

His laugh was husky with emotion.

He loved me! A tumble of emotions filled me and spilled out of me—a waterfall of wonderful. *I love you.* I sent him some of that energy his way—the overwhelming, zinging, trembly feeling. *I love you.* I felt the pull of his eyes—the warmth of them. I opened my mind further, filling Trevor with more of that giddy, silver-white glow. A reddish pulse of power came from him, a dizzying tingle that caught my breath. I fell into his eyes and the world disappeared.

It was as though our souls were connecting, pulling together. His love washed over me, and mine over him, twining together again and again. Intense power built deep within our cores. There were no boundaries between us. We could feel what the other felt as if we were extensions of one another. The energy grew between us, pulsing and growing. It shifted, becoming stronger, pulling within us. Our lungs forgot to breathe and our hearts forgot to beat until this energy exploded between us, crashing in waves that rocked us back, pulling us apart as we both collapsed back onto the couch.

My heart pounded crazy quick against my chest. What had happened? I could feel the vibrations throughout my entire body—like aftershocks. Dizzy. Hyperventilating. I trembled so intensely that my teeth chattered. Even turning my head to look at Trevor seemed to take an incredible effort. I'd melted into a pile of quivering jelly.

Trevor's wide eyes met mine. He was breathing as hard as I was. Words didn't form when he tried to speak. He gripped my hand more tightly in his. He was shaking, too.

I wanted to make a joke or something, but it seemed wrong to lighten the intensity—the sacred feel of the moment. I couldn't think of anything to say that wouldn't trivialize the connection. We just looked at each other. Our clothing was still on. We were still in the empty library, although the light coming through the windows from outside had changed. We hadn't even been so much as kissing at the moment it'd happened.

A single word bubbled up within me. It floated there, waiting for me to notice it, to figure it out. Slowly, I realized what it was and what it meant. I sent it to Trevor. *Soulmates.*

Soulmates. He rolled the word around in his head, pondering it as if he were trying the different meanings on for size. *Soulmates,* he agreed.

Whatever had passed between us had affected us intensely. We were both still trembling, overwhelmed by the emotions—the energy—that still reverberated though us.

How much time had passed? It was getting dark outside.

Whoa. Hours.

My stomach rumbled.

Hungry? he asked.

You heard that?

Felt it.

Wow. I looked up at the clock; it was nearly five. *Four hours.*
What?

Slightly embarrassed about it, Trevor needed to take a quick
shower and change clothes. We decided to meet back at the
church.

Downstairs, I avoided other people as I grabbed several
sandwiches and a couple of cans of soda for us from the
kitchen. Apparently, Sunday dinner was a casual thing after the
elaborate brunch. I slipped the sodas into my bag and balanced
the sandwiches on a plate. Outside, the dark clouds made dusk
come early. My feet squelched into the rain-soft ground and the
grass dampened the bottoms of my jeans as I walked the now-
familiar path. Blackness engulfed me inside of the church. I set
the plate of sandwiches down in the coatroom, and then went to
the sanctuary and ran my hands along the floor until I located
Trevor's flashlight.

The sickly, orange glow from the near-dead batteries faded
further when I jostled the casing. I sat on my cot, alone with
the dim light and my turbulent thoughts. Without the touch of
Trevor's mind, I started to feel exposed and insecure. What had
happened between us? I'd never experienced anything like it.

My heart caught when I felt him returning. The beam of the
penlight in his hand flashed across me as he stepped in. His hair
still dripped shower water onto his shoulders. Trevor was as
preoccupied as I was, his own thoughts knotting within him. We
looked at each other. What were we supposed to say?

Awkward.

Neither of us knew how to do this. Fortunately, Trevor's
stomach chose that moment to rumble.

I held up the plate. "Sandwich?" I said, brightly. He cracked a
reluctant smile.

Trevor pulled over two cot mattresses for us and we ate sitting on the floor in the sanctuary. With the first taste of food, our hunger overwhelmed us. We polished off the plateful in a few minutes.

"That was the most amazing, most incredible thing..." he broke off, unable to complete the sentence even in his mind.

I nodded. *For me, too.*

Your first time?

I nodded again. *Yours?*

He nodded back. *Maybe for anyone. What did we do? I mean, it wasn't like a physical...* He trailed off.

It's hard to put into words, isn't it?

Yes! I don't know what to say; it's like it was—

—beyond words. Like we came together—

—as souls, he finished.

Exactly! I was relieved he felt the same.

Are you all right?

I felt my face go hot. *Better than all right.* I felt... *Wow.* A humming contentment wrapped around me. Colors shone, newly vivid. Everything was beautiful. Alive. I felt more alive than I ever had before. I slid over to sit next to Trevor. *You?*

He put his arm around me, pulling me close. *I'm amazing.* He blushed pink again, right up to his hairline.

Darn straight you are. I put my hand up to his face, pulling him down into a slow, sweet, deep kiss. I felt my insides go liquid, and crackling red power sparked through me.

Looking into his eyes again, silver light surged between us and the world fell away.

This was *Trevor.* I loved him and he loved me.

The energy pulsed between us and our souls connected power-fully again. Building; filling us; crashing over and through us until we collapsed, exhausted and beautifully, beautifully overwhelmed.

CHAPTER 10

I moved in the dark toward a distant light. It became brighter and warmer until my feet sank into a white, sandy beach. The vivid sky matched the turquoise waves that tugged at the shoreline. Two beach chairs faced the water under an umbrella made of palm leaves.

The empty chair was for me.

I slid in beside Trevor and he reached for my hand. Dressed only in knee-length shorts and sunglasses, he gazed out at the water as though hypnotized. I felt the urge to run my hand over his bare chest.

I got it. "So, is this Heaven, Aruba, or a dream?" I asked aloud. The movement of the waves was entrancing… relaxing… calming.

"Take your pick," he said after a moment.

"Nice work. I like what you've done with the place." I looked down and found that I wore a flattering black bathing suit with a short wraparound skirt. Definitely a dream—no bathing suit in the real world ever fit this well. I nodded with approval. I even had a tan. How thoughtful of him.

Trevor's thumb stroked gently against my hand. Soothing. Warm. We stayed like that, not talking, not even thinking anything much, just being together and enjoying the closeness. Peaceful— the opposite of our nightmares. And Trevor had created it for us. *Magic.* Contentment filled us both up and made us whole. We relaxed and enjoyed being whole together.

Eventually, the edges of the world seemed to unravel and we both felt ourselves being pulled out of the fantasy and back into the reality. I squeezed my eyes shut and concentrated on committing the dream to memory. I stored up all of the details: the warmth of the sand; the contours of Trevor's bare chest; the smell of the sea air. When I opened my eyes, I was back on my cot in the cold church.

Trevor looked down at me with concern. "What are you doing? Are you okay?"

Got it! I grinned as I flashed my newest memory to him.

A huge smile broke across his face and he laughed with delight. "It worked!"

"That was the real you?"

He nodded excitedly.

"You actually did it!" *The man of my dreams.*

"Yup. It was the third time I tried it, too. You didn't come for the first two. I think we must've been dreaming at different times."

I usually didn't remember many of my dreams. But this one… this one I'd never forget. I knew I'd treasure the memory for the rest of my life.

It seemed pathetically anticlimactic to have to get up and go to class after such an experience. We lost track of time, and then had to rush to get to our respective dorms to shower and dress. I would've gone hungry, but Trevor came into psych class with a cup of coffee and half a bagel, which he surreptitiously placed on my desk as he slid into the seat next for me. A lump of gratitude filled my throat. I knew I didn't deserve this incredible guy, but darned if I wouldn't rip the still-beating heart out of anyone who got between us.

We hadn't done the readings yesterday. For a non-telepath, this might have been a problem. Luckily for me, though, the answers to the instructor's questions floated clearly in his thoughts. Really, it was almost as though he wanted me to read his mind. I raised my hand and answered the first two questions he asked, simply repeating the answers he expected. I had no idea what I was talking about.

Surprise flashed through Trevor. *When did you do the reading?*

I flashed him a smile. *Does mind reading count?*

Discomfort tingled within him. *It feels like cheating.*

But we're not being graded on answering questions in class.

The instructor—whose name I'd forgotten—called on Trevor. Perfect timing.

I picked the answer from the Mr. Whatever's head and tossed it to Trevor. *Operant Conditioning! Operant Conditioning!*

"Um… Operant Conditioning?" Trevor said after a moment.

"Correct." The instructor continued on with his lecture.

I feel so unclean. He wasn't entirely joking.

Ah hah! I have now sucked you into my web of lies! Welcome to the dark side!

He laughed aloud, and then had to cover it with a couple of fake coughs.

We'll do the readings today so we won't have to stoop to such underhanded tactics again, okay?

He felt better with that plan in place.

We paid dutiful attention to the instructor for a while, but the lecture was so dry I soon plotted an escape. I leaned against Trevor's shoulder and shut my eyes. *This is boring. Meet you in Aruba!*

His silent laughter shook the shoulder I was using as a pillow.

The instructor called on me again. Apparently, I didn't look like I was paying attention. "Skinner Box," I said, hoping the phrase meant something to him. Fortunately, it did.

What's this guy's name again? I made a concentrated effort to sit upright. Falling asleep in class was a bit rude, after all.

Trevor's brows knit in concentration. *You know, I don't think he's ever told us.*

Must not have been in the book.

We somehow managed to stay awake through the rest of class. We hung back for a moment as everyone else filtered out. *See you at lunch.* He gave me a toe-curlingly delightful kiss and headed down the hall to thermodynamics.

Once I remembered how to breathe again, I returned to the main building for Spanish. Today's class was not as animated as the previous one. We practiced if-then statements like, "If you are hungry, then we will go to the restaurant." Since this was a class full of charms, I kept coming up with what they might actually say in Spanish one day like, "If you tell us where the diamonds are, then we will let you live."

Perhaps I was being unfair. I had most of Ganzfield's charms in range right now; I could check them out. Gretchen and Michael were beyond help, but what about the rest of them? I focused out, filling my mind with their thoughts.

Ugh. Headache. I quickly stopped trying to read the charms in German and Mandarin. *Too much.* After two minutes of listening to the French class, I started mixing my French and Spanish vocabulary, so I pulled back to the eight charms in Spanish with me.

Alex and Josh thought about my threat every time they looked in my direction, so they tried to avoid doing that. I suppressed my smile when I realized they hadn't spoken to each other in the past two days. Each worried the other would think he was coming on to him.

I put them in my mental "maybe" pile. They might be salvageable… with work.

As for the rest of the class … hmm. The two other guys both had the same dirty-blond hair and cleft chin, so I figured they were closely related, possibly even brothers.

The one named Kurt was closer. I focused into his mind. What I could tell about him from his current thoughts? It would be great if I could just pull up some of his memories to see if he had the same cruel streak I'd seen in Michael and Gretchen, but it didn't work that way. I would have to place a thought into his mind and read his reaction, like I'd done with Gretchen's worst memory.

Wait… maybe I could do something more subtle here. In the police station that first day, Dr. Williamson had drawn up my memory of the van with a quiet thought. At the time, I hadn't recognized it hadn't been my own. Could I do the same? What would I put into this guy's head?

It's wrong to use charming ability to hurt other people.

Was that subtle enough? Yes! Kurt didn't recognize it as coming from any source but his own mind. Several memories flashed through his consciousness. All of them were of other charms. Either Kurt hadn't used his ability to hurt others, or he lacked self-awareness to an alarming degree.

What are you doing?

Dr. Williamson's mental contact gave me a guilty start and hot embarrassment stained my cheeks. Why did I feel guilty? Was I doing something wrong?

Come upstairs to my office.

Now?

Right now.

I raised my hand. "Señora Lopez? Dr. Williamson just called me to his office." I gathered my books into my bag without waiting for permission. Normal rules didn't apply, after all. This place didn't use anything as mundane as hall passes.

Half the students thought I was faking. *Not a bad way to get out of class.* Josh already planned to use that excuse with other instructors.

The third floor of the main building was smaller than the lower two, with lower ceilings and less ornate woodwork. I found Dr. Williamson by following the sound of his mind. He sat at a polished mahogany desk in an office decorated in shades of dark red. The room reflected his immaculate appearance. The roofline cut into one side, angling the wall inward around the dormer windows. I suddenly realized that Dr. Williamson's office sat directly above the library.

Thank heavens he hadn't been in here yesterday when Trevor and I had been downstairs.

Why? What happened in the library?

Without thinking, I pushed him as hard as I could out of my mind. *No!*

Dr. Williamson's eyebrows shot up in surprise. Had he seen my memories of Trevor? Of what had happened between us?

Did you just block me?

"I guess so," I replied aloud. "Welcome back. Did you have a nice trip?" I asked, desperately hoping to change the subject. I forced myself to think about something—anything—other than what had happened in the library. No other memories came up. Crap. Why was my brain letting me down like this? I settled for picturing a brick wall. Maybe the image would keep Dr. Williamson out.

You're blocking after less than a week? He seemed proud. He tried a second time. *What happened in the library?*

I pushed back hard. *No!*

Very good. You're the only other telepath I know who can put up a mental shield. You're a natural. He changed the subject. *What were you doing down in Spanish class just now?*

I smiled. *Redrawing the lines.*

He frowned. *The charms need to be able to use their abilities without hesitation.*

I've been checking out their minds. Many of them aren't usually cruel, and a few would stop if it wasn't tolerated. Let them practice on people without harming them.

Is that what you were doing?

My jaw dropped. If Kurt had been aware that I was planting ideas in his head, would he have minded? Probably. Even though my "suggestions" wouldn't carry a charm's compulsion, I wouldn't want people influencing me that way.

Exactly.

I felt like I'd caught him in a double-standard, which was funny because he thought the same thing about me. *So they're allowed to charm other people—humiliate and hurt them—but I'm not allowed to use my ability to influence them into behaving better?*

Oh, you're allowed. I just want you to be aware of what you're doing. Don't get carried away.

Is that why I'm here?

Partly. I heard you playing around downstairs and I thought I'd check and see how you were settling in. Have you been able to sleep?

Umm… Seth must've told him I wasn't staying in the dorm.

I have a cabin for you now, if you need it. I caught a brief glimpse of his other thoughts—the thoughts he wasn't trying to broadcast. It had been his niece, Ann's, cabin. She'd left Ganzfield this morning, throwing away her specialness in favor of an average life. He'd resigned himself to the empty-souled feeling this gave him.

No, thanks. I don't need the cabin. I braced myself to push him from my mind again if he wanted to know about my sleeping arrangements.

What's this about nightmares?

Dr. Williamson had already seen my memory of the attack in the van, so I didn't have a problem with him seeing my nightmare. *I seem to throw dreams when people are in range. I sent a nightmare to half of Blake House a couple of nights ago.*

Where have you been sleeping since then? He caught a glimpse of the church in my mind before I could shut him out.

"Where Trevor Laurence stays?" he asked aloud.

I nodded, inwardly cringing. I was sure that his next words were going to put a stop to my staying with Trevor. However, Dr. Williamson's thoughts were not on the obvious issues of an underage boyfriend and girlfriend sleeping in the same room.

What about his throwing things?

My bed's in the coatroom.

And your nightmares?

I shared the dream in which Trevor had appeared and saved me. He assumed it was an invention of my own subconscious until I showed him that Trevor's mind had also registered the dream.

His eyebrows shot up. *How did you two manage to do that?*

I shrugged. *Your guess is probably better than mine. I'm new here, remember?*

This dream-sharing with Trevor… it's the first time I've ever seen that.

The time in the dorm? Sending my nightmare to all those other people?

Oh, I do that all the time. He smiled. *It's a side effect of projective telepathy. That's why I get this big house all to myself at night. Have you done it any other time?*

I pushed him out of my mind again, but I think he caught a glimpse of Aruba. Dr. Williamson seemed thoughtful.

Whoa. Dr. Williamson *seemed* thoughtful. I couldn't hear any actual thoughts that he wasn't specifically aiming at me.

Okay, so I wasn't the only blocking telepath in the room.

He came to some conclusion, and then shifted his attention back to me. *Anything else?*

You went away to recruit someone?

He nodded.

Did you bring anyone back?

Yes. A new girl. She's in the infirmary.

Another telepath?

I wish! He smiled broadly before toning down his obvious favoritism. "Another charm. Play nice," he said aloud, dismissing me with a wave of his hand in the general direction of the door.

"I always do!" I gave him an overly innocent smile as I turned to go.

Maddie, Dr. Williamson called as I was leaving. *One more thing. Come here for your practical this afternoon.*

I had no idea what to expect from that, but I was sure that whatever he planned to teach me would almost certainly be worth learning. *Cool.* I started to return to class, but a sudden impulse changed my direction. I could meet the new charm before she felt the full effects of dodecamine. Maybe I could convince her to avoid the cruel and cliquish charm culture.

Matilda was in the front room of the infirmary with Hannah and a dark-complexioned boy I didn't know. They were taking each other's vitals, and then laying on hands and comparing what they could sense. *Healer training.* It was the most animated that I'd seen Matilda. She and her students flashed with pale-pink excitement; all three got a charge out of using their healing abilities.

Matilda looked up at the sound of the door. *Is something wrong?* "Hi, Maddie. Do you need something?"

Hannah gave me a thoughtful, disapproving look. *Maddie didn't sleep in her own bed last night.* The other healer, Lester, mentally undressed me.

I focused on the guy first. *Knock it off.* He dropped his eyes, embarrassed. Most teenage boys had these kinds of thoughts. I'd been hearing a lot of them recently. The decent guys, at least, were embarrassed when caught at it. Lester was probably all right.

I then focused on Hannah. Evasive response time—I didn't like her well enough to tell her everything.

I can't get any sleep with everyone else's thoughts so near. She jumped slightly at the voice in her head.

I answered Matilda aloud. "Sorry, I didn't mean to interrupt your training. I heard there was a new girl and I thought I'd say hi."

Matilda's surprise splashed across her mind. I guess Ganzfield didn't have a welcome wagon. Maybe that was part of the problem. She opened the door to the annex—the room with the cots where I'd spent my first night. "Grace, this is Maddie," she said, leaving us and returning to the lesson. Grace sat cross-legged on one of the cots. She held a book in her hand, but her mind wasn't processing the words on the page.

"Hi, Grace." I smiled. "Welcome to one of the freakiest places on earth."

She laughed. Nervous energy jumped within her, tinting her thoughts orange. She was petite, and her hair was chin-length, smooth, and glossy black. She was the first Asian-American I'd seen here, and it confirmed my suspicion that G-positives came from all backgrounds, even though most of Ganzfield seemed to be Caucasian or African-American.

"Where are you from?" I asked.

"New York City. How about you?"

"New Jersey."

"Oh, I'm so sorry," she said with mock sympathy. Dissing me about Jersey after less than a minute? I liked her already. She impressed me as an outgoing, cut-to-the-chase kind of person—when she wasn't sitting in a strange medical facility waiting for her superpowers to emerge, that is.

"Hey, New Jersey is a great place to be from…" I replied. "Far from."

She laughed.

"What happened to bring you here?"

"No clue. I'm still not sure how Dr. Will—I want to say Williamsburg, but that's a bridge."

"Williamson."

"Thanks. Dr. Williamson convinced my mom and dad to send me here."

"Did he have someone else with him?"

"Yeah."

"Probably a charm."

"Charm?" she asked. "What's a charm?"

I thought for a moment. I had to explain it in a way that didn't sound too creepy since she probably was one. "Charms have the ability to... say things that... that people feel compelled to do."

A strange look crossed Grace's face. "Like hypnosis?"

"Yeah, but stronger. Mind-control."

"Charm," she said, trying out the word. "Are you a charm?"

"Oh, no!" I replied, startled at the thought. Then I quickly added, "But you might be."

There must be a mistake. Maybe I don't belong here. Grace's thoughts raced. Part of her hoped that was the case.

"Have they given you dodecamine yet?" I asked.

"What's that?"

"Did they give you a shot?"

"No. They took a blood sample, though."

I recalled that Matilda hadn't followed procedure with me. Apparently, Grace was coming in by-the-book.

"Grace, here's the deal. There are some really amazing, wonderful people here. There are also some unbelievable jerks. If you're a charm, you'll see a lot of the jerks. You don't have to become one of them to fit in. You know what I mean?"

She actually seemed to understand. Her lips pursed and she nodded. "Yeah, I do."

"If any of them give you a hard time or try to make you do something you don't want to, let me know, okay?"

Her eyes scanned my face, trying to figure out what was behind the offer. "You can do something about it?"

I nodded. "I can make them stop. And I will if they give you any trouble. I don't... I don't want the jerks to run this place anymore."

The bell rang. End of class. I jumped up. "Gotta go. Do you need anything?" I looked around. Computer, books, snacks—she seemed all set.

"No, I'm fine. Thanks."

I left quickly—waving goodbye to Matilda as I passed her—and joined the throngs headed to the dining hall. *Trevor!* I rushed to catch up, mentally calling his name.

He lit up with sparkly energy when he saw me. I caught up with him and the sparkly stuff turned crackly red as it flared between us. Did anyone else see emotions like this—as colored energy? I really liked it. Our own private fireworks. Trevor wrapped his arms around me and lifted me off my feet, setting me down only as the "ooohh" sounds of several amused sparks penetrated our little bubble of bliss. Maybe we should cut back on the public displays. That would be hard. I felt so pulled to Trevor—like we shared our own personal gravity.

We no longer had our table to ourselves—Drew, Harrison, Sean, Ellen, and two other red-headed McFees joined us. The Fireball match seemed to be the point when I'd been accepted into the tribe. Lively conversation overflowed to the next table, which was also full of sparks. They set up another game of Fireball for this afternoon. It was supposed to rain the rest of the week and the sparks wanted to play while they could.

"What do you do when there's snow on the ground?" I asked.

Drew grinned hugely. "Fireball... *on ice!*" I could see the image in his mind of the sparks out on the frozen lake, using holes melted into the surface as goals. "We came up with it last winter. It's great!"

Ellen groaned and rolled her eyes. "That's not *real* Fireball."

"Nice!" I said with a grin. "All the violence of hockey, but now with the added fun of playing with matches!"

Drew laughed. "You got it, minder!" He turned to me. "So, what do you do for fun?"

I sent a quick flash of Aruba to Trevor. He dropped his eyes and grinned as he flushed right to his hairline. I loved doing that to him.

Aloud, I said to Drew, "You know, the usual. Go to movies. Read books. Fight crime with my amazing superpowers."

The table laughed. "Have you seen any of the movies since you learned you were a G-positive? They're hilarious!"

"Like *Firestarter*?" I asked.

"A classic!" Drew laughed. Several other sparks nodded enthusiastically. "Required viewing for all sparks. I don't care that it's, like, fifty years old. Can you imagine giving dodecamine to a spark toddler?"

"No way. I am *not* volunteering to baby-sit," I said emphatically.

"*X-Men* is pretty good," Harrison chimed in with his mouth still half-full. He swallowed, and then continued, looking at me. "I always thought it was lame the way they showed telepathy, though. Like you guys have to touch your foreheads and squint."

I'd seen that in enough movies to know what he meant, although now it took on new relevance. It was like a "tell" in poker—something that showed the audience that the telepath was reading someone's mind. What good was that in the real world? The true advantage came from stealth.

Squinting at Harrison, I put two fingers to my temple. He actually paled a little when I did it. I stopped then flashed a little "just kidding" smile.

"*Fantastic Four* annoys me," Drew said.

Sean joined in. "The Human Torch? Can you imagine what it'd actually be like?" He suddenly grew thoughtful, and I didn't like the direction his thoughts were taking.

"Not worth it," I said to him. He looked at me, confused. "Be something else for Halloween."

"What was that movie? The really old one with the girl who set the prom on fire?" asked one of the other McFees. It was Beth, who looked like a smaller version of Ellen.

"*Carrie*?" Harrison offered with his mouth full again.

"There are some days I wouldn't mind going all Carrie-at-the-prom on that lot." Beth indicated a table full of charms.

The conversation jerked to a screeching halt. Sparks were expelled if they intentionally lit up indoors, so of course that was where the charms got to them—usually waiting until one was alone. I suddenly realized the sparks seemed to always travel in protective packs.

"Hey," I said. "From now on, if they do anything, just let me know, okay?"

All eyes were on me. Gulp. Wait a sec. Did I really want to take this on? Did I have much of a choice? No one else could do it.

The six sparks at the table regarded me with a mix of gratitude and disgust. Having someone else fight their battles for them did not appeal, but they liked the idea of someone cutting their tormentors down to size.

We don't have to put up with this crap anymore. The sound of my voice in their heads surprised everyone but Trevor.

"Easy for you to say." Grant, a gangly McFee cousin, gave me a disgusted look. "You're immune."

"I've been checking this out. Not all of the charms are doing this." I swallowed hard, trying to knock the lump from my throat.

"A lot of them would be happier if the ones like Michael and Gretchen were gone."

"Are you going to get rid of them?" There was enough enthusiasm in Drew's voice that I was afraid he was going to offer to help me bury the bodies.

"I think we can isolate the worst ones. Get the rest to, I don't know, *police* themselves. Most of them aren't too bad."

"You've only been here a few days," Grant snapped back. "What do you know about them?"

I raised my eyebrows and looked sidelong at him. *Hello! Telepath!* I said into his head.

"Oh," he said, deflating, "Oh, yeah."

"She's a minder." Beth elbowed him in the ribs. "Duh!"

He elbowed her back—hard.

"If only we could go public." Sean thought aloud. "There're not a lot of ways to secretly use pyrokinesis. If we could go public, we could make Fireball a pro sport."

"ESPN, baby!" Drew laughed. The sparks' conversation drifted to what they would do with their wealth and fame.

I looked across the table to Trevor, giving his hand a squeeze. I was getting better at eating one handed. *You've been very quiet. What are you thinking about?* Although I already knew.

He rewarded me with a smile, a blush, and a warm, sandy beach in Aruba. I closed my eyes with a sigh.

If Dr. Williamson wasn't giving me a practical this afternoon, I'd blow off the rest of my classes and meet you there.

I have to go into town after class today or I'd join you.

My eyes flew open. *You're leaving?* I frowned. Was that safe?

Just for an hour or so. We have a standing order for supplies at one of the local stores. Usually Greg goes and picks it up, but he just got back from driving Dr. Williamson this morning so he has the rest of the day off. I sometimes help out when they need an extra hand.

They don't deliver? A remembered flash of the car outside the gate made me frown. I didn't like the idea of Trevor going somewhere without me.

He laughed aloud, which surprised Drew next to him. It took him a second to realize that Trevor and I were having a silent conversation.

You should come sometime. I'd love to know what they really think we're doing out here.

What do they think we're doing?

It's possible they think we're some kind of cult. They're always kind of freaked out when I go in there, like they expect me to start chanting or trying to convert them or something.

I laughed at that idea. *Hey, if we wanted to start a cult, we could just send a few charms out to evangelize.*

You know, you'll be running this place in no time. He was only half-joking. *You're a minder who can stand to be around other people, and now you've got half the population of Ganzfield looking to you to protect them.*

I can stand being around everyone else because you're here. A silver spark pulsed down my arm and through Trevor. It was true. Ever since I'd started to experience the effects of dodecamine, I'd felt like I was in a crowded theater and everyone in the audience was talking during the show. When Trevor was with me, I could focus on him and the noise of the other minds faded into the background.

I felt the now-familiar energy flash between us and the edges of my vision started to dim. We both reacted with a gasp as it began, but simultaneously pulled ourselves out of it. Breathing hard, we avoided looking each other for a moment. We didn't want to start doing whatever it was we did right here in front of everyone.

Drew thought we were hilarious. "What's she doing, Trev? Whispering sweet nothings into your brain?" We both blushed further but didn't answer him. That just confirmed his suspicions.

Give us a minute, okay? Drew jumped and I gave him a quick half-smile to show I wasn't mad.

He returned to the rich-and-famous-spark discussion. Drew planned to become a stuntman in Hollywood, doing fire stuff for the movies, and he explained how that would place a good-looking and talented person such as himself in the position to become a movie star. Something called a "fire fountain'" would decorate in rich-and-famous Drew's front yard.

That sounded tacky, even by the standards I was used to— and I was from New Jersey.

Afternoon classes passed without leaving a lasting impression on me. I hoped that they hadn't covered anything I might need to know someday. I caught a quick moment with Trevor as he went to the old barn. The person-sized entrance on the side had a sophisticated-looking keypad lock that seemed out of place on the old building. Instead of entering a code, Trevor stood in front of the huge double doors for a moment, concentrating. A scrape of metal and wood came from inside and the tall doors opened into the equipment area. The large wooden bar that had held them closed swung gently from its enormous hinge.

Trevor didn't need a keycode. *Cool.*

The old, run-down barn façade camouflaged a full modern garage. Dr. Williamson's town car, a silver sedan, the riding lawnmower took up one side. Three large, black vans stood ready along the other. Each probably could hold about ten or twelve people. Did Ganzfield take us on field trips or something? I couldn't imagine where they'd want us to go.

Trevor grabbed a set of keys from the rack on the wall. Then he pulled me into a kiss that made my insides melt and run out of my toes.

"Do you need anything from the store?" he asked aloud as we reluctantly broke apart.

I tried to make my brain work again. "Breath mints. I want to be able to kiss you in the mornings."

He laughed, delighted. "I put that one on the list already."

"Flashlight batteries."

He nodded, making a mental note.

I walked out through the big doors as he started the engine and inched the van out. As soon as the vehicle was clear, Trevor leaned back around the driver's seat, as though reaching for something in the back of the van. The huge barn doors slowly pulled shut. The scraping sound of the latch completed the process.

Wow. Fifteen feet at least. He did have a big mental reach. I watched until he drove out of sight down the gravel drive toward the main gate. With a sigh, I turned toward the main building and tried to pull my melted insides back in before my meeting with Dr. Williamson.

CHAPTER 11

I didn't get all the way to the front porch.

Maddie!

Dr. Williamson had Grace, the soon-to-be charm, run Zener cards with me out in the field. It was awkward and uncomfortable as soon as Grace figured out I was a telepath. I felt guilty when I realized I hadn't told her before. The omission hadn't been intentional.

Grace's thoughts brimmed red with hostility and stress. *I don't want to be here. I don't want to do this. I want to go home. I want my normal life back. I don't want this freak in my head.* She was angry at Dr. Williamson for bringing her here; angry at her parents for letting her be taken; angry at me for being a mind-reading freak.

"Don't worry," I said again, trying to keep myself from feeling hurt. I'd been nice to her! No one else had made the effort. "In a few days, you'll be able to tell people to go to hell and they'll just grab shovels and start digging."

I looked at Dr. Williamson. *Is this still going to work if she's like this?*

He looked at Grace thoughtfully for a few seconds. *It should. It's not like she can block. What happened in the library?* He thought quickly, but I'd tensed as soon as he'd mentioned blocking. I was ready for him. He hit a wall in my mind and bounced off.

Once we reached a distance where I could no longer hear her thoughts, Dr. Williamson rejoined Grace and checked the tape measure in her hand. From there, I could still hear his mind, even though Grace was indistinct. As a telepath, he sent out a stronger signal or something. *Only sixty-five feet.* Apparently, I had the shortest range of any of the minders. His disappointment caused a hot flush of shame to fill me, like I'd done poorly on a quiz in my favorite teacher's class. Was there something wrong with me?

Maybe that's why I can still stand to be around other people.

Perhaps. He considered that. *And you may gain range over time.*

Part of me actually hoped that wasn't true. I was hearing plenty now—more than I wanted to, in some cases. Grace avoided my eyes as she passed me without speaking and headed back to the infirmary.

Trevor's face flushed as he handed me a single, red rose.

A rose.

A rose with shiny, green and white paper with a sprig of baby's breath and a little plastic vial on the base of the stem. I choked up and I felt my hand lift to my mouth, as though it could hold back my overflowing emotions.

Oh, yeah. I could get used to being cherished like this.

Thank you. It's beautiful. Good thing I no longer needed to speak aloud.

I'm glad you like it. His mind flushed with vicarious joy.

No one has ever given me one before. I held it to my nose and inhaled the scent deeply, sharing the sensory experience with him. His nostrils flared in reaction.

Then it'll be something that I do.

We'd both been such lonely people before we'd found each other. How had we ever survived?

After dinner, we went back to the church together. The bloom of my rose swayed with each step; I carried it in a glass of water I'd taken from the dining hall. Trevor held the battery-operated camping lanterns he'd bought in town. We set three of the cot mattresses up against one of walls to make a kind of couch, and then placed the four lanterns strategically so we had enough light. *Homey.*

I leaned against Trevor's shoulder, and we threw a sleeping bag over us against the October cold. It was already frigid in the church. How much worse was it going to be in January?

We both started with the psychology reading. My book lay open in my lap, but I closed my eyes and listened to Trevor as he read silently. He was a quick reader and he readily understood everything. I felt him pull the material in and organize it in his mind. Extremely intelligent—even smarter than I'd thought. I loved the way his voice sounded, even when I wasn't listening with my ears.

Next, Trevor switched to thermodynamics. I tried to concentrate on Spanish, but I had to give up. I could still hear him reading in my head, and this time the material didn't match the book in my hand. It was like trying to read with someone talking to me, and rather than let it frustrate me, I simply closed my eyes again. I listened to the words flow through his mind, felt the beating of his heart, the warmth of his arm around me, and I drifted in the sense of peace and the feeling of completeness. I didn't wake when Trevor lifted me in his arms and carried me out to my cot, wrapping the still-warm sleeping bag around me.

I heard the music before anything else registered... then I smelled the roses.

My slinky black dress sparkled in the candlelight as I moved across the circular, parquet dance floor. Flickering candles blazed in huge, free-standing candelabras. The star-filled sky floated above me and hundreds of red roses decorated the edge of the circle.

Trevor strode up wearing a tuxedo and a delighted smile. He took my breath away. He passed through the flowers, just like the one he had given me... when we were awake.

Another dream? Oh, he was good.

Trevor reached me and held out his hand. I took it and he pulled me into his arms. The music swelled and I recognized it: a classic. I twined my hands around his neck, laid my head on his shoulder, and followed his lead.

Wise men say,
'Never pools rush in'
Since I can't help falling in love with you
Shallots stain, when they're made of tin
So I can't help falling in love with you

I looked up at Trevor, feeling the beginnings of a smirk on my face. "Are those really the words?"

He ducked his head. "Sorry. I think I need to work on learning the lyrics."

I shook my head. "Don't. I like your words better."

He grinned, twirled me elegantly, and then pulled me close again.

Like the bah-dah-boe
Slowly da-duh-dee
Darlin', blow my nose
Some things I'd like to see
Shake my hand,
Take my whole life, too
Cuz I can't help falling in love with you

"Do you know how to dance when you're awake?" I asked after the song had ended.

"Not at all. That's how I know we're dreaming."

Another slow song started. I thought I recognized it as "Unchained Melody." He liked the oldies.

Oh, my darlin', my love
I hunger for some lunch…

Trevor twirled me again, slowly, and then pulled me into a kiss. Confident. Sure of himself, here in our private paradise— just the two of us.

I never wanted us to leave. He dipped me slowly, his hand moving down my back, pulling me up… pulling me close.

I felt the dream dissolving and drifting into oblivion. I looked at him, feeling the impeding loss of something precious. A sudden thought flashed back to that first night. "Throw something! Wake us up so we can remember this!" He glanced around, then used his ability to pick up one of the candelabras and throw it as far as he could into the surrounding night.

There was a clatter in the sanctuary. I felt the threads of reality pulling at my mind, trying to unravel the dream. I tightened my mental grip—holding on to the details and fixing them in my memory. I got up in the dark of the coatroom, but stopped when I realized I couldn't hear Trevor's mind. Groping for the flashlight, I opened the door and shone the light inside.

Trevor's face was slack with sleep, making him look younger and more vulnerable. Had he even been there? Had it just been a regular dream, after all? I swung the flashlight around the room. My breath caught when I saw the shattered plastic of the lantern in the corner.

Confirmation. Trevor had been there, but bittersweet because he hadn't woken up. He'd have no memory of the magical experience he'd given me. I could share the memories I'd saved, but they'd be secondhand to him.

In the morning, I felt the gentle touch of Trevor's fingers stroking my hair. The tingle of contact with his mind warmed me before I'd even opened my eyes. I drew a deep breath and shifted, smiling.

Good morning. His lips brushed against mine. Minty fresh.

Do you have any more of those mints around? I want to be able to kiss you properly.

I don't mind.

I opened one eye and arched my eyebrow. *If the situation were reversed…*

He acknowledged my logic and a pack of mints flew gracefully to me. A few seconds later, I was able to kiss Trevor properly, so I did. Repeatedly. Blissfully.

Trevor had no memory of dancing with me, although last night it'd been his intention to try it. A wistful longing filled him when he realized he couldn't recall it himself. *Then we'll just have to do it again.*

A warm glow filled me. *Oh, yes.* Our eyes met and we felt the energy flare up between us. Classes? Ugh. I didn't want to go to my classes. I wanted to stay here with Trevor. How long could we go without food?

I had a theory that sex was an attempt to forge the same kind of connection that Trevor and I shared. Other people used their bodies because their minds couldn't connect directly. Of course, I didn't have any basis of comparison.

I silently explained my theory to Trevor. His eyes flashed; he thought the idea deserved further study. Comparative study. The images this evoked in his mind made my heart beat rabbit-fast in my chest. A deep red buzzing energy traveled through us. We pulled closer to each other, our bodies pressed against each other on the narrow cot. The sleeping bag fabric made little whishing noises as we moved. Eventually, we broke apart, breathing hard. My whole body tingled and hummed.

He was in a similar state, trying to will himself calm. *Not yet.*

Not yet. I agreed. A little laugh escaped me. We had come to this agreement in a church. That seemed appropriate somehow.

Do you believe in God?

His surprise splashed over me. *Where did that come from?*

I shrugged. *We just decided not to fornicate. We're in a church. Natural progression.*

He laughed, but he was thoughtful—distracted. *I'm not sure. I'd like to think so. It would really be great if there was a plan, you know? When I'm in here*, he indicated the church, *I sometimes feel…*

something holy. I feel the connection to all of the Eatons and Blakes who came here, all those years ago.

What happened to them?

He startled. *You don't know? I keep forgetting how new all of this is to you. You remember Ann, from the cookout?*

I nodded.

She's Dr. Williamson's niece. Her mother was the last of the Eatons. Ann's mother was one of the founders of Ganzfield. They developed the program here after she inherited the land from her parents. I think they also bought up the other houses in the village. I know my dorm wasn't originally owned by the Eatons.

But the church was?

Yeah. It was built on Eaton land. No one has used it in more than thirty years.

Except us.

He smiled. *Except us.* He took my hand, the first contact we'd had since we'd broken apart to control ourselves. *How about you? Do you believe in God?*

I'm kind of like you, I guess. When my dad died, my mom stopped going to church. I think she still believed, but was mad at God for taking him.

How did he die? His sympathy stroked gently against my consciousness, soothing me.

Car accident.

How old were you?

Four. I barely remember him, and most of what I do is tied up with photographs, you know?

Trevor squeezed my hand.

Finding you, though… I looked into his eyes. *Finding you… it feels like there has to be something—someone with a plan.*

He tenderly touched my cheek and then pulled me to him for a slow, gentle kiss. Trevor existed. Trevor loved me. I considered that strong evidence of a Higher Power at work.

Once again we had to rush through the morning to make it to class on time. Nothing from the lectures left an impression. I was too much in my head—talking to Trevor when he was near enough, daydreaming about him when he wasn't. That afternoon, I headed up to the third floor for my practical in a happy little bubble.

What happened in the library? Ugh. My bubble burst. I hadn't even closed Dr. Williamson's office door yet. I blocked with a mental shield, then narrowed my eyes and glared at him.

"That's none of your business!"

Well, your shielding is pretty good. It feels like I'm running into a wall in there.

I nodded. *Good.* I liked picturing a large, brick wall when I blocked.

Try a more subtle technique. Eventually, you might be able to block without another telepath knowing you're doing it.

Like you do. It wasn't a question.

That startled him. *You could tell?*

No, I just guessed. Sometimes your thoughts disappear. I just noticed the absence, more than anything.

Oh. He still seemed disturbed, like someone who'd tried to show off his juggling skills but kept dropping the pins.

I changed the subject. *Can you teach me the financial stuff?*

He wasn't expecting that. I was just full of surprises today. *Why do you want to learn that?*

I flashed him an image of Trevor in the cold, dark church.

And you want to learn the financial stuff—

—to buy him a new place to live that can be heated, but is still big enough that he can't break down the walls in his sleep.

Dr. Williamson regarded me silently, his thoughts behind his shield.

Seriously, what happened in the library?

I blocked again. "Enough!" I was tired of this discussion… this invasion of my privacy. *Are you going to teach me the financial stuff or not?*

The remainder of my practical involved a detailed explanation of how the stock market worked—how to buy, sell, and short. Dr. Williamson gave me some books on investing and I silently wondered how I was going to keep up with all of the readings I already had and plow through these, as well.

As I left at the end of the lesson, he said, "Tomorrow we'll start on how to get good trading information." He smiled and I could feel his almost-paternal pride. I just might be his new protégée. Cool. I could live with that.

Trevor walked through the front door as I came down the stairs. Invisible hands caught me at the waist and flew me down the staircase into his arms. Several other people gasped; even in a place as strange as this, people usually didn't fly.

He looked into my eyes, smiling. *How was your practical?*

My master plan to take over the world is finally falling into place. Mwah ha ha ha.

Master plan? he asked, then nearly fell forward as Drew clapped him on the back.

"I'll tell you about it later," I said as we joined the sparks entering the dining hall.

I really enjoyed the meals with the sparks. When Trevor and I wanted to speak privately, we could think at each other, but could still share the camaraderie that being with a group entailed—like being part of the tribe. I hadn't had much of a social life in New Jersey. I'd been a peripheral member of the loose-knit clique of honors-track "smart kids" who'd tried to avoid overt nerdiness and the resulting social targeting. I'd had a place at a lunch table and people to commiserate with over Mr. Storrs's evil essay questions. But my friends in New Jersey were more like coworkers than close friends. I hadn't even thought about them much since I'd come to Ganzfield. Now I was part of this group and I felt like I belonged here. It was a new and unexpected experience.

Drew asked Trevor about going into town. "Why did Williamson send you?"

"I volunteered."

"It was so you could drive, right? Man, I haven't driven in months!"

A sudden image in Trevor's mind caught my attention. *You sometimes drive with your ability, don't you?*

Dr. Williamson specifically told me not to.

I cracked up. *You do it anyway! You rebel!*

He grinned back. *I take the fifth.*

I'd like to see it.

Trevor considered. *I wonder if I could take you out with me.*

Let's try it sometime.

Drew threw a friendly punch into Trevor's arm. "Hey, you two crazy kids. What are you talking about?" I realized that Drew's discretion on that first day had been really out of character for him.

The guys started talking cars. I had zero interest, but Trevor joined in the discussion. Drew used to work on old cars with his dad. He now realized, sadly, that he probably couldn't work with them anymore. Being around open fuel lines wasn't a good idea for sparks on dodecamine.

I considered the other things we'd had to give up. Most of the charms and RVs went on to college after Ganzfield. Dr. Williamson provided some kind of school records—possibly forged—and a single visit by a charm to the admission's office usually ensured acceptance at the institution of their choice. Dr. Williamson paid their tuitions in full, and then he helped them get specific jobs where they could use their abilities to further his agenda, whatever that was. I still had a lot of unanswered questions about that. There was something else, too—a sense of danger. *Stay hidden and secret while we make ourselves powerful.* What was Dr. Williamson afraid of? What did he think might happen?

I shook myself out of my current line of thought. I remembered hearing that he planned to send Hannah and Lester to medical school, as well.

Not fair.

The sparks, Trevor, and I could never live in college dorms. We might be able to commute to classes or take them online, but that'd be the extent of our college experience. Living in a city would be difficult, as well. The sparks would need to do a lot of fireproofing and Trevor would need so much space that a place like New York would be prohibitively expensive. I'd never get a quiet second in a city; the internal voices of thousands would press down on me.

Later on, having kids would be hard. Since it was recessive, the kids would probably inherit the G-positive trait. That would mean if one of us had a child with another G-positive, the child definitely would have the mutation. I wondered if dodecamine would be harmful for pregnant women. If I wanted to have kids someday, would I have to give up my ability to do it? Yikes. Our lives were going to be even more restricted than I'd previously imagined. I began to wonder if Ann had had the right idea.

I watched Trevor as he talked with his friends. At least there were compensations. If I could be with Trevor, it would be okay. No, better than okay.

Perhaps I could help some of my new friends to be happy, too. *Trevor.* He had paused in the conversation to take another bite. *Is Sean a good guy?*

Sure is. He's kind of quiet, I guess.

I smiled. *Everyone's quiet compared to Drew.*

He grinned back. *True enough.* At the moment, Drew enthusiastically described a 1968 Camaro he had worked on with his dad. Apparently, this was a big deal classic car.

Whatever. I had zero interest in cars.

Thanks.

Rachel sat with some other RVs at the last table in the dining hall. I focused in on Sean's thoughts. Nice guy. Not as into the car conversation as he pretended to be. I floated a very subtle *Do I want a girlfriend?* into his mind and listened as he contemplated it.

Yes, he did.

So far so good.

What do I think of Rachel? I asked into his head and risked sending a mental image of her. Stealth was harder with images than with the little voice. I bit my lip as I concentrated. Subtle. Nudging, not prodding.

Sean played with that idea while he chewed. When he considered her, he thought she was pretty. He'd never really noticed her before. I heard him thinking, *Should I go talk to her?* I gave him a tiny, affirmative push. *Score!* A little thrill of success shot through me as Sean pushed back from the table and walked over to Rachel. Her excitement at his approach fluttered into my mind, noticeable even from across the room.

Suddenly, a feeling of sick horror cut into me—a sword in my gut. Trevor's face was furious. *What did you do to Sean?*

What? Dismay. Anger. Trevor's distress twisted into me painfully. I was going to cry, scream, or throw up… or maybe all three.

Trevor thought I'd compelled Sean, like a charm would.

He thought that I was the kind of person who'd force others to do things they didn't want to do. He felt sick at heart and his pain and distress overwhelmed me.

I started to shake. *No, it's not like that!*

I can't believe you did that. Trevor stood up, left his meal on the table, and stalked from the dining hall. He felt I'd betrayed him… betrayed his trust. But I'd just made a suggestion! Was it really so bad? Trevor actually believed I'd manipulate someone like that— *Oh my God.* I felt all of the energy drain from my body.

What have I done?

I left the table as well, ignoring the curious looks the remaining sparks directed at me. I had to get away—to be alone. I had to get everyone else's thoughts out of my head. They were pressing in on me too strongly.

Too loud.

Once outside, I half-ran toward the lake, avoiding everyone. I reached the path that wound through the woods along the water's edge and kept going, my arms wrapped tightly around me, as though I could physically hold in the overflow of emotion.

The cold seeped into me. It was getting dark. Collapsing in the middle of the path, I sobbed and couldn't stop.

CHAPTER 12

I felt hollow. I'd been sitting on the cold ground for hours, and my legs felt painful and stiff with a numb patch on the side of my thigh from pressing against the near-frozen earth. I'd been so wrong. If Trevor ever spoke to me again, that was the first thing I'd tell him. The lump in my throat seemed permanent. It hurt to swallow.

Fumbling in the dark, I slowly worked my way back toward Ganzfield. I really didn't have a plan for what to do next. Maybe I could sleep in my bed in Blake House, although I didn't want to share another nightmare with everyone. I hadn't had a bad dream in a while, but I was pretty sure Trevor was the reason for that. It was after midnight, according to the glowing red numbers on the clock on my bedside table. I felt drained and exhausted.

Cold dread hit me when I saw that Rachel wasn't in her bed. I listened for her, finding her mind far below me, terrified. *What the...* I'd been so wrapped up in my own problems that I hadn't even heard her. Now, her mental voice screamed to me.

I flung myself down the stairs, finding the door that led to the basement. My feet thudded hard on the wooden boards. The basement walls were rough fieldstone—old and unfinished. It was warm and damp down there.

Creepy.

Naked bulbs hung from wires at intervals from the low ceiling. At a folding card table in the far corner, Michael and another charm named Victor played strip poker.

They were making Rachel and Grace do the stripping.

Tears flowed in tracks down Rachel's face. She wore nothing but a bra and panties, and her bare skin puckered with gooseflesh despite the humidity.

Grace still had on her shirt and underwear. Her jeans lay balled on the floor at her feet and her impotent desire to kill Michael and Victor rolled off her statue-rigid body.

The too-familiar anger filled me, flowing blood-red. I hated Michael… hated his smug cruelty. I now knew that the obscene things I'd seen in his mind weren't fantasies—they were plans.

Michael and Victor looked up when they'd heard me coming.

Victor tried to charm me with a command of, "Don't move!" This wasn't the first time these two charms had brought girls down to the basement, but they'd been able to charm-silence any previous interruptions.

Well, that wouldn't work this time—not with a minder.

Michael knew his voice wouldn't stop me. He stood up quickly. New plan: I'd have to be silenced in a more final way. Cold, lethal thoughts filled his mind. *She's small and I'm pretty fast. I could break her neck before she could stop me.*

Son-of-a—! Dark red power roared within me. Without hesitation, I blasted Michael's brain. I wanted to kill him. I really, really wanted to—but I didn't.

Michael fell to the earthen floor, writhing in pain and clutching his head. I turned my attention to Victor, blasting him as well. My hands clenched with the effort, but the effort was to restrain my ability, not to enhance it. It would've been so easy to kill them. I still could. I felt like an avenging angel, filled with righteous fury. It hurt to hold back the energy. I wanted to fry them until smoke billowed from their ears.

WHAT THE HELL ARE YOU DOING?

I felt Seth's mental connection as he started running full out toward Blake House. I had no idea how much he'd sensed, but it was enough to get him booking over here in the middle of the night.

Blake House basement. I forced myself to think words. *Bring Dr. Williamson. Now.*

The next few minutes felt eternal. If my mind had been a gun, it would've been pointed at the two figures on the floor. They started to recover and I blasted them again. My jaw hurt from clenching my teeth. I had to hold myself back.

Don't kill them.

Rachel and Grace remained charmed in doll-like stillness, as silent and unmoving as the stone pillars that held up the house, creating small pockets of space and shadow between them.

Dr. Williamson came down the stairs. Out on the grounds, I heard Seth's internal muttering as he listened in. He paced like a panther out there in the cold, circling without getting too close. I felt his anger at Michael and Victor; it improved my estimation of him.

Dr. Williamson took in the scene silently for a few moments, his mind touching briefly into each of ours. Then he mentally called Cecelia from her room upstairs. I felt a quick pang of jealousy that he could reach sleeping minds when I couldn't. The killing energy simmered back slightly within me, now that he was here. Dr. Williamson would handle this.

A minute later, Cecelia came into the basement, still tying a black bathrobe around herself. The traces of sleep fled her mind as she processed the scene. Anger flavored her thoughts, mixing with my own. *Too far. Way over the line. How dare they!*

She quickly released Grace and Rachel with a charm command. "Stop doing what Michael and Victor told you to do."

Rachel collapsed to the floor, sobbing and inconsolable. Her anguish overwhelmed her. I winced and drew a quick breath as the overflow hit me.

Grace slowly picked up her jeans and put them back on with deliberate care. Her anger mixed with relief—I'd come in time.

"Thanks," she said to me. She looked down at Victor shuddering in pain on the floor, processed the situation, and controlled her emotions with surprising outer calm. All of her wariness about me had vanished. Compared with people like Victor, I was definitely the lesser of two evils.

Whatever. I was still working on tamping down the last of that killing energy.

A strong image suddenly filled Grace's mind. She wanted to kick Victor in the head until he was dead.

A mirthless laugh escaped me. I could relate. "It's not worth it," I said. "You might ruin your shoes."

She gave him a long look, deciding. Finally, she exhaled. "You're right." She headed up to her bed in the infirmary. She wasn't going to get much sleep; her mind still twisted with what-ifs.

Dr. Williamson dragged first Victor, then Michael, across the stone floor. A long room—about twenty feet by ten and heavily insulated—huddled under the infirmary. I hadn't noticed it when

I'd first come in. The thick door had the same modern keypad as the barn. It looked out of place in the old cellar. I heard the door code in Dr. Williamson's mind as he hit the keys. *9-7-5-3-1*—an odd-number countdown. Huh. Too simple. I'd expected something more sophisticated from him.

The room was a cell. Bare mattress. Metal toilet. Thick, soundproofed walls. Apparently, Michael and Victor weren't the first charms to occupy it. Dr. Williamson was prepared for situations like this.

I was fairly sure that imprisoning teenagers in a custom-built basement cell was grossly illegal, but at the moment, I didn't care. I felt a sense of righteousness as the door closed, anticlimactically quiet. I would have preferred the metallic clang of a prison door— or perhaps a dungeon.

Once they were locked in, I met Dr. Williamson's eyes. *They're gone, right?*

They're gone. As soon as the dodecamine wears off, they'll be out of here forever.

I nodded. The worst of the tension slid away as the killing force finally fell silent within me.

Cecelia bent over Rachel. Her compassion surprised me. I knelt next to them and Cecelia's gaze met mine over Rachel's sobbing shoulders. She still didn't like me, but she gave me a nod of acknowledgement. We were women here, and we both understood.

Dr. Williamson felt it, as well. *You've got this?* He headed up the stairs.

What? Was he kidding? He was leaving *me* in charge of something like this? What the hell was I supposed to do? I felt completely out of my depth. I heard him double-check the lock on the front door as he left the building.

Now what?

I slowly gathered up Rachel's clothes. There would be no police involvement... no investigation. How could we explain what Michael and Victor could do? How could we explain what I'd done?

No, this was something that we'd have to handle ourselves.

Cecelia and I got Rachel back to the room upstairs. Our entry woke Hannah. Her initial flash of surprise at seeing Cecelia and me changed when she saw Rachel. Concern flowed through her. Rachel's lack of clothing and her intense distress clued her in very quickly. I grabbed a fuzzy bathrobe from the hook on the back of the door and covered Rachel as we moved her onto the bed.

Rachel jumped at Hannah's touch, then calmed as Hannah used her ability to soothe her stress reaction. After she'd finished, Hannah looked between Cecelia and me. "What else can we do?"

I shrugged as I wondered the same thing.

We thought for a moment. Rachel lay fetal on her bed. She was screaming inside and her pain hit me like a bitter wind. I forced myself not to cry.

"I could charm her into forgetting it ever happened," said Cecelia.

I shook my head. "No. She needs to know."

"Would you want someone to do that to you and have no memory afterward?" Hannah asked Cecelia accusingly. "It would be like being drugged or something."

"Maybe we could tell her about it afterward."

"The emotion," I said.

Both Hannah and Cecelia looked at me, confused. Maybe I was being selfish, but the emotion that Rachel felt was the part that threatened to overwhelm me. Rachel needed the emotion turned down so she could deal with the memory. Right now, her mind overflowed with anguish and a jumble of terrible images. It was hard for me to focus, and I only felt it second-hand.

I gritted my teeth and tried to concentrate. "Charm commands work like hypnosis, only stronger, right?" I asked.

Cecelia nodded.

"So let her keep the memories, but tell her that whenever she recalls them, she won't feel the pain."

Hannah still looked uncertain, but Cecelia considered it. "It should work," she said, finally.

"Rachel?" I asked, tentatively. *Rachel?*

I focused in more closely on her mind, fighting my way through the silent, cringe-inducing scream billowing out from her. Tears ran down my cheeks. *Rachel? Do you want us to do this?*

"Take the pain away," she whispered. If I hadn't been in her head, I wouldn't have heard her clearly enough to understand.

I nodded to Cecelia. "Do it."

"Rachel," she said, using her charm voice, "when you remember what Michael did to you tonight, you will only feel it distantly, like you're watching a movie, okay?"

A sick feeling hit me as I felt something else in Rachel's mind. *Oh my God.* Cold stone filled my voice. "Get the other times, too," I said to Cecelia.

What I saw in Rachel's head made me regretful—regretful that I hadn't fried Michael's brain to hell when I'd had the chance. Cecelia's previous words, "You can stop doing what they told you to," also had released Rachel's forcibly-silenced memories of other nights—nights when no one had stopped Michael.

Hannah gasped as she understood.

Cecelia repeated, "When you remember what Michael did to you before, you will only feel it distantly. It'll be like you saw it in a movie, like it happened to someone else."

Rachel shuddered, and then exhaled slowly. The pain left her mind with that single breath. After lying still for a few seconds, she sat up, which surprised us.

"Thanks," she said quietly.

Good work, I thought at Cecelia.

"You stay out of my head."

CHAPTER 13

I didn't sleep that night. After Cecelia left, all three of us lay down in our beds and pretended. Too much ran though my head—my own thoughts and those of Rachel and Hannah. At first light, I grabbed my coat and walked down to the sparks' buildings. I pulled up a metal folding chair on the tiny beach and watched the stillness of the lake. The brilliantly turning leaves showered reflected colors onto the silent water. I waited for Sean to wake, listening in on a few fiery dreams that flickered in the sparks' minds behind me.

Sean staggered out to his locker for new clothes. I'd forgotten how little they could keep where they slept. He'd wrapped a cotton blanket around his shoulders for warmth against the morning chill.

"Sean," I said, surprising him. His mind still felt sleep-drunk. "I need to talk to you."

I had no intention of saying anything about the events in the basement; that wasn't my secret to tell. "Last night at dinner, do you remember having the thought about wanting a girlfriend?"

Sean's eyes narrowed as he looked at me. "Yeah, what about it?"

"And the one asking yourself what you thought of Rachel? And whether you should go talk to her?" I asked, steeling myself. This was painfully hard.

"Yeah."

I took a deep breath. Just do it—like ripping off a band-aid. "I… I put those in your head. I'm really sorry. I won't do it again. I just… I just thought you might like to get to know her better."

Sean considered this for a long minute, and then he nodded. "Okay."

"You're not mad?"

"Not mad."

I closed my eyes and exhaled in relief. "Thanks."

"Hey Maddie, next time you have something to tell me, just tell me, okay?"

"Absolutely. I'm really sorry, Sean."

"She's your roommate, right? Rachel?"

"Yeah."

"She's nice."

"She *is* nice."

Sean looked at me, processed that I had nothing left to add, and then went back to getting clothes from his locker.

That'd gone better than I'd hoped.

I felt the emotional burden slip from me. Suddenly my eyes drooped and my shoulders sagged. I needed sleep and I had no idea where I could go to get it. My room in Blake House? I doubted that I'd be able to sleep with everyone in class right below me, broadcasting their thoughts like a roomful of too-loud TV shows. Were Michael and Victor thinking venomous things about me in the basement? The cell might be soundproof, but that wouldn't suppress their thoughts. Also, I didn't think I'd share my dreams with people when they were awake, but I didn't know for sure. Ugh. That would be even worse; everyone would remember the details that my twisted subconscious threw out.

I dragged as I headed back.

"Maddie!" Panic filled Trevor's distant voice as it carried across the tall grass.

I'd never seen someone move so fast. Trevor pushed off with his ability as he flung himself across the field to me, so he took bounding leaps as he ran. He wrapped me in shaking arms. "Are you okay?"

I met his gaze and started to cry. *I'm so sorry. I was wrong. I've already apologized to Sean.*

Trevor pulled me even closer. His giddy relief quelled the aftertaste of sick-grey fear in his mind. His anger at me wasn't even a memory. *I heard that Michael attacked you last night. I was afraid that—*

Michael's not going to be a problem anymore.

Trevor went rigid. "It's true? Are you all right? What happened?" Twisting, hot nausea seemed to burn within him. *If I hadn't—*

He was... hurting someone else. If we hadn't been fighting, I wouldn't have been in Blake House and... it would have been worse.

Trevor took my face in his hands. It felt as though his eyes examined every pore. "You're exhausted."

I tried to nod—it was hard to do with his hands on my face.

Trevor swept me up in his arms and carried me back to the church. The rocking of his steps was primally soothing. I leaned my head against his chest and closed my eyes. He placed me on my narrow cot in the coatroom then lay down next to me, wrapping himself around me protectively.

Safe.

I turned my head into the crook of his neck, inhaled the warm, woodsy scent of his skin, and fell asleep in seconds.

How long had I slept? It was hard to tell what time it was. The reflected daylight coming through the cracked sanctuary door made a pale line on the floor. My rose, still in its glass on the floor by my cot, caught the light. It seemed to hold some profound meaning that I was still too sleepy to register.

Trevor sat on the makeshift mattress couch in the sanctuary, trying to read. His mind tumbled his concerns over and over like mismatched socks in a dryer. I could tell he hadn't left the church all day. He'd been eating cereal straight from the box in dry handfuls, and a half-finished six-pack of soda rested within reach. The light filtering in through the broken shutter made me think it was early afternoon.

I pulled the sleeping bag around my shoulders as I padded in to join him. It was cold in the church, probably only about ten degrees above freezing. I must've spent more time in the cold since I'd arrived at Ganzfield than I'd spent all last winter in New Jersey. I joined Trevor wordlessly, sliding down next to him, and helped myself to a handful of his cereal and one of the caffeinated sodas. The crunching sounded unnaturally loud as I chewed, and the continual fizz sound from the soda can seemed to fill the space around us.

I didn't feel alert enough to form sentences. My free hand absentmindedly reached for Trevor's, just feeling the contact. Trevor put his arm around me, comforting me, sensing my need for quiet companionship. His thoughts calmed. *Maddie's all right. We're together. Everything's okay.*

"You skipped class." I felt the caffeine take effect and my soul reconnected to my brain. Ah, caffeine—the *other* drug that enhanced my mental powers.

"I needed to be here." His eyes flicked to mine. Guilt had gnawed at him over his reaction in the dining hall. While I'd been sleeping all morning, he'd been going over what had happened and what could've happened, again and again.

It was my fault, Trevor. Please don't spend another second thinking about what you could've done differently, okay?

If I hadn't walked out on you at dinner… I'm so sorry. He pulled me into a hug. Bitter regret flavored his thoughts.

I wanted to let him off the hook and lighten the mood. "Is this the part where we both say, 'Let's never fight again!' and kiss a lot?"

He laughed, and we put that plan into immediate action.

Over the next few days, the telepathic tone of Ganzfield shifted. Michael and Victor's removal created a power vacuum in the charms' social hierarchy. But rather than trying to outdo one another in bids to become the most feared charm, a strange truce took hold among them. At first, I wasn't sure what had caused the change, but I was grateful for it. I later learned that the morning after the incident in the basement, Cecelia had entered the dorm room of every male charm, early enough that most had still been asleep. Using carefully constructed phrases, she commanded them, "You will *never* use your ability to make anyone have sex with you. You will *never* use your ability to cause harm to someone who is both unwilling and innocent. You will *not* make any attempt to have this order removed."

The next morning, she'd done the same with the female charms, just to be fair.

The extent of the new reality hit me when I first saw Rachel in an animated discussion with Cecelia at one of the charm tables in the dining hall. *Rachel? At a charm table?* I stumbled at the sight, but Trevor's invisible hands steadied me and kept my tray from spilling. I recovered gracelessly, then waved hello to both of them. Rachel smiled and waved back. Cecelia acknowledged me with a cool nod. I noticed for the first time that their blonde hair was nearly the same color. They could've passed for sisters. I wondered how they were related. If we went back far enough, most of us probably shared a few common ancestors. G-positive was a genetic trait, after all.

Two days later, I invited Grace to join us for lunch at one of the sparks' tables. I could feel the social walls of Ganzfield crumbling. Grace's arrival caused flickers of interest in several of the male sparks and apparently she didn't need telepathy to feel it. Their initial wariness of her charm ability faded as she flirted lightly with Drew, Harrison, and Sean in turns. I realized that they'd relaxed around her because they trusted me. *Maddie won't let her pull any of that charm crap on us when she's around.* Grace wouldn't do that, though. Her experience in the basement had left her with a strong sense of right and wrong regarding her ability.

Dr. Williamson stayed in residence on the third floor of the main building. The incident with Michael and Victor had made him realize that he'd been neglecting important aspects of running Ganzfield. He was determined to keep things in better order in the future. Our daily practical lessons covered improving my range, understanding the emotional nuances in other people's minds, and how to get the best insider trading information during a short elevator ride in an investment bank.

But the best part of every day was the part I spent with Trevor. The touch of his mind alternately filled me with a giddy, spinning-like-a-fool joy and a warm sense of peace that beckoned me home. I found myself entranced by little things: the long fingers of his hands; the way the morning light brought out deep-reddish highlights in his hair. My breath caught when he thought about me: *dazzling, amazing, wonderful.*

The intensity of our physical attraction threatened to overwhelm us. He had these awesome, heart-racing daydreams in which he'd slowly remove my clothing, kissing every inch of skin as he exposed it. They made everything inside me go liquid. When our eyes caught, the energy jumped between us, pulling us into one another. Every cell of our bodies hummed with a silver glow.

I'd read once that sex was ninety percent mental. We were just leaving out the other ten percent—but that other ten percent was probably overrated, anyway.

The intensity of our connection grew stronger each time we "soulmated," as we'd begun to call it. Beautiful… wonderful… magical.

If only I'd known how fragile everything was.

CHAPTER 14

This sucks.

Seth hated taking food to the prisoners in the basement, and he frequently broadcast his mental complaints to me. Only three of us in Ganzfield could be near Michael and Victor; anyone else would immediately be charmed to unlock the door and help them escape. Good thing Seth was doing it, though. I wasn't sure I could've kept from hurting them. Rachel's memories still haunted me, mixing with my own trauma from the van. At least Dr. Williamson recognized that, which was why Seth was stuck feeding the prisoners.

The corrosive, painful presence of Michael's simmering anger filled Blake House. How could other people not feel it? It was like the noise from a jackhammer, pervading everything. Attending class became an exercise in endurance, making me squeeze my eyes shut and rub my temples. The morning he left Ganzfield felt like a holiday to me.

Victor remained in the cell; the dodecamine hadn't fully left his system. I heard his thoughts beneath me during classes in

Blake House and when I went to the infirmary for my weekly blood draw. Matilda didn't discuss what had happened in the basement with me, although I knew Grace had told her. Wild rumors roamed the halls of Ganzfield. I got a mindful in class and the dining hall for several days, pretty much whenever someone looked at me.

And they looked at me a lot.

—*said that lasers flashed from her eyes when she—*

—*know Michael and Victor both had it coming—*

—*after what they did to me last spring. I wish I could have seen—*

—*that she's picking off the charms, one by one, until—*

—*were going to wait for her to go to sleep so she wouldn't hear their thoughts when they—*

Since the three minders weren't talking, no one could get accurate information. At least people didn't connect Rachel or Grace to the incident. I could deal with my role in the rumor machine but, thankfully, they didn't have to worry about what people were saying.

I'd been at Ganzfield for just over three weeks when Matilda pulled me out of psychology class. It was Saturday morning—it still felt strange to have classes on Saturday. Her thoughts hummed with controlled anxiety as I followed her to the infirmary.

Trevor's mind followed mine. *Is something wrong?*

I'll tell you what she says in a few minutes.

"Maddie, your blood work came back," she said as soon as the infirmary door had closed behind us. "Dodecamine is a slowly absorbed molecule in most G-positives. However, your absorption levels are unusually high."

"All right." I listened more deeply to her mind. What about these high absorption levels caused her concern?

Seizures. Catatonia. Permanent brain damage.

A chill started in my chest and spread through my torso. "Brain damage?" Crap. I was rather fond of my brain. I really didn't want to damage it.

Matilda sighed. "I was going to tell you more gently than that," she said, "but yes. There's an increased risk of serious complications in people with high absorption rates."

"Am I going to have to stop the meds?" My nails dug into my palms. Would Trevor feel the same way about me if we lost the special way we communicated? I was getting used to being a minder, and I suddenly realized at how strongly I wanted to remain that way. I didn't want to lose my ability. It would be like being blind all my life, getting my sight for a few weeks, then losing it again.

"I want to try something new—give you lower, more frequent doses." *Weekly injections might even out the absorption process and lessen the risk of severe side-effects from the sudden spikes.* She'd never tried it.

What should I do? If I stopped the medication, I could have all of the aspects of a normal life back—the ones I had been mourning only a little while ago—college; living with and around other people; a family someday; silence within my own mind.

Oh yeah, and the no-brain-damage thing.

Alternatively, I could stay here. I could be with Trevor. I could do exciting and unusual things with my life. Maybe I could do important things, and I could make a difference in many lives.

Definitely worth the risk.

"Let's try the lower dose," I said.

Matilda hesitated.

"I'm sure," I added.

Had they gotten my charmed mom to sign a waiver, allowing the Ganzfield people to give me experimental medical treatments? I suspected they had; Dr. Williamson seemed to have that sort of thing covered. For all I knew, my mother had signed a form saying the Ganzfield staff was allowed to lock me in a soundproof cell in the basement. If a charm had asked her to, my mother probably would have relinquished custody. In fact, I wasn't a hundred percent sure she hadn't.

After Matilda gave me the injection, I returned to psych class.

What's going on? Trevor asked before I even sat down.

Blood work. I needed another shot of dodecamine.

He frowned. *Everything okay? It's only been* —he did the math— *three weeks.*

Apparently, I burn through it faster than most. Matilda's changing my dosage. I didn't want to worry him, but I knew that if the situation were reversed, I'd want to know about any risk to him. *If I start acting weird, tell Matilda, okay? So she can tweak the injection rate or something.*

Weird? We're having a mental conversation. Define weird.

I smiled. *Okay, maybe we've raised the bar on weird. If I seem disoriented or something… that sort of thing. There's a risk I might have a seizure.*

Trevor's concern flooded over me. *Seizure?*

No, thank you. Maybe I'll have one later, though.

Don't joke around about that, Maddie. You're too important to me.

That's why I told you. I'd want to know if it were you. Look, we won't worry about it unless something happens, okay?

Trevor was not mollified. His thoughts took on a new layer of protective concern and he watched me when he thought I wasn't paying attention.

I would've been the same way if it'd been him.

Williamson's gone.

What? I recognized Seth's voice in my mind, mostly by its rudeness. I pulled the sleeping bag closer around my shoulders and squeezed my eyes shut in moot protest. Seth was somewhere outside and he'd woken me painfully early. It was still dark. I couldn't sense Trevor; he must still be asleep in the sanctuary.

He's fundraising in New York. Left this morning. We both knew that "fundraising" meant gathering inside information from the minds of investment bankers. I was looking forward to trying it myself. Dr. Williamson planned to give me a small account to manage soon.

It was a grey Monday in mid-November, my fifth week at Ganzfield. I was beginning to wonder why someone with as much money at his disposal as Dr. Williamson would set up shop in such a cold climate. It had been below freezing every night for the past week, and it was never got significantly above the high thirties during the day. Trevor and I huddled together for warmth each night.

Actually, I really, really liked that.

We found wonderful ways to generate heat, but then we'd go to our separate beds, doubly-cold because of the lack of the other. Wasn't there a private, tropical island Dr. Williamson could use for his secret training facility? I tried to focus more professionally before I touched Seth's mind again. *I take it you're in charge?*

Yeah, and now you get to feed Victor. Don't kill him.

That's not funny.

Not meant to be. He should be out of here in a few more days. Take food twice a day, mornings and evenings. Best to do it when everyone's at meals—fewer people in the building if he charm-yells. Sandwiches are in the kitchen. Tray slot is at the bottom of the cell door. Check his mind before you open the trap, and remember to latch both sides when you're done. That's important. Don't go in, even in an emergency. Got it?

Even the thought of Victor made me sick… and really, really pissed off. A flash of killing energy flared up within me and I forced it down. *I don't want to do this.*

Welcome to my world. It's only for a couple days. Suck it up.

I was left with the distinct impression I wasn't being given a choice.

I groaned as the cold hit me, even through my extra layers of clothing. Trudging back toward the main buildings, my shoes left prints in the light frost that dusted the faded remains of summer grass. At least it hadn't snowed yet.

Snow. Winter in New Hampshire. I was going to need some boots.

Oh. Wait a minute. If Dr. Williamson was gone, then his driver, Greg, was also probably gone. That meant Trevor might be going into town today to do the weekly supply pick up. This might be a good time for me to go, too. I could get some boots.

Hey, Seth! I called mentally.

What? He sounded closer than I thought he'd be. Did he have to stay near the main buildings when he was in charge?

I'm going into town this afternoon.

No, you're not.

Yes, I am. Look, I'm taking over your job of feeding Victor, and I need boots. I don't have any and it's going to snow soon. Trevor's going in to pick up supplies this afternoon, right?

I felt Seth's sullen conflict as he considered this. *Fine. Go.*

The day suddenly looked brighter. I was getting out with Trevor. It even made taking food to Victor bearable. First, though, I needed coffee. Off to the dining hall.

Once I'd fortified my daily intake with essential caffeine, I loaded up a tray with a couple of sodas, a bottle of water, and the two wrapped sandwiches in the kitchen. They'd been set out separately, right where Seth had said they'd be.

The Blake House basement felt as *Silence-of-the-Lambs* creepy as I remembered, and I absentmindedly rubbed at my arms to get rid of the goosebumps. Victor's depression made his thoughts sluggish and dull. They barely registered. His precious charm ability was fading and he felt the loss deeply.

I opened the tray slot and slid in the food. Victor's mind sparked. *That's not Seth's hand! This is my chance!*

I heard his intention to lunge. *Oh, hell!* I pulled back just ahead of his grasp, falling onto my butt on the rough, stone floor. The door shook with the impact of his shoulder.

Crap! Move, move, move! I scrambled back out of reach as his arm extended from the slot. His hand closed on my ankle and I kicked at him, slamming my heel hard against his fingers until he let go.

"Let me out!" he commanded, putting as much of his charm ability in his voice as he could.

"No," I said in a half-whisper. The sound of my harsh breathing echoed from the stone walls and seemed to drown out the word. A wave of cold fright washed over me, and I wondered what had taken it so long.

Victor recognized my voice and he shouted angry curses at me. His renewed despair sucked the energy from him. His thoughts turned grey again.

I almost pitied him. *Almost.*

After a minute, he slowly withdrew his arm from the tray slot. I waited, listening to his thoughts for any further intentions of an ambush. When I was sure he'd given up, I darted forward and quickly latched both sides of the slot.

I needed a shower. I needed to wash the physical and emotional dirt off from the basement. I bolted upstairs. The water felt deliciously, stingingly hot against my skin, and it washed away the last of the fear about the time I rinsed out the conditioner. I put a bit of extra effort into getting dressed.

"Want anything from town?" I asked Hannah and Rachel. We'd settled into a routine as cordial faux-roommates, but we really didn't spend much time together.

Rachel's thoughts were clearer now, like springtime had taken hold of her mind. Everything was growing, green and strong. Her timid fragility had faded, melting away. I was surprised at how helpful Cecelia had been to her. I'd learned from Rachel that Cecelia should've gone off to college this past fall, but she'd been unmotivated to do so and had taken what she called a "slacker year." She accompanied Dr. Williamson on most of the recruiting trips because she had no other obligations. Now she planned to start classes at the University of New Hampshire in the spring term and officially enroll at UNH starting next year, studying clinical psychology. I thought that was a brilliant plan. I'd seen her in action. She'd be able to help so many people—hundreds or even thousands. Now *that* was what a G-positive ability was for!

"Did Cecelia go with Dr. Williamson today?" I asked Rachel.

"Yeah."

"Want to join us for breakfast?" Rachel had been hanging out with Cecelia so much recently. Would she be lonely?

"Sure. Thanks!"

"Hannah? Want to join us?"

"Thanks, but I can't eat in the morning." The thought of food so early in the day sent a little spiral of queasiness through her.

Unsurprisingly, Rachel took the empty seat next to Sean at our table. Trevor caught my gaze as she joined us. *Did you... ?*

I just invited her to join us for breakfast. That's all!

Trevor relaxed, convinced.

Sean also silently questioned my part in the situation. I wasn't going to put any thoughts into his head at a time like this. I shook my head slightly and mutely held up my hands as if pushing away his suspicion.

Rachel actually got Sean to engage in a real conversation. Little tendrils of interest seemed to grow from him as they talked, making Rachel bloom. I suspected that Rachel's nebulous fear of Michael had been holding her back. Now that the source of her fear had been removed, she was blossoming, becoming stronger and more confident.

I smiled.

What's making you so happy? asked Trevor.

Life. You. Everything. Oh yeah, and I can go with you into town this afternoon.

Great!

Now both of us were having a good day.

The drive into town took less than ten minutes; we just followed the only road for a few miles until we came to a T-intersection. Little giddy thrills of joy flicked through me. Trevor and I were out! Just going into town seemed like an adventure. At first, the only mental contacts I had were the flits of birds and the dull, warm thoughts of a few cows standing at a fence bordering the road. Trevor demonstrated his hands-free driving skills to me. The minds of people started filtering in quickly as we approached the town. It surprised me that the rest of the world was so close.

The houses and stores of North Conway looked as though they'd been built to hunker down against the cold winters. Moose- and bear-themed signs decorated many storefronts. The ski shops were open, while shutters covered the ice cream places and canoe rentals. Several art galleries and quaint bed-and-breakfast places gave the town a more upscale charm, while quirky little restaurants advertised things like burritos and lobster on the same sign. Some places already displayed Christmas decorations. I'd forgotten how close we were getting to the holidays. It was as though I'd been living in a country where Christmas wasn't celebrated.

We parked the black van—which seemed larger inside without the three passenger benches—then walked into town. In one store, I picked out a pair of unfashionable but warm snow boots in less than ten minutes. I dug though my purse for cash. When was the last time I'd had to pay for anything? My mom had given me two hundred dollars when I'd left. I discovered that I still had it all.

Trevor and I held hands and strolled the along the main street. We passed a park with a playground and a Victorian-looking train station used for a scenic railroad line through the Mount Washington Valley. It now had some sort of Christmas theme. There were a few people going in and out of the shops, usually hurrying against the chill. Their minds seemed a little duller, their thoughts less distinct, than the G-positives up at Ganzfield. Was there actually a difference or was I being a G-positive elitist?

We drove back to a strip mall we'd passed on our way in. Trevor pulled around the back and stopped at the loading area of the Shur Fine supermarket. A burly, middle-aged man came out when Trevor honked. "Hey, Travis."

Travis?

Yeah, or sometimes Tyler. He never gets it right. "Hi, Billy. This is my girlfriend, Maddie."

Girlfriend. A tingly little thrill passed through me. This was the first time Trevor had introduced me that way. Everyone at Ganzfield had just kind of figured it out.

Billy looked at me with concern. *She's just a kid, about the same age as my Beth. What are they doing up there at Ganzfield? Are they really some kind of cult? Has she been brain-washed? Do her parents even know where she is? Does she need help?* "Do your folks know where you are, honey?"

"Of course! I talked with my mom this morning." That was the truth. I used the phone in Dr. Williamson's office whenever he wasn't there. No one else dared to go up to the third floor, so I had the place to myself. There was another phone in the hall at Blake House that the other girls used, but I preferred the privacy and sense of minder privilege I got from sneaking calls from the third floor office.

I loved my mom, but I also felt detached, like she was part of a life that was no longer mine. In truth, my mom was the only person I truly missed. The surreal part was that she really wasn't worried about me, thanks to Cecelia's charm commands. My mom still loved me, and she usually mentioned how proud she was of me, but she wasn't concerned that something bad might happen to me. My whole life she'd peppered conversations with warnings, telling me to be careful crossing the street, not to talk to strangers, that sort of thing. This non-worried version of mom was a lifetime first.

I stressed about hearing her thoughts for the first time. What if my mom thought something horrible about me, something she would never say? Or what if she thought some guy looked hot? Ick! I shuddered.

Trevor looked into my eyes as we waited for Billy to bring out the order. *So, what does he think?*

Cult.

Billy and a younger man with a scruffy, yellow beard brought out several cases, and then went back for more. I was surprised at how much food we all went though in a week; the supplies filled most of the van, even with the seats removed.

And the younger guy thinks we might be a coven of Wiccans.

Wiccans… witches? His eyes widened with surprise.

Apparently, the Eatons were a little… unusual. We may have inherited some of the legends that started with them. Unenhanced G-positives do strange things from time to time. I thought about how I'd been able to stop Del and his friends. We might be unreliable without enhancement, but with enough adrenalin and incentive, we sometimes caused remarkable events. Were G-positives responsible for all the stories of witches and other supernatural stuff?

Should we be thinking at each other like this? Won't they notice?

My attention flickered to their minds briefly. *They just think we're making goo-goo eyes at each other. Beard-guy thinks we should get a room.*

Trevor nearly cracked up.

Don't laugh! I thought at him. His eyes danced with suppressed mirth. I bit my lip. Everything just seemed so much funnier when I wasn't supposed to laugh.

Billy cleared his throat to get our attention and Trevor signed the invoice.

"Nice to meet you, Bobby!" I called out brightly as we were pulling out.

It's Billy, Trevor corrected me.

I know.

"You too, Maggie. Bye, Travis," said Billy.

As soon as the door shut, I burst out laughing. Billy was annoyed I hadn't gotten his name right.

Trevor took my hand again, and I grinned at him. *Hey, just as long as you keep three hands on the wheel.*

At the turn to the lonely road back to Ganzfield, I had a sudden, strange flicker of contact.

Him.

Someone recognized Trevor.

Frowning, I tried to find the source—but it was distant, at the end of my range. I didn't see anyone. Goosebumps spread across my arms. Something just felt… wrong. *Do you know anyone else in town?*

A few people. I sometimes pick things up from other stores. Why?

Someone just recognized you. I didn't get a good… it didn't seem right. I didn't like it.

Jealous? He teased.

I squeezed his hand, relaxing as the strange contact faded. *Absolutely. You're mine!*

Darn straight.

Back at Ganzfield, Trevor keyed in the code to the gate, 0-9-8-7-6. I laughed.

What?

Dr. Williamson also uses an easy code.

He rolled his eyes. *Well, they're all easy when you pick them out of someone else's mind.*

I shrugged. *True enough.*

Trevor drove the van around the main building to a kitchen door I hadn't known existed. He unloaded the entire van in less than a minute. Since we were back home, he could use his ability openly.

Home. That was the first time I'd really thought of Ganzfield as home.

But it was.

I think I've figured out a way to extend your range. Dr. Williamson and Cecelia had returned yesterday, after nearly a week's absence. I sat in his office, unenthused by the prospect. At least Victor was finally gone. His mental presence had grated against mine whenever I was in range. Every time I'd brought food to him, I'd felt sullied by the contact, like he'd left greasy fingerprints in my mind. My gut churned at his lack of remorse and at something that might have been my own guilty conscience. My enthusiasm for keeping people in basement dungeons had waned.

...It involves Trevor Laurence.

That got my attention. *Trevor?*

Since you two are so fond of each other, it might be easier for you to extend your range if you focus on him.

I had to admit, the idea had appeal.

As we left the main building, we both reached out and found Trevor's mind in the basement of his dorm—the exercise room. How sexist was it that the boys got a cool workout center in their basement while we girls got the creepy soundproof dungeon? Maybe now wasn't the time to bring it up. Dr. Williamson registered the thought anyway. A twitch of his lips was his only comment.

Dr. Williamson's driver supervised Trevor's practical lesson with the rigor of a drill sergeant. I had forgotten his name, but I'd seen enough of his memory to know he'd once been in the military.

Greg—that was his name. As we came down the stairs into the overly-warm room he looked up, annoyed at our interruption.

My jaw dropped and I froze. I even stopped breathing. Trevor stood shirtless, encircled by the various pieces of equipment. He didn't hear us arrive. Concentration tightened the muscles of his face and body as he used his ability to manipulate each of the machines in rapid succession. The exertion caused perspiration to run in a line down to his abdomen. His lean, muscled chest gleamed and crackling red energy sparked through me as I drank him in. I felt dizzy as I imagined—

Ahem.

I squeezed my eyes shut and flushed absolutely red. Crap. Everything I'd been thinking had been absolutely clear to Dr. Williamson. I covered my face with my hands. Trevor suddenly noticed us. The weights fell with a crash that caused Greg to cringe.

"Maddie! Are you okay?" Concern painted his thoughts with yellow energy.

Um, I just had some really, really provocative thoughts about you, and Dr. Williamson heard me.

Oh.

Yeah.

Would it help if I had some really provocative thoughts about you? He was joking, thank heavens. I laughed. It was out there. I'd just have to live with it.

Dr. Williamson followed our exchange with interest. "Your connection's very strong. This might just be the thing."

The thing? Trevor's brow furrowed.

He thinks I might be able to follow your mind from greater distances than I can with other people.

Trevor flushed happily at the thought that he was special to me. *What do you need me to do?*

I looked at Dr. Williamson. *Do we have to use Zener cards this time? I am so sick of the stupid plus signs and wavy lines!*

"I suppose not."

This was getting better and better.

Just talk to me. Tell me something about you. I'll see how far away I can get and still hear you.

Trevor kept up a running mental monologue. *One day, on my home planet of Tatooine, Obi Wan Kenobi rescued me from the Tuscan raiders. Then we went to Mos Eisley Spaceport where we booked passage on the Millennium Falcon. Sadly, Alderaan had been destroyed before we got there.*

If you get to the part where you kiss your sister in the Death Star, I'm going to be grossed out.

Did about I tell you what Ron, Hermione, and I did at Hogwarts?

Those were my favorite books when I was growing up! I was getting farther from him, already upstairs and out the front door. I could still feel him strongly. *I loved the way all the character names and magic words had second meanings. When I was a kid, I thought that J.K. Rowling had to be a real witch to be able to write so well.*

How about I tell you about training at Battle School to fight the Buggers in an interstellar war?

What's that from?

Trevor's astonishment jolted through me. *You've never read Ender's Game? It's amazing!* He started to fill me in on the details. His mental voice grew fainter. I couldn't make out most of what he said about the book. When I could no longer feel his mind, I signaled Dr. Williamson. He'd gotten out of range so that his own abilities wouldn't give me a false boost. I shook my head, but he already knew I'd lost the connection. He measured the distance from the house, and then added the ten feet from inside.

One hundred and forty three feet. I could hear Trevor's mind twice as far as I could anyone else's. Dr. Williamson's mind glowed of triumph. Success!

At the end of the practical lesson, Dr. Williamson gave me one of my first assignments at Ganzfield. *Spend more time mentally connecting with Trevor.*

I quickly blocked my thoughts before Dr. Williamson got a mindful of how Trevor and I "mentally connected." I couldn't stop grinning, though.

Best. Homework. Assignment. Ever.

CHAPTER 15

Dr. Williamson and Cecelia left on another recruiting trip a few weeks later. It was the first week of December and snow covered the ground in a thin layer that had half-melted, and then refrozen overnight into a crusty, treacherous sheet. I broke in my new boots as I joined Trevor on his Monday afternoon supply run into town.

Trevor had a problem. *But it won't be a surprise!* His dismay colored his emotions green-grey.

I could see no solution. There simply was no way for Trevor to give me a Christmas present that would surprise me. *Don't buy me anything—just take me to Aruba.*

But I do that all the time. I want to give you something special.

Aruba really was our favorite REM-sleep destination. Trevor had skills—mad, lucid-dream skills. I'd liberated a few oversized jingle bells from the dining hall's Christmas decorations a few days ago and we'd put them in cardboard boxes around his mattress. The jingle-boxes woke us up very reliably when he threw them, so our memories of shared dreams grew even stronger and clearer. We seemed to be dreaming in-synch more often, as well.

For some reason, though, I still couldn't share any lucid dreams with Trevor. At first, I'd tried to take him to New York, since he'd never been to the City. Then I'd tried other places and simpler images. Nothing worked. It made no sense; wasn't I the telepath in this relationship?

I was able to share a few more of my van nightmares with him, however. Yippee. Apparently my sadistic subconscious had no problem sharing trauma and horror with Trevor, but when I wanted to share a slice of decent pizza and a walk through Central Park, I was outta luck.

Each time I had the nightmare, Trevor rescued me from it. The sickening fear no longer overwhelmed me; I knew now that he'd make everything okay. In the most recent version, Trevor had gathered me up in his arms and flew Superman-style to Aruba.

Like I said: mad skills.

You have no idea how special that is to me. The man of my dreams, Trevor made everything just seem to glow. Waves of emotion swelled out through our mental connection and wash over him.

The van swerved dangerously and I hastily pulled my feelings back. I didn't want to kill us both with my love for him. Once we straightened out, I took a deep breath and settled for holding his hand. Trevor might be able to drive with his ability, but he still needed to be able to concentrate on the road.

We parked on the main street again and spent less than an hour window shopping. Quilts; wooden bears carved with tiny chainsaws; maple syrup in little beige jugs. None of it really seemed to be what we were looking for. In a quirky little gift shop, though, I pulled a black, long-sleeved t-shirt off the rack. I started to laugh.

"I *have* to get this for you." I held it up for Trevor to read.

Those who believe in telekinetics, raise my hand. —Kurt Vonnegut

Trevor cracked up. I took the shirt up to the checkout.

We ended up getting a bunch of cold weather camping stuff at Eastern Mountain Sports. Even practical stuff like hand warmers seemed like romantic gifts to us. The church had gotten so cold that for the past few mornings, the frigid air had condensed my breath into a delicate layer of frost on the sleeping bag around my face.

Walking back, I saw a pretty handmade scarf in one of the store windows. I ducked in and bought it for my mom. My shopping was done. My mom loved that color blue and I knew it would look good on her.

Christmas. My mom. Yellow-brown trickles of anxiety seeped through me and I bit my lip.

What's wrong? Concern swept through Trevor as he sensed my mood change.

My mom was coming to New Hampshire for Christmas. Since I was still throwing nightmares, Dr. Williamson thought it was a bad idea for me to be away overnight. *I'm just... I hope my mom can handle all of this stuff.*

Do you think she can?

Well, if she freaks out, Dr. Williamson's going to get one of the charms to have a short talk with her. Yup, I might be setting my mom up for a brain-washing this Christmas.

Ho, ho, ho. Merry Christmas, Mom.

What will Maddie's mom will think of me? The thought flashed through Trevor's mind.

I wrapped my arms around him. *She'll love you.*

Trevor raised his eyebrows as grey trickles of anxiety flickered through him. *You think she will?*

Absolutely. She's a great judge of character. I flash or two of G-positive insight about you and she'll think you're wonderful.

Trevor hadn't been back to Michigan since he'd come to Ganzfield. His family hadn't made an effort to keep in touch with him in the more than a year he'd been gone. Why wasn't he angry? I was pissed off at them on his behalf and I'd never even met them. But Trevor still wanted their acceptance—their approval. He yearned for the sense of belonging he'd never felt from them.

Oh. A trembly-sick feeling hit me in the gut. Trevor didn't buy any presents for his mom or his grandparents. No wonder he wanted to give me a surprise. He didn't have anyone else to shop for. I squeezed his waist and leaned closer against him as we walked back to the van.

So… what's Christmas like at Ganzfield?

Trevor smiled. *Last year, the McFees took over the place. It was great.*

I knew that most of the charms, RVs, and healers traveled home for two weeks at Christmastime. Apparently, the minders interrogated the charms upon their return to ensure they hadn't used their abilities inappropriately. Charms could "ask" for some very disturbing gifts. I'd be conducting my first interrogations in January. Ugh.

How come all the McFees know about Ganzfield? I had to bug Dr. Williamson for weeks to let me tell my mom. Why all the secrecy? Shouldn't all our families know? G-positive was a genetic trait, after all.

Trevor frowned. *The McFees are a special case. But as for the secrecy, I heard that a few years ago there was this guy who killed off a bunch of G-positives. He's dead now, but Dr. Williamson wants to keep a low profile so we don't get targeted again.*

I remembered Rachel talking about her aunt—how someone had experimented on her. She'd also mentioned the Sons of Adam, the group that thought we were dangerous mutants. I looked out the van window, watching the strangers around us with a new sense of concern. What would people do if they found out about us?

I shook off the creepy trepidation as we brought the van to the loading dock of the supermarket. This was America. We hadn't had witch hunts here in centuries.

"Hi, Bobby!" I called out when Billy stuck his head out the door in response to our honk.

It's Billy, I heard in stereo from both Trevor and Billy. I suppressed my laugh.

"Travis. Maggie."

"I'll be right back," I said, giving Trevor's hand a quick squeeze. I wanted to grab some feminine hygiene stuff in the store. Trevor didn't need to be with me for that. "Can I cut through?" I asked Billy. He nodded, and I went though the storeroom and pushed open the "Employees Only" door into the supermarket.

Want some Doritos? I asked Trevor as I passed the display.

Sure! Our junk food supply in the church was running low. I grabbed a bag.

At the end of the seasonal aisle, I saw a box containing a sprig of mistletoe. I felt a little thrill and impulsively picked it up. I had someone I wanted to stand under the mistletoe with this Christmas. Another row over, I found the shampoo and turned down the aisle. What I was looking for should be around here somewhere.

An electric feeling of panic hit me as something stung Trevor in the shoulder—hard. *Trevor? Trevor!* I felt his pain and then cold shock.

What the—? Trevor fell as his mind flickered and went dark.

Oh, my God in Heaven. I dropped everything and ran full out. *Trevor! Trevor! TREVOR!*

The employee door slammed against the wall with a gunshot-loud bang as I ran through. Tires squealed on the pavement outside. I was closer now, close enough to sense four minds inside. One checked the site in Trevor's shoulder where the tranquillizer dart had penetrated. The other holstered his weapon efficiently—probably ex-military. He grabbed the seat back as the van tilted through the turn.

The mental images from the front passenger caused my knees to buckle. *Oh my God. No!* I fell heavily at the end of the loading dock. I couldn't make my legs move. Shaking. Crying.
Billy came though behind me, pushing a hand-truck stacked with milk crates.

"What's all the noise out here?"

Experimentation. Vivisection. The front passenger's thrill—he would finally see the basal ganglion structure of a telekinetic.

I fell forward onto my hands and heaved up my lunch. *No, no, no. No. No. No! No! No! NO!*

I tried to think. The van. I had to get to Trevor. I made myself move, limping to the driver's door of the vehicle. The keys were gone. Trevor must've pocketed them.

I needed help. Ganzfield. Five miles away. I started running.

Billy called out after me. "What's wrong?"

I couldn't even begin to tell him.

Sweat had soaked through my winter clothes by the time I arrived at the front gate. Nearly an hour had passed and sick terror overwhelmed my thoughts. *Trevor, Trevor, Trevor.* I couldn't get enough oxygen. It felt as though something squeezed my chest. My shaking hands wouldn't work the keypad. I had to force myself calm and try again, thankful that Trevor's code was easy. *0-9-8-7-6.* The gate started to roll. I squeezed through the open slot and ran toward the main buildings.

Seth! Seth! SETH!

What?

Trevor. They took Trevor! I flashed my memories at him in a confused jumble. I was sure I wasn't making any sense. *We have to go after them. Now!*

I ran past the main building toward Seth. I needed help to get Trevor back. Seth was in charge. He would help. I nearly smacked into Drew and the other sparks on their way up to the main building.

"Maddie? What's wrong?" Drew's brows knit together with concern.

"It's Trevor." My breath caught in sobbing gasps. "I need help. We have to go get him."

It's too dangerous. Seth tried to talk me down. *Let me call Dr. Williamson and we'll see what he thinks should be done.*

No! We need to go now! Vivisection. They wanted to cut Trevor open and they wanted him awake when they did it.

"Let's go," Drew said without hesitation. He hadn't heard my exchange with Seth, but my earlier comment was enough to get him moving.

"Rachel. We need Rachel." I'd put that much of a plan together while running back. "She can find him."

I turned back and desperately scanned the buildings for her mind. Yes! She was in our dorm room. I ran. Drew followed.

"Rachel! I need your help!" I burst into the room, startling both Rachel and Hannah. "Someone's taken Trevor."

"Taken?" she asked, confused.

"Kidnapped. Like the people who took your Aunt Lucy."

Rachel paled. The word *vivisection* had the same awful resonance in her mind. She grabbed her coat.

Hannah followed. "Maddie, you're hurt."

I looked down. Blood soaked the fabric around the ripped knee of my jeans. I shook my head. "Doesn't matter. We have to go now!"

"I'm coming with you," she said, grabbing her own coat.

We ran to the barn. I tried Trevor's code in the keypad. It didn't work. Trevor didn't use this keypad so he didn't have access. Aaargh! I felt like ripping the door off its hinges. I could ask Drew to burn though the door… No. Wait! I knew another code. Dr. Williamson's code. Another easy code. At that moment, I thanked God I was a minder. I punched in 9-7-5-3-1. The door lock clicked and we were in the barn.

I heard Seth's mental voice calling me. *Stop! Wait! You can't go! We have to talk to Dr. Williamson!* He was running, determined to stop us, to make us wait until we understood the situation better.

"The crossbar!"

I grabbed the two remaining van keys from the rack as the others unbarred the big doors. I jumped into the driver's seat of the nearest van. The first key didn't work. I threw it to the barn floor and tried the second. The engine roared to life.

"Get in!" I called. Drew grabbed the shotgun seat next to me. Rachel and Hannah piled in the back. I gunned the engine, making the van lurch forward and throwing everyone against their seats. Gravel spewed from our back wheels as we shot though down the driveway toward the main road.

I got the code into the security keypad despite my shaking hands. The gate seemed to take forever to roll out of the way.

Move, move, move! I gunned the gas again as soon as the opening was wide enough. A harsh metallic squeal came from the back panel—I hadn't waited quite long enough. Not important right now.

Drew cringed at the sound. "Um, Maddie? Do you even know how to drive?"

We barreled down the main road toward North Conway at twice the legal speed limit. "I have my learner's permit," I said, with annoyance. I couldn't be bothered with such mundane issues. Trevor was in danger!

"Maddie, let me drive," Drew said calmly. How could he be calm? I focused on the road. "Maddie, we can't help Trevor if we get killed in a car crash."

Okay, that made sense, and part of me could see that I was being dangerously reckless. I pulled over and jumped out of the way. Drew moved into the driver's seat. I started to take shotgun, but Hannah said, "Sit back here and let me fix you up."

Rachel squeezed past me into the front. In her mind, I saw the golden line—the golden line that led to Trevor. It took the edge off my panic to see it. Rachel could see him. We would find him.

"Take the 302. I think they're driving south on 91." I suddenly realized who at Ganzfield went on field trips: the RVs. Rachel focused further and I could see the vision in her mind—the backs of two heads in front, a pair of ex-militaries hunkered down in back, and Trevor lying unconscious on the floor between them. Thick plastic binding cuffed his hands together. An IV bag hung from a hook in the ceiling. The clear tubing snaked into Trevor's arm and swayed with the motion of the van. *Drugged. Unconscious.*

Rachel concentrated on the view out the windshield. She saw the road signs she'd been looking for and relaxed slightly. "Got them. They're on 91 South."

A strong tingle jolted through my knee and I nearly jerked away from Hannah's hands. The still-seeping wound closed and the bruises faded. The electric sensation spread further down both my legs, relaxing the overused muscles and traveling into my feet. I'd run more than five miles in new boots. She healed the blisters.

Once I could focus again, I told them what'd happened and what I'd seen. Drew and Hannah's shock washed over me as a distant sense of cold. Rachel seemed prepared. This was a world she'd inhabited all her life; she knew more about the dark side of G-positive existence than the rest of us.

I kept mentally touching that golden lifeline in her mind. We were going to get Trevor back. We wouldn't be too late. We couldn't be.

Rachel watched tirelessly, saying things like, "They've turned west on Route 11;" "They've gone south on 7;" "Right on Grange Road." I memorized each direction, noting, with gratitude, that Drew was doing the same. He had an intense, calm-in-a-crisis strength. Perhaps that was another reason the McFees made good firefighters.

We'd been on the road for more than three hours when Rachel announced, "I think they're stopping." I scrambled out of my cocoon of anxiety and into her thoughts to see where Trevor was. The van had pulled up to a guard booth—a little island of brightness in the twilight. The driver spoke to the guard but we couldn't hear their words. A large sign lit by two small spotlights read, "Eden Imaging."

Eden Imaging. Eden Imaging. I committed the name to memory.

Streetlights illuminated the rolling, campus-like grounds. The glassy sheen of ice-topped snow reflected and brightened the view as the van pulled up to the entrance of a boxy, three-story building.

Vivisection Man held the IV as the two ex-militaries pulled Trevor out of the back of the van. They set him on a wheeled gurney, and then Vivisection Man typed a code into another keypad lock. Rachel and I both saw his fingers in her vision: 5-7-5-9-2.

"5-7-5-9-2. 5-7-5-9-2. 5-7-5-9-2. Somebody write that down," I commanded. Hannah pulled a pen from her coat pocket. Since she had no paper, she hesitated then wrote on the leg of my jeans. No problem. They were already ripped and bloody.

Vivisection Man rolled Trevor's gurney to an elevator. He pressed three. *Third floor.* I compiled my internal map. Down the long corridor and into room 318. *Room 318. Got it.*

Rachel's mind exploded in pain and shock. *Oh, no. No, no, no!* Her concentration failed.

I gasped as the connection was severed. *What happened? Trevor!* I'd been so focused on Trevor and laying my trail of mental breadcrumbs that I hadn't seen what else had been in the room. I found the answer in Rachel's mind. There'd been a second gurney in the brightly-lit, cold-looking place full of medical equipment where they'd taken Trevor.

A dead body lay on the gurney, its head still held by a metal circle. Screws dug though his flesh and into his skull to hold him immobile. A mint green sheet covered his grey, heavyset body from the waist down. The dead man's open eyes stared into eternity, the horror of his final minutes still somehow evident. Even with the top of his skull missing, the dead man's face was recognizable in profile. It was Rachel's Uncle Charlie—the one who'd been in Cancun.

Rachel tried to use her ability again, but her emotional distress kept overloading it. She swept out with her golden touch but it fizzled, crackled, and short-circuited. She cried with a twisting mix of grief and frustration.

"What? What happened?" asked Drew.   I suddenly remembered that neither he nor Hannah had seen what we'd seen.

"They've put Trevor in some sort of operating room." My voice sounded dead. Dead... like Uncle Charlie. *Oh my God.* What was happening to Trevor? I felt blind and helpless, and the need to *do something* caused me to clench and unclench my fists repeatedly. I had to keep it together. I had to keep it together for Trevor. "Rachel's Uncle Charlie's in that room. He's dead. They killed him."

Drew's shock splattered like grey slush against my mind.

Hannah's thoughts lurched sickeningly, as though she might faint. She closed her eyes for a minute of silent prayer, which steadied her. "Switch with me, Maddie," she said, as she took the seat directly behind Rachel and laid her hands on her shoulders. Pins and needles passed through Rachel, calming her.

He's dead, he's dead, he's dead... Grief filled Rachel's mind.

I inhaled deeply, steadying myself, forcing myself not to give in to the screaming panic in my head. We were going to get Trevor back. The alternative was unthinkable. I needed to focus—to plan. "Drew, do you know where we're going?" I asked.

He nodded.

We were forced to stop for gas; the van was running on fumes. I found my purse on my shoulder. It must have been there all afternoon. I hadn't noticed. Between my financial contribution and Drew's, we had enough cash to fill it up.

Hannah came back from the little shop with some granola bars and fruit juice. Even the thought of food made my stomach threaten mutiny. I shook my head when she offered.

"Drink the juice, at least. Keep your strength up." I made myself down a bottle of orange juice. She got Rachel to do the same.

The stupid gas pump was so slow! It took forever to top off the tank. Then we started moving again, gliding through the night on the dark country road. Rachel finally reconnected to Trevor. This time, the image was harder to make out, like looking though a smudged window into a half-grey dawn.

A metal ring had been fitted around Trevor's head. Screws dug into his skull. I started to shake. *Oh, my God in Heaven...* I knew I was really, really praying; this was not just an empty phrase. *Please, God. We have to get there in time. Please.* I couldn't see Uncle Charlie; the edges of Rachel's vision had trailed into darkness. Trevor lay there, helpless and alone in the dark. I squeezed my eyes shut as I dug my nails into the edge of the vinyl seat.

I had a plan. It was a simple plan.

We would drive up and use the code to get inside. We would get Trevor and bring him back.

And I would blast the minds of anyone who got in our way.

I quietly explained this to the others.

"Too bad we don't have a charm along," said Hannah, disapproval tingeing her voice. "You wouldn't have to hurt anyone."

I really, really wanted to hurt the people who were doing this to Trevor, but I didn't say so. However, Hannah's words worked on me. I couldn't go in like an angel of wrath, harming everyone indiscriminately. I could read minds; I'd be able to separate those responsible from the innocent. I didn't want to harm innocent people. Someone might feel about them the way I felt about Trevor. Those innocent people might be their whole world.

I felt my internal rage slow from a full, bubbling boil down to a simmer. I didn't have to kill. I could immobilize people with pain. I was fine with causing pain to the people who stood between us and Trevor. No problem.

"We could disable their cars, too… so they can't follow us afterward," Drew suggested.
He thought a series of engine fires would be more than sufficient.

Good thinking. "How close do you need to be?" I asked. Drew was turning out to be a good person to have around in a crisis.

My throat tightened when I saw the sign for Eden Imaging. "Drive past the front entrance," I told Drew.

"I know."

I concentrated hard as we went by the security booth, mentally reaching across the distance, searching out other minds. The solitary guard listened to some kind of grunge metal on his iPod. No one else was in my range. Good. That'd make things easier. Rachel intensified her focus and her vision of Trevor sharpened. The golden line shifted toward the building we could see outside the van. We were so close!

Hannah wavered, her emotional distress spiraling within her. She didn't want to hurt anyone and she had the good student's aversion to getting into any kind of trouble. Breaking into a medical facility was never something she'd even considered doing.

"Hannah?" I forced calm into my voice, even though something inside me screamed, *Get in there! Do something!* "Do you need to stay in the car?"

The temptation to stay behind pulled at her. Finally, she shook her head. "If he's hurt, you'll need me."

We turned the van around and headed back toward Eden Imaging.

"Everyone ready for this?" My voice sounded low and controlled. That surprised me, because everything inside my head seemed to be on fire.

Drew seemed almost eager. "You bet."

"Yes," Hannah agreed.

Rachel nodded and her golden link to Trevor brightened further.

We pulled up to the security booth, stopping just in front of the barrier that crossed the drive. The guard paused his music and looked at our van without concern. Nothing about kidnapping or vivisection tainted his thoughts. *Weird time to come here. Probably another one of Dr. Hanson's patients.*

In that second, I decided that we were. "Hi," I said, leaning slightly over the surprised Drew. I tried to use my friendliest tone and keep the tremors out of my voice. "We're here to see Dr. Hanson."

"Name?" he asked, picking up a clipboard and scanning through the unchecked patient names. I picked the first one out of his mind. "Weaver?" I inwardly cringed. I probably should've sounded more confident giving my own name.

The guard didn't seem to notice anything. He checked the box. Next to me, I felt Drew surreptitiously melt the phone connection to the wall.

Don't forget the radio, I directed his attention to the walkie-talkie on the guard's belt. I felt Drew's focus shift and the speaker emitted a tiny puff of grey smoke.

The guard waved us through as the barrier swung up. I didn't realize I was shaking until we pulled away.

"I thought you were planning to hurt him." said Hannah.

"He just works here. He's not in on this. We still might be able to get in and out again without anyone knowing."

Hannah's relief brightened her thoughts and strengthened her resolve.

Drew pulled into a parking space, choosing a spot near the door so the van could drive out quickly. Five other vehicles occupied the lot: one van and four cars. It was after nine at night, so I guessed that one car was the security guard's, and the van might belong to the company. That left at least three other people inside. We were closer now. I could focus in and feel them. One was at the front desk just inside—another security guard. The other two were upstairs, on the third floor.

Hot nausea passed through me as I recognized the mind of one of them. In a book-lined office, Vivisection Man discussed preparations for surgery on Trevor. *"Cut the sedative in the subject's IV drip in half,"* he said to the lab tech. *"We need to wake him easily when the other freak arrives."*

Why was he doing this? His cold thoughts reeked of cruelty. He had a charm coming—the "freak" in his terminology. The charm was going to use his ability to keep Trevor immobilized. *Oh my God.* Vivisection Man wanted Trevor conscious but unable to use his ability when he cut his head open.

A voice inside me started wailing.

Dr. Hanson, the one I thought of as Vivisection Man, planned to knock the charm out with a tranquilizer after the experiment. Once the lab tech had left his office, Dr. Hanson stuck the dart gun into the pocket of his lab coat. The charm would be his next test subject. Dr. Hanson smirked. *I won't even need to pay the freak all that money I promised him.* He felt proud that he was such a savvy businessman. I tasted bile in the back of my throat.

"Guard at the front desk on the ground floor and two people upstairs. They're both bad guys," I said. The monitor at the guard's desk showed our progress through the parking lot. We tried to look calm and normal as we walked from the van.

The keypad glowed with a soft green. The code! My heart froze within me. It was too dark to read the ballpoint ink against the blue of my jeans.

"Drew, I need a light to read these numbers," I said, fighting to keep the panic out of my voice. Drew whipped off his glove. A tiny flame flicked up from his fingers, which he held cupped behind his palm next to my leg. "Got it. Thanks." The flame winked out.

I kept my own winter gloves on as I hit the keys. Better not to leave fingerprints: that was how the cops had found me the last time.

5-7-5-9-2. I stopped breathing as I stared at the little red status light.

It flipped green and the door clicked. Drew pushed it open.

"Can I help you?" asked the guard. He was middle-aged and going grey, with the build of an old soldier—barrel-chested and heavily muscled. He got to his feet behind the half-moon of the reception desk as we came through the door. *Something's not right. What are these kids doing here?* The guard's mind flickered to the gun in the holster on his hip.

"Dr. Hanson's expecting us up on three," I said. I tried to stay behind Drew since I looked sweaty, ripped, and bloody. Actually, we all seemed too young to belong here—too young for Dr. Hanson to expect us. Doubt flickered through the guard's mind, building momentum like a rockslide. *Why would a bunch of kids show up at a medical center? Are they medical students or something?*

Medical students? That'd work.

"We're the med students," I continued.

"Oh." *That explains it. And they had the door code.* He sat back down as his suspicions deflated. "Elevator's on the left."

"Thanks." Drew lingered near the desk just long enough to fry the phone and walkie-talkie here, as well. Hannah pushed the button and we waited what felt like years for the elevator to ding and the door to slide open.

How are we going to carry Trevor past the guard on the way down? Hannah wondered.

Got any ideas?

She jumped. *That sounded like a ghost in my head!* Hannah let out a quick, nervous laugh. *Hey—*

I agreed. *Ghost voice. Good plan. I'm on it.*

Ding. Third floor. We moved as quietly as we could to the end of the dim hall. It gave me a strange sense of déjà vu—an echo from Rachel's mind. Locked door. Keypad. I put in the same code, 5-7-5-9-2, hoping that Dr. Vivisection had used the same one on this door as he had below.

The tech's head shot up in surprise as we entered. I channeled all of the energy from the anxiety of the past endless hours into overloading his mind. He crumpled into a heap on the cold, white linoleum before we'd even closed the door behind us.

Trevor. He lay on an operating table, stripped to the waist. From the metal ring, four screws stuck obscenely into his head. I couldn't feel his mind, but I put my hand on his chest, trembling with relief that I could feel his heartbeat and his slow, even breathing. My own breath caught in bursts as I closed my eyes for a second of silent gratitude. *Thank you, God. Thank you, thank you, thank you.*

I pulled the IV from his arm, then turned my attention to the screws.

Hannah, ever the healer, couldn't help but check to see if I'd left the lab tech alive. I felt the tech's mind start to work through the pain of the overload.

If you can put him under further, I won't have to hurt him again.

Hannah nodded, put her hands on his head, and pulsed a quick burst of energy into his brain that knocked him deeply unconscious.

Rachel stood over her uncle's body. She didn't want to touch him, as though physical contact with his cold flesh would make it real. Her shoulders quivered with silent sobs.

We need a screwdriver, I thought to Drew, looking at the restraining ring. My throat felt painfully tight. I couldn't make my voice work.

Drew started pulling open cabinets and drawers. Surprise sparked though him and a stack of papers started to smoke before Drew thought out the hot spot. "Isn't this dodecamine?" he asked, indicating a supply of bottles with bright orange labels.

Grab 'em. We'll check them out later.

He pocketed the vials then found the tools in the next drawer. "Here." He tossed a screwdriver to me. I caught it and set to work loosening the screws. The metal made a sickening squeal as it started to come out of the bone. The threads pulled at the skin of Trevor's forehead, causing the circular marks to bleed freely as the screws came loose. Drew found a second screwdriver. Three down. I cradled Trevor's head in my hands as Drew started on the final screw.

The silent strains of "Ride of the Valkyries" floated in from a mind down the hall.

Dr. Hanson's coming!

The others froze as we listened to his approaching footsteps. Drew worked on removing the last screw from Trevor's skull.

Dr. Hanson. *Vivisection Man.* I'd seen his thoughts and the man was sadistic.

No, more than that—evil.

I'd seen the Frankenstein screws sticking into Trevor's head—the screws Dr. Hanson had put there. This one I was going to kill. The burning energy of my pain and anger channeled itself into an electric force, building to a dangerous point behind my forehead. It felt like a laser was about to shoot out from between my eyes.

Hanson came closer. The code for the keypad rose in his mind.

The last screw came free from Trevor's head. Blood trailed down and dripped slowly from dark, wet spikes in his hair. Drew tossed Trevor over his shoulder in a fireman's carry.

Energy surged through my mind like a pack of wolves running down prey, searching for the kill. I tried to focus it into Dr. Hanson's mind, to hone in on his thoughts and blast him. I could hear him there, so close. The eerily evil opera music acted like a beacon.

It wouldn't go. *Why won't it go?*

I squeezed my eyes shut and tried again. Nothing. What the hell was wrong? The rising panic threatened to overwhelm me, pulling the breath from my lungs. What would Dr. Hanson do if he found us in here? How many darts did he have in the gun in his pocket?

Line-of-sight. The thought came as though it had been flung into me. Maybe I needed to be able to see him. The door swung open without a sound.

Dr. Hanson took two steps then froze as he registered our presence. *More test subjects!*

That final thought focused my rage into a white-hot beam that fried every circuit in that evil, evil brain. His lifeless body dropped to the floor in a tangle of limbs.

Hannah gasped, horrified. *She killed him!*

Rachel looked down at her uncle's murderer lying lifeless at her feet. Fury burned red hot in her mind. *Good. But he should have suffered more, after everything he did.*

I stood stock-still, my nails digging into my palms, trying to pull the power back. The energy didn't want to stop. It kept pulsing into his dead, silent mind.

Kill. Overkill. Overwhelming.

What if I couldn't stop? Pain shot behind my eyes. I felt dizzy and weak. *Focus.* Focus on Trevor. We needed to get Trevor out. My runaway energy snapped back and I drew a shuddering breath.

"C'mon!" said Drew.

We tumbled into the hallway as the elevator dinged. "Stairs! Run!" Drew pointed to the glowing exit sign at the far end of the hall.

Oh my God. I recognized the mind in the elevator—the mind of the charm who was coming to hurt Trevor. *Oh, no.*

The security guard from downstairs was with him, too. He'd tried to call up to Dr. Hanson and the line had been down. He'd come to investigate.

The elevator door opened as we passed it. Michael's shock of recognition hit me like a splash of acid. "Shoot them!" he screamed at the security guard. The charm resonance gave his voice extra depth.

The guard drew his gun and pulled the trigger.

CHAPTER 16

Lethal energy flooded through my mind again with each quick-beat of my heart. *Kill.* The intense overload flashed through Michael's brain like a firestorm. His consciousness whimpered away as his body hit the floor, convulsed for a few seconds, and then was still. I felt the ache behind my eyes as the energy burned itself out, dying back to a simmer within me.

Only then did I realize that the guard's gun hadn't fired. *What happened?*

Drew's trembling hand extended in concentration as his mind frantically suppressed the spark within the gun from igniting the powder.

The guard clicked his impotent weapon wildly as his mind babbled with confusion. *Oh, Lord, please help me. What happened to that kid? My gun won't fire—but I have to shoot them! Help me, please. God, this is a nightmare!* His vivid yellow terror slashed sharply through me.

Run, I planted the suggestion into his mind. *Hide. Stay alive.* I picked up his daughter's name from his frantic thoughts. *Stay alive for Caroline.*

The security guard bolted, still trying to shoot us as he ran. We thundered down the stairs. Drew took the lead with Trevor still over his shoulder. I was right behind them. A queasy tingling started in Trevor's mind. He was waking up.

Trevor?

Maddie? His thoughts felt like wet sand—amorphous and gritty. *Maddie?*

Trevor! I felt like crying with relief. *Oh, my love. Oh, Trevor. Hang on. We're getting you out of here.*

We popped out of the staircase and shot through the door to the parking lot in seconds. I jumped in first and helped Drew slide Trevor onto the bench behind the driver's seat, pulling his head into my lap. I stroked his hair and his face with my hands, reassuring us both. Dizzy, blurry nausea filled him as he pushed through the last of the sedative. He opened his eyes and tried to focus. *What's going on?*

Hold on. We're not safe yet.

Rachel hopped into the front passenger seat; Hannah slid across the seat behind us. *Let's go!* We had to get out of here. Now! I felt Drew's mind flicker to the earlier plan: to damage the cars so we wouldn't be followed. *No need! Dr. Vivisection's dead. Let's go!* Drew jumped into the driver's seat and turned the ignition. Everything seemed to be taking so long!

The first shot hit the van just as we started forward. The bullet pinged through the thin metal of the roof, thunking into the base of the driver's seat. A puff of white foam sprayed from the bullet hole. I broadcast my realization without knowing it. *Gunshots! Go! Move!*

I leaned across Trevor's head and upper body, shielding as much of him as I could. Drew floored it. A second after the first bullet hit, another came through the roof and tore into Drew's thigh. He and I both yelled at the sudden burst of pain. Trevor brought his invisible arms protectively over me, pulling me closer to him.

The security guard peered down from the roof, out of range of my ability and Drew's. I felt his next three shots before I heard them. Trevor shuddered with the impact. His mind winked out, falling away from me with horrible, overwhelming suddenness. "NO!"

Oh, my God in Heaven. No, no, no!

Drew crashed the van through the barrier at the entrance. We were out.

The invisible arms dissolved around me. *Oh, Trevor. No. Don't die. Please don't die!* I felt the chunks of burning metal land on my back with a detached awareness. They rolled off and fell to the floor—chink, chink, chink—before rattling away under the seats. Bullets. My mind tried to wrap itself around their existence and significance. Understanding made me gasp.

Thank you, God!

Trevor hadn't been hit. He had caught the three bullets and had stopped them with his ability. He'd stopped them to protect me. I stroked his face and hair. My tears dripped down from the tracks on my face and splashed onto his. *Oh, my love. My love, my love, my love.*

Had it injured him to do it? Would Trevor be all right?

Drew's leg throbbed. The pain finally intruded into my bubble of panic about Trevor.

"Pull over, Drew." My voice sounded ragged.

What? I felt Hannah and Rachel's identical reactions: *don't pull over! We need to get as far away as possible!*

"Not yet," he said.

"Drew, you're going to pass out soon. Pull over."

Rachel gasped as she caught sight of the gunshot wound. Blood pulsed from it with each of Drew's rapid heartbeats.

Hannah took charge. "Rachel, can you drive?"

"I've got a permit."

"Good enough." We were breaking all sorts of laws tonight.

Drew rolled the van to a stop and we maneuvered him back to the second bench seat. Blood ran in a dark stream across the van floor.

Rachel focused intently on driving; she didn't want to think about anything else. A raw, ripping sound came from Drew's jeans as Hannah exposed his wound. Drew didn't even let out a whimper, but purple-hot, excruciating pain screamed darkly from his mind into mine. Hannah used her ability to heal the tissue beneath the imbedded bullet, forcing it from his flesh as it inched toward the surface.

It took a very, very long time.

Drew's entire body tensed as she worked. His skin shone clammy-white and sweaty in the light from passing headlights, making his blotchy freckles stand out as though they'd been painted with ink.

"How's Trevor?" he asked me, breathing hard through gritted teeth.

"Unconscious." My voice shook. "I don't know… he stopped three bullets."

"What?"

"With his ability." I sounded little and weak, like an eight-year-old. "He stopped them from hitting me." *And now I can't feel his mind and I don't know if he's unconscious or in a coma or if he's ever going to wake up or…* I could feel the hysteria bubbling up inside of me. Tears ran down my cheeks again. I squeezed my eyes shut, trying to stop the flow. I couldn't brush them away because my hands were covered with blood—Trevor's blood. The lights from the highway seemed to tilt, like they were spinning around me.

When I was a kid growing up in my old neighborhood, we sometimes used to play games where we'd go on rescue missions. Those games were fun and exciting. But this wasn't fun and this wasn't exciting. It was painful and sickening and scary as hell.

Hannah inched the bullet back up through the wound in Drew's leg. The wound burned with raw agony, even secondhand. My clenched teeth caught my breath like a sieve. What would happen now? There would be all kinds of fallout from this. Oh, hell. Seth was probably furious at me. Was I going to be kicked out of Ganzfield? Yeah, probably.

My last shot of dodecamine was two days ago. I'd have at least a week or more before the effects wore off, even with the lower dose. Would I have to stay in the cell in the basement? Actually, could anyone make me? It's not like they could charm me in or force me somehow. And I didn't plan to go in willingly.

Would there be police involvement? Doubtful. The Eden Imaging people would then have to explain why they'd been kidnapping and experimenting on Trevor. They'd have to explain about Charlie Fontaine, too. No, they weren't going to call the cops.

Who were the Eden Imaging people? What were they trying to do? Were they simply unethical researchers trying to discover new technologies to enhance the brain? Eden was a biblical name. Were they religious extremists who wanted to destroy people different from themselves? What could possibly have motivated them to kidnap Trevor?

I looked down at Trevor's face, in deep shadow except when the lights of passing cars rolled through the vehicle. I stroked his hair, listening for a tingle of consciousness. Nothing. He wasn't even dreaming. *Oh, Trevor.* I didn't know why they had started all of this, but I knew, without a doubt, that anyone who tried to hurt Trevor like this was wrong. Absolutely wrong.

Evil.

Were there more people like them out there? Did Dr. Hanson work alone, or was he part of something bigger? I had to know. We all had to know. All of the G-positives were at risk.

I curled protectively over Trevor, pressing my forehead to his... trying to connect to him. I needed to feel his mind—to know that he was going to be all right—but the only sensation I felt was the sharp, hot ache as the bullet in Drew's leg slowly slid to the surface. Hannah finally moved it close enough to pull out with her fingers. Drew bit his tongue to keep from crying out against the pain of her digging nails. Once the bullet was out, Drew relaxed, even though the wound continued to throb.

"Yeah, but now your tongue hurts," I said to him. The remark sent Drew into semi-hysterical laughter. In his mind, Drew catalogued the events of the night. He looked forward to sharing the story. I heard him trying to find all of the bullets: two in front, including the one that had hit him. Trevor had stopped three. One had barely missed Hannah; the seat still shed small bits of foam from the impact. The last two had punched through the back door. It wasn't hard to find the places where the van had been hit; frigid wind whistled though the holes.

The bullets were smaller than he'd thought they'd be. Good thing, too, since larger rounds probably could have gone through the floor and hit the fuel lines or some other useful mechanical bits. *I stopped that gun from firing. How cool was that? Why hadn't we figured out that sparks could do that before now?* A world of new possibilities seemed to open before him. He could do exciting things with his ability. Hostage negotiation. Bomb squad. Counterterrorism.

Drew was such a *guy*.

The five-hour drive through the night seemed to take much longer. My energy had drained away, replaced by a sad, sick anxiety for Trevor. I was helpless. Useless. I couldn't do anything for him but hold his head in my lap and take him home.

The pain ebbed away from Drew's leg. Hannah moved up next to me and laid her hands on Trevor's head. Lines furrowed between her eyebrows. *Why won't he wake up?* There was nothing else she could do except heal the damage from those hideous screws. The holes closed into shiny, pink marks on his forehead that faded as I watched. Afterward, she slid into the back row of the van and stared out the window at nothing. Tonight, Hannah had discovered that the world was a more dangerous, horrible place than she'd previously known. Most of her thoughts on the long trip back were prayers. *Please, Jesus, guide us. Please protect us from those who wish us harm. Please comfort us in our time of need. Help Rachel in her grief, and please take the soul of her uncle unto You.* She even prayed for the souls of Dr. Hanson and Michael.

I felt her prayers flutter against my thoughts, but I couldn't join in. If Hannah's worldview was right, and God and Heaven and everything were as she believed them to be, then I was quite sure I'd sent two more people straight to Hell tonight.

And I was fine with that. It was scary how fine I was with that. But I didn't feel clean enough to pray.

Rachel focused on the road. She kept forcing the horrible thoughts down when they bubbled up. A brittleness seemed to turn her insides into tiny little sticks that rubbed against each other. She didn't want to think about what had happened tonight. *Ever.*

Maybe Cecelia could help her with that, or at least with the emotional fallout. But I knew that Rachel could get through this. She'd gotten through worse.

CHAPTER 17

We keyed the code into the front gate at Ganzfield just after 4 a.m. Before we'd gotten halfway up the drive, Seth was in my head, ranting. *Of all the reckless, stupid things to do—*

I interrupted him with a sharp, vivid image of Trevor, his head held by screws in the metal circle. Then I showed him Uncle Charlie lying dead in another metal ring with the top of his head cut away.

I knew there would be fallout from my actions—I would accept the consequences—but I was going to make sure that Seth and Dr. Williamson understood the entire situation before those consequences occurred.

The images stopped Seth's rant cold, but it didn't give me the satisfaction it should have. I was too empty inside.

Rachel drove directly to Blake House. She stopped the van, got out, and then closed her eyes and leaned her forehead against the cold metal side. Hannah put a hand on her arm. They headed upstairs without speaking.

Drew carried Trevor into the infirmary where Matilda placed her hands on Trevor's head, searching for the problem. "There's no inflammation and no injury." For some reason, she thought that would be a comfort to me. I chafed my fingers across his unresponsive hand and followed her mind. My head swam with exhaustion and the effects of the emotional burn.

Matilda gazed at me piercingly, as though trying to read my mind to see my emotional state. Ironic. "Why don't you go and get some sleep?" I knew I must look horrible, and I felt like fuzzy death.

I shook my head. "I'm not leaving." *Not open to discussion.*

Matilda gave me another assessing look. *Maddie's in bad enough shape. She probably should stay in the infirmary, anyway.* Drew shook with exhaustion. After a quick assessment of his freshly-mended wound, Matilda sent him off to sleep, excusing him from classes in the morning.

Classes. I couldn't believe there were still things as mundane as classes in the world.

I slid in next to Trevor on the narrow cot, wrapping my arms around him. Matilda's disapproval floated to me like someone nagging through an unattended telephone, but she didn't say anything aloud. I fell asleep with my head on Trevor's chest.

CHAPTER 18

Thoughts from dozens of minds babbled around me. I squeezed my eyes tighter, listening for the only one I wanted to hear.

I couldn't find it.

My eyes flashed open. I still lay curled against Trevor on the narrow infirmary cot. I'd often imagined sleeping next to him—being able to lay in his arms all night—but I'd gladly trade this reality for one in which he'd wake up and talk to me.

I might never mentally connect to Trevor again. Even if—no, when—he woke up, I'd be kicked out of Ganzfield. Once off dodecamine, I'd be unable to read his thoughts or share mine with him. No more intimate, direct connection without misunderstandings or ambiguity. No more "soulmating."

I held back a sob. I knew that if Trevor lost his ability, it wouldn't change how I felt about him. But would he feel the same about me? My telepathy played such an intense part in our relationship. If I weren't special—if I no longer knew him better than anyone else—how would he feel about me?

Should I break it off with him? I pushed the thought away in disgust. *Stupid idea.* I'd *never* break up with Trevor. I'd take whatever little bits of him I could still have. I was too selfish to cause him the pain of rejection; it would hurt me too much to hurt him.

I pressed my forehead to his temple. *Please, wake up. Please.*

All around me, the buzz of minds ramped up as people started leaving the classrooms. It was already lunchtime. Someone had started an IV in Trevor's arm. I stared at it. The innocuous medical equipment looked vaguely sinister to me after seeing similar things at Eden Imaging.

Drew came in a few minutes later. He carried a tray filled with food and drinks. I sat up, perching on the edge of Trevor's cot, still holding his hand.

"You've been here the whole time?"

I nodded.

"Eat something." He offered me a sandwich.

I bit and chewed dutifully, not tasting it. I started to feel better, though, as soon as the food hit. Less drained. I took a soda, popped the top, and drank half the can.

"How's he doing?"

I shook my head. "No change."

We sat in silence for a while. Drew struggled to find the right words. *What should I say to her? I'm sorry? I know he'll be okay? But what if he isn't? I'm glad we tried? There's still hope?*

"Thanks, Drew," I said. "Thanks for coming... for everything. For keeping me from driving off the road... for stopping a guy from shooting us—"

"He still shot us."

A lump filled my throat and I gasped back a sob. "And if I'd killed him in the building, Trevor would be awake and—"

"Whoa, slow down." He put his hand on my arm to comfort me. The unexpected contact caused me to jerk away. "Trevor's gonna be okay. You know he is."

I didn't know any such thing, but I nodded.

"Why don't you go and get cleaned up? Grab a shower and some fresh clothes. I'll stay with him 'til you get back."

I looked down at the rips and bloodstains on my clothes. My hair had plastered itself to my head and it was stiff with dried sweat. I felt sticky and gross, like the floor of a movie theater.

Even going upstairs to shower felt like abandoning Trevor. Being away from him simply felt wrong—like a too-tight rubber band stretched between us, threatening to snap. Listening for the stirrings of his mind, I stood in the shower stall, still in my clothes. I tried to figure out what steps I'd missed in the normal shower process. Okay, clothes off. Water on.

The hot water stung my skin. I closed my eyes and let the spray revive me. I was finally breathing again. I quickly brushed my teeth and my still-wet hair, and then put on the first clothes I put my hands on. Jeans and a sweatshirt. Oh. This was the outfit I was wearing the first time I ever saw Trevor. I grabbed a book and my laptop and ran down the stairs.

The rest of the day, I sat on the cot I'd pulled up next to his. I tried to read, tried to work, tried to do something other than poke my little mental feelers into his head, searching for the man I loved. But Trevor's mind remained silent… unchanged.

Morris checked Trevor several times, taking a blood sample along with his vitals. Rachel and Hannah briefly stopped in together. Rachel's brittleness had morphed into anger. *Wasn't that one of the stages of grief?* The fiery power of it made her feel stronger—more in-control.

Hannah avoided me and stayed in the other room, talking with Morris. *Afraid.* Afraid of me and what I'd done. Not for herself: she didn't think I'd hurt her. But she'd seen me kill with my mind and that made me dangerous… too dangerous.

Drew returned with several of the sparks before heading out for their practical. Drew planned to hijack the lesson and teach some of the others his newfound skill at disabling firearms. I half-smiled, feeling like something was wrong with my face as I did.

"Where are you going to get the gun?" I asked Drew. Several of the sparks startled. Disturbing question to hear out-of-context.

"No problem. This is America," Drew said, with a return of his wide grin. An hour later, the distant sound of intermittent gunfire seemed to indicate that his optimism had been well-founded.

In the late afternoon, having had several waking hours to build up his irritation again, Seth mentally yelled at me from outside. *We've had to put the whole compound on lockdown! You irresponsible, reckless, little brat! You've just escalated a war, and we don't even know who's trying to kill us!*

Eden Imaging.

Who?

Eden Imaging. Dr. Williamson tracks companies for investing. If he investigates Eden Imaging, he'll find the people who did this.

Why didn't you say anything before?

I rolled my eyes and fought to hold back my irritation. I lost the fight. *Because I was exhausted and bloody and the man I love more than life itself is lying here in some kind of coma! I've got a lot of other things going on! If you want a debriefing or something now, ask away!*

Let me make a couple of phone calls first. Anything else that Williamson should check out?

Yeah, find out how they recruited Michael.

Michael Quinn? The charm? He was there?

He was working for them. He probably told them all about us. And he'd gotten his ability back so he must've been on dodecamine again.

That's impossible. We control the supply.

No. We saw the vials. Drew probably still has the ones we took from the lab.

Seth turned thoughtful. *I'll tell Williamson.*

Thanks.

Seth's mental voice faded as he moved out of range. I sat next to Trevor, stroking his hair back off his face. I tried to touch his thoughts with my mind, tried to pray, tried not to cry. I tried to find something I could do to fix this—to make Trevor be okay again. In the fairy tales, the sleeping person always wakes to his true love's kiss. I closed my eyes and touched my lips to his, channeling all of the magic that Trevor made me feel—all my adoration for him—into the connection.

Nothing. Without Trevor, there didn't seem to be any magic left in the world.

Seth came back after a while and I gave him the full mental PowerPoint presentation, complete with all of the graphic images I'd flashed to him before.

Williamson will be back tomorrow. We'll deal with everything then. He no longer blamed me… or rather, he was no longer holding me entirely to blame. He still thought I'd been reckless, and could have gotten myself or the others killed.

I agreed with him, but I'd needed to go. I couldn't have *not* gone. However, I could see his point about involving the others. My thoughts seesawed back and forth over it. I couldn't have gotten Trevor out without help. A hot lump formed in my throat. Even lying here, unable to respond, Trevor was better off now than at Eden Imaging with Dr. Hanson's sick plans for him. No regrets on that score.

Drew brought food again at dinnertime and we ate together, keeping vigil. Morris checked Trevor once more before switching off duty with Matilda. They still didn't know why he wasn't waking up. I bit my lip to keep from screaming. How could they not know? They were doctors with superpowers!

Drew left when Morris did. Matilda parked herself at the desk in the next room with a biography of a woman who'd become the president of Liberia. The cadence of Matilda's internal voice soothed me as she read. I slid down onto my side next to Trevor, gazing at his still profile in the low light. *Wake up! Please, please, please wake up!* I put my hand over his heart, feeling the slow, strong beats pulse against my palm and the even rise and fall of his chest. I drifted down into sleep.

The sugar-white sand nearly blinded me. The water sparkled, vividly blue and inviting. I knew exactly where I was. Aruba. Dream-Aruba.

Trevor sat in his usual chair under the palm frond umbrella. He stood to face me, pulling his sunglasses off and smiling with warm welcome in his eyes. I flew into his arms. He gathered me close, my cheek pressed against his bare chest. I closed my eyes and breathed him in. He smelled vaguely of coconut.

"I've been so worried," I said. "When you didn't wake up…"

Trevor gently tilted my chin up so I met his gaze. His beautiful eyes—brown and warm and perfect—made me feel like everything was going to be okay.

"Even when I can't be with you there," he said, "I'll always be here for you." He kissed me on the forehead tenderly, and then grew fainter, transparent. Ghostlike, he faded out in the bright, tropical sun.

"Trevor!" I cried out and woke myself up. The dream echoed vaguely, tugging my mind with half-remembered strings.

Trevor was still unconscious… not dreaming. I lay back with a groan, feeling my heart pounding rapidly in my chest. Three people upstairs, including Hannah, had also seen Trevor disappear in their dreams. Ah, hell. Even down here in the annex, I was still in range to throw nightmares around the dorm.

It was just a regular dream. I tried to convince myself. *Just a regular dream.*

Matilda stood silhouetted in the doorway, responding to my shout. I didn't want to talk about it so I pretended to go back to sleep. It was a while before I drifted off again with my hand still on Trevor's chest, rising and falling with his slow, even breathing.

A sharp pain shot through my right elbow when I landed on the floor. Ow! What the hell? Trevor was dreaming.

Trevor was dreaming!

"Trevor. Trevor!" My soul seemed to re-inflate as I scrambled back up, determined to get to him, to wake him, to see him again.

I put my hand on his face. His eyes opened and met mine. Every fiber of my being sang, and sparkling white energy danced across my skin. *Trevor!*

"Maddie?" his voice was hoarse, and he was groggy and confused.

I was shaking, sobbing, and generally incoherent. *Oh, Trevor!*

"What's wrong? Are you okay?"

I nodded and hugged him. I wanted to never let go. His arms wrapped around me and cradled me against his chest.

I really hope this isn't a dream.

"Reality testing?" He kissed me.

That won't work. I kiss you all the time in my dreams.

But I knew he was real because his breath was horrible after two-days without brushing. Bad breath had never been as wonderful as it was at that moment.

Matilda heard the commotion and came in to investigate. She insisted that I stop lying on her patient while she examined him. *Stupid rule.* I stroked the side of Trevor's face with one hand while clasping his with the other. I couldn't stop touching him. My chin quivered so I bit my lip to stop it, blinking quickly to clear away my tears.

Once Matilda had gone, we lay side-by-side, gazing into each other's eyes. It was nearly morning. Echoes of dreams floated through the building. I kept touching Trevor's face, feeling the rough stubble on his chin, the firm bones of his cheek and jaw, the little emotional thrill that each caress caused in him.

I thought I'd lost you.

What happened? Everything is a blur. Did someone shoot at us?

I nodded. *You stopped three bullets from hitting me.*

His hand tightened on mine as a burst of cold shot through him. "Someone tried to shoot you?" His voice was steel. In his mind, trying to injure me was an obscenity.

I gave him the mental replay. Dawn sent spokes of sunlight through the window by the time I'd finished.

Trevor clasped my hand tightly against his chest. "I can't believe you did that for me. I'm not... it's just... I..." He choked up. *I hate the thought of you being in danger like that.*

I feel the same way about you. That's why I had to do it.

Trevor considered that. *No more danger then—for either of us.*

Good plan. *That part may be easy. There's a good chance I'm going to be kicked out of Ganzfield today.* I tried to downplay how worried I was about that.

What? No!

Dr. Williamson's coming back today. According to Seth, I'm the reckless "brat" who put several other people in mortal danger; stole a van and trashed it; and, oh yeah, provoked a secret war against an unknown adversary who wants to destroy us all.

If you go, I go.

My heart brimmed as silver energy welled up within me. *I can't let you throw away your future like that.*

You threw away yours for me.

Where would he go? Back to Michigan, to the grandparents who looked at him as an embarrassment? Would he come with me if I went back to New Jersey? I could see it now. *"Hi, Mom. This is my soulmate, Trevor. He's going to be living with us from now on."* Not likely. Unless I could somehow convince Cecelia or one of the other charms to have a little talk with my mom first...

It wouldn't be all bad. At least if we were no longer taking dodecamine, we could do normal things. College. Sleeping in heated buildings. Living close to other people. These things all would be possible again. *Silver lining.* I wouldn't share my nightmares with those sleeping near me, and Trevor wouldn't throw anyone across rooms. I could sleep in his arms every night.

If he still wanted me.

Would you still love me if I... if we couldn't talk like this? I cringed as soon as I thought it to him. Dammit. I hadn't wanted to ask him that.

Trevor gathered me close. "I'll *always* love you," he said simply.

I started to cry. I knew it was true. That was more than enough, even if the rest of everything fell apart.

I'll always love you, too.

CHAPTER 19

"If you two are going to be all mushy like that, I'm leaving," Drew said. He'd stopped into the infirmary to bring me breakfast and to check on Trevor. The tray dropped in his enthusiastic "whoop" at seeing Trevor awake. Trevor had grabbed the food before it hit the floor and replaced everything on the tray, all without visibly moving. Despite stopping three bullets, Trevor's ability seemed to be undamaged.

He's bringing Maddie breakfast? A little voice stung Trevor's mind.

I nearly did a spit-take with the coffee and had to cover it with a quick, mental *hot*.

Drew wasn't interested in me. Drew had the stirrings of a crush on Grace, an emotional bond of gratitude toward Hannah, and regular sexual thoughts about at least half a dozen other girls at Ganzfield. I wasn't one of them, and that was a good thing. In Drew's mind, I'd become like a sister when I'd started dating his best friend. I slid closer to Trevor, leaning against his side and alternating bites of a shared bagel with him.

Morris put an end to the visit; he needed to do a neurological exam on Trevor. Since he believed my ability might interfere with this, Morris banished me from the infirmary for the duration. I left reluctantly. I still felt a twitchy sense of wrongness whenever I was away from Trevor. But if I had to go, at least I could make myself presentable. I used the time to take a shower and clean myself up. And if today was our last day at of freedom at Ganzfield, then I certainly wasn't going to squander it by going to class.

I checked in from upstairs, hoping my occasional mental touches wouldn't mess up the test too much. When I recognized that Morris was about to release Trevor from the infirmary, I reached for my winter coat. One quick look at it changed my mind. Three burn marks had been singed across the back from the heat of the bullets that had fallen on it, and the dark stains on the front—ugh. Almost certainly blood. I'd rather freeze than wear it again. I grabbed my other jacket—even though it was too light for the weather—and the heavy coat soon overflowed from the trash can in the hall.

I'd never been to Trevor's dorm room before. His "official residence" was on the first floor of the house across from the main building. It'd probably been the living room when this had been a single-family home. There were three beds, and it was obvious that Trevor spent almost no time here. Folded clothing and a few books lined the shelf.

Just a place to change clothes.

I looked at the spines of his books, absentmindedly feeling Trevor brushing his teeth in the bathroom down the hall. We were alone in the building; everyone else was in class. Trevor's thoughts came to me strongly. His mental touch filled me with a warm glow. I closed my eyes and smiled, drifting in the reassuring contact.

Oh, my. My eyes flashed open and my breath caught as Trevor peeled off his clothes. There were no other minds here that I could focus on—nothing to distract me. Not that I wanted to be distracted. I felt his thoughts very clearly as he stepped into the shower, sharing his keen sense of pleasure as the hot water ran over his bare back and streamed over his—whoa.

No, this was wrong. This was such an invasion of his privacy. Wrong, wrong, wrong. I had to get out of range, but I really didn't want to. Trevor's bare skin in the hot water… My breath came in quick, panting gasps. Trevor soaping up and lathering his chest…

No. I couldn't violate his trust this way.

I practically fell down the front steps in my rush to get out of the dorm. I stumble-ran until I was halfway to the main building. The cold air of a New Hampshire December still wasn't enough to immediately cool my overheated body. I paced with quivering energy, moving back and forth at a discrete distance from where Trevor was probably still feeling the shower running over his—

No, no, no. Wrong. Not without his permission.

I waited, hugging my arms tightly around my body as the cold finally penetrated my thin jacket. I cautiously moved closer, tentatively reaching out with my mind to glimpse if it was all right for me to return.

Trevor pulled a shirt over his head.

Okay.

I knocked on the door to his room before entering.

His questioning, *you went somewhere?* made me blush scarlet and confess the whole thing.

If it would make you feel better, I could watch you in the shower. His eyes twinkled and red flashes danced over his skin. It thrilled him that he'd had such a strong effect on me. *Then we'd be even. It's a sacrifice I'm willing to make.*

My heart fluttered like a caged bird as I thought about taking him up on his offer. Another flush of red hummed though me, staining my cheeks. Trevor kissed me then, channeling and building that energy into an overwhelming, dizzying vortex. His arms wrapped around my waist. Through my clothes, invisible hands caressed the bare skin of my back. I moaned and leaned in closer, deepening the kiss, wanting to—

A door slammed just outside the room, shocking Trevor and me back to awareness. We stepped apart, still gazing at each other with hungry eyes.

Hungry. Lunchtime. It was later than we'd thought. A cheer went up from the sparks' tables when we walked into the dining hall. Trevor ducked his head and smiled. The mental bombardment I received left no doubt that we were the talk of the entire school.

I'd just grabbed a tray when I felt a strong, silent voice from above. Third floor. *Oh, crap.* A message from God would've been preferable.

Come up to my office in ten minutes. Bring Trevor Laurence, Rachel Fontaine, Drew McFee, and Hannah Washington. I had a difficult time swallowing around the lump that'd suddenly formed in my throat. I squeezed my eyes shut and took a deep breath.

This was it. Game over.

Trevor noticed my sudden freeze. *What's wrong?*

We have to be in Dr. Williamson's office in ten minutes.

If you go, I go. He didn't just mean going to the office.

I bit my lip to keep myself from crying. *I don't deserve you.* The thought flashed through my mind but I didn't share it. I looked at the miracle of Trevor—alive and healthy. *I love you so much.* I'd face the consequences of my actions. Without a doubt, no matter what those consequences were, it'd been worth it. Trevor was worth it.

I conveyed the summons to Drew, Rachel, and Hannah. The wooden steps thudded loudly as we trooped up to the third floor together.

"Come in," Dr. Williamson said before anyone could knock.

Oh, hell. Dr. Williamson looked stern—more serious than I'd ever seen him. I could read nothing from his shielded mind. In his expensive suit, he gave off a strong predatory feel—like a lion, or shark, or really high-priced lawyer. I felt cold and exposed as he met my eyes. His unsmiling lips pursed into a tight line and the sudden burst from behind his shield made me flinch. *Keep your thoughts to yourself until I tell you differently. Be quiet and listen.*

Stunned, I could only nod like a wide-eyed idiot. I hadn't expected him to be so angry; Dr. Williamson was usually so emotionally controlled and cool. My stomach churned sickly at the thought of disappointing him. I hadn't realized how much his respect mattered to me.

Trevor stepped close behind me and put his hands on my upper arms. *Standing with me. Supporting me.* I closed my eyes for a moment and took a deep breath as I drew on his strength. Trevor was here. Trevor was worth it. No regrets.

Dr. Williamson turned to Hannah. "Tell me what happened." Startled at being singled out first, Hannah spoke with cautious hesitation. Her thoughts and mental images supplemented her account, although she wasn't aware that Dr. Williamson and I were in her head.

He repeated the question to Rachel. When she got to the part about seeing Uncle Charlie in her vision, Dr. Williamson said,

"I'm sorry. Charlie Fontaine was a good man and a good friend."
Grief left a hollow ache within him.

Drew gave his version. Dr. Williamson listened without
interruption.

I barely recognized myself in their memories. It was like I
was watching someone else or a character in a movie. Hannah
thought of me as a dangerous killer… excessively dangerous.
Her feelings reached over and slapped me.

Rachel thought I'd been too restrained—too weak. She'd
wanted revenge for Uncle Charlie and felt that killing everyone
at Eden Imaging and burning the building to the ground would
be a good start.

The others had no idea what I'd seen in the minds of the
people at Eden Imaging that night. Why hadn't I thought of that
earlier? Hannah hadn't known the twisted evil of Dr. Hanson's
plans. Rachel hadn't seen the innocence of the security people.
She didn't understand that the guard who'd shot the van was
still under the influence of Michael's last charm-command to
shoot us. Was this the real reason that minders were in charge?

Drew thought I was an action hero. He also thought he was
an action hero. He thought Hannah was an angel of healing, and
that Rachel was okay to have around, too, in case we needed to
find stuff. The memories of that horrible night had morphed into
an amazing tale of adventure in his mind.

Dr. Williamson turned to me next. "Anything to add?" Cold.
Detached.

I nodded, and then silently showed all of them the things
the others hadn't seen: Dr. Hanson's evil objectives; Michael's
sadistic intentions; the ignorance of the guards. I showed them
how Trevor had stopped the bullets that would've killed me. My
arms crossed in front of me protectively and my hands found

Trevor's on my arms. My fingers twined with his. Once I'd finished, Dr. Williamson sat at his desk—unmoving and silently pensive—for what seemed like the first half of eternity.

"You could've all been killed," he said, shaking his head. "You could've been captured and used for experimentation."

He turned to me. "Maddie, you didn't call the police. You could've called them when Trevor was abducted or when you located him at Eden Imaging."

I said nothing. I hadn't even thought of calling the police. What could the cops have done? What could I have told them?

He looked at me again with that opaque shield covering his thoughts. I braced for the worst. "I am actually amazed at your success," he said, looking puzzled. "You either got very lucky, or you're naturals at this."

Huh? That sounded strangely like a compliment rather than the preface for an expulsion.

"You did nearly everything right. You could've exposed us if you'd involved the police. You accomplished your objective and you got all of your people out alive. You also found the connection to Eden Imaging—that was the key. I've been able to follow their money trail. It led to someone very dangerous, someone I thought was dead."

What?

"And you brought back proof that a leak in our pharmaceutical plant has been smuggling out dodecamine and giving or selling it to him."

Wait a minute. This wasn't a reprimand. Dr. Williamson was smiling, although it was rather restrained and tight. The anger flowing from him wasn't directed at me; it was for this other person. I hadn't lost Dr. Williamson's respect. Cool relief flooded over me and I closed my eyes as my lungs seemed to re-inflate properly for the first time in a while.

"Who's Isaiah Lerner?" I asked aloud, having heard the name in a flash of memory. Dr. Williamson's shield seemed to be dropping; his thoughts grew clearer to me.

"Isaiah Lerner was a U.S. Congressman back in the 1980s. He was a junior member of the House Intelligence Committee, the one that oversaw Project Star Gate, among other things."

Star Gate? Like the movie? Trevor and Drew's thoughts flashed simultaneously.

"The government project to use extrasensory abilities. It led to the discovery of the G-positive mutation and the development of dodecamine. Isaiah Lerner left Congress shortly after we developed the genetic test for G-positives. I later learned that he'd gotten one of the Star Gate doctors to run the test on him. Isaiah is also a G-positive."

Dr. Williamson leaned forward. "From time to time, people learn about our abilities—people who wish us harm. Some want to use us to make themselves wealthy or powerful. Some want to eradicate us because they see us as abominations or threats. These people are usually very easy to deal with."

"Charms." It was the first time Trevor had spoken since we'd arrived.

Dr. Williamson nodded. "One of our charms has a short talk with them and they decide to devote their time and energy to other purposes."

"He's a telepath," I blurted as the realization hit me.

Dr. Williamson nodded. "Isaiah Lerner is an extremely powerful telepath, so sending a charm to have a little chat with him doesn't work. In fact, he's killed several of them."

He's like me. He can kill with his mind. I shivered as something twisted in my gut. Trevor tightened his grip—reassuring me—although he hadn't heard the thought that'd caused the reaction.

Dr. Williamson met my eyes and nodded. *You're the only other person who can do that.*

Was I being trained as an assassin? Was I now supposed to kill this Isaiah person for Dr. Williamson? An angry surge passed though me and I opened my mouth to protest. The protest died—unspoken—as Dr. Williamson flashed a vivid series of images to me. The people killed by Isaiah Lerner—dozens of people. Their lives and their deaths bombarded my mind, my soul.

Reflected grief hit me as anguished, physical pain. Oh my God. Elise—Dr. Williamson's wife. He'd loved her intensely, and her loss was a silent, howling ache that was still strong after years without her. Although the memory flash of her was brief, I could tell that Trevor and I hadn't been the first to soulmate.

The visuals of the decade-long secret war made me stagger. Trevor's grip on my arms tightened. Stormy protectiveness filled his mind. "Stop it!" he yelled. *What are you doing to Maddie? You're hurting her!*

The intensity of his feelings penetrated Dr. Williamson's focus. He snapped shut the window to his memories and I could breathe again.

I'm okay. I tried to give his hand a giving a reassuring squeeze, but I think it just came out weak and clammy. *Elise.* Dr. Williamson had had a soulmate, too. Even the small flash of his dizzying, aching loss sent sadness to my core. It was worse than awful. How did he stand it?

"Isaiah has been using aliases and phony corporations to hide himself and his activities. We thought we'd gotten him four years ago, but it now looks as though he faked his own death. That's why we never had another RV try to locate him. His newest alias is Jonas Pike and he's the CEO of the holding company that owns Eden Imaging," said Dr. Williamson. "He wants to kill the rest of us simply because he wants to eliminate the competition."

In the land of the blind, the one-eyed man is king. The quote floated into my mind from somewhere.

Dr. Williamson nodded. "If Isaiah gets his way, everyone here at Ganzfield—everyone even related to the people here at Ganzfield—will be dead."

You're not getting kicked out. Dr. Williamson explained. *You're not even going off the property until we determine how much Isaiah knows about you. You wouldn't be safe.*

I never would've thought that I'd be so happy to be the target of a power-mad, telepathic sociopath. *Trevor, we're staying.* His sparkling green joy spread over me as he pulled me back into a relieved hug.

"So…" Dr. Williamson turned to talk to the whole group. "Given your success with this unplanned rescue mission, I want you to start training together. Once you know what you're doing, you'll be a formidable team."

My eyebrows shot up. With Isaiah Lerner targeting us, I had to admit the idea made sense. We needed something like this. Protection for Ganzfield. *Protection for all of us.* Working together, we might do some impressive stuff.

Drew thought it was the coolest idea ever. X-Men. Hall of Justice. Fantastic Four. I winced at his enthusiasm. Why didn't the scary and horrible stuff haunt him? Ugh. Speaking of scary, his thoughts suddenly filled with ideas for superhero names… and costumes.

I rolled my eyes. That was *so* not going to happen.

Rachel felt grim determination. This would be a way for her to channel her anger. To fix stuff that was wrong.

Hannah held back. She'd need some time to think about it and to process everything; WWJD and all of that.

Trevor wondered if he was included.

Of course you are. We'd both intended to avoid danger for each other's sake. But now *that* plan was out the window. Isaiah Lerner was bringing the danger to us. If we were at risk, we needed to learn how to handle it, and we could do that together.

"We'll probably add a charm, as well," Dr. Williamson said, nodding. The others didn't like that much, but I already knew who I wanted to ask.

Grace.

Dr. Williamson dismissed the group, then added, "Maddie, Trevor, stay a moment longer."

Uh-oh. I squeezed Trevor's hand.

Dr. Williamson came around from behind the desk and closed the door with an ominous sounding click. He turned to stand face-to-face with Trevor, peering intently at him over crossed arms.

"Trevor Laurence, what are your intentions toward Maddie Dunn?"

My jaw dropped. What? I hadn't expected the father-to-daughter's-date-to-the-prom thing from him. I'd never really known my father, but suddenly I could see how Dr. Williamson might fit the part. Apparently, he looked on me in much the same way.

Trevor looked Dr. Williamson right in the eye. Unfazed. Calm. "I plan to cherish her for the rest of my life, sir."

Sincere.

My heart exploded a little bit in my chest and I choked back tears.

What happened with you and Maddie in the library? Dr. Williamson asked suddenly.

Cold shock. *No!* I mentally shouted, mortified. *Private!* How dare he? My face flamed red and I glared at him.

Trevor couldn't block the way I could. His thoughts were absolutely clear and his hand tightened on mine. *That's when we discovered we were soulmates.*

Dr. Williamson ignored the wrathful comments simmering in my thoughts, the ones telling him to stay out of our private stuff. His eyes narrowed as he focused on Trevor's mind, determining his character at a deeper level.

Yikes. Scarier than any protective father.

Trevor looked right back, meeting his gaze calmly—silent strength. I suddenly realized that these weren't two males in a power play over a piece of female property. These two people both cared about me. They were each making sure the other one knew it, knew that he wouldn't let the other one harm me.

In a sick, macho way, it was actually kind of beautiful.

"No sex," said Dr. Williamson. I squeezed my eyes tightly shut as my cheeks burned. "If you two are going to continue to room together, I want your word on that." *And I'll know if you break your word.*

Trevor nodded. "You have my word," he said solemnly.

I sent an ugly, red thought to Dr. Williamson. *Mind you own damn business!* Apparently, Trevor's word was the only one he wanted; he didn't even ask for mine. His gaze flicked to me and his lips twitched. Why did he seem to think my reaction was funny? *Seriously pissed off here!*

Wait… continue to room together? As in, I can stay in the church? My eyes widened. *Really?* Never mind. Bad feelings gone!

Dr. Williamson laughed at my reaction. I was too happy to care. "I don't think we'll get that new building you wanted anytime soon," he said to me, "but I think we can make that church a little more livable. If you need it, Maddie, you can always have Ann's cabin. We're upgrading the sound system there and at Seth's while the electricians are here."

Wait a second here. Trevor had been living in the frozen dark last winter, and Ann had already been using a sound system that was upgradeable?

I didn't know. He doesn't complain. The guilt of not being on top of every problem at Ganzfield twisted at Dr. Williamson, making him feel inadequate. But he was trying, trying to fix things, trying to make them right. And he'd found a way to make things right for Trevor.

I gasped. *Seriously?* "Can we go see?"

Dr. Williamson nodded and gestured to the door, dismissing us. A ghost of a smile touched his face as he watched us go. A flash of Elise, of what they'd had together, wrapped his mind in grief-tinged nostalgia. He pulled up a mental shield to be alone with her memory.

"Go see what?" Trevor asked as I practically pulled him out of the building. "What is it?"

"An early Christmas present," I drew a deep breath as the cold hit me through my too-thin jacket. I ignored it. Not important right now.

Trevor's first clue was the electric power line that now ran along the path to the church. He quickly made the connection and his eyes widened. "Seriously?"

If you'd made a fuss last year, they would've done it then.

Seth interrupted me. *I can't believe you're still here.*

Always a pleasure to hear your thoughts, too, Seth. I hoped my sarcasm adequately transmitted telepathically.

Well, now you can keep track of the work crews and I can go home. He started to give me a mental inventory but I cut him off.

You know I can't. My range doesn't go far enough.

Then what good are you? Seth thought sourly.

C'mon, aren't you getting a new sound system out of all this? I wondered if the music could drown out other people's thoughts effectively. Was that why the minders had gotten that particular perk?

Seth brightened at the mention of it. *Installed this morning. And a new plasma TV.*

I didn't need a fancy sound system or TV, but perhaps I could get a new set of earphones so I could try to read when Trevor did.

Lights shone from inside the church, glowing through the slats in the shutters. The electrical crew hauled out the last of their equipment as Trevor and I skittered to the side to get out of their way. In back, a "Granite State Geothermal" truck blocked the door to the brand new addition. The gunmetal grey furnace hummed as two guys adjusted whatever needed adjusting.

Several wall panels still hung open, flashing patches of insulation along with some pipes and wires. A toilet flush came from behind us, echoing around the unpainted walls. A workman left the new bathroom, tucking in his shirt as he headed out to the truck.

Heat. Indoor plumbing.

Inside the sanctuary, newly-installed light fixtures blazed behind black, wrought-iron scrollwork covers, protection from whatever Trevor might throw at them. Heating vents ran along the length of one wall. A woman in a Granite State Geothermal jacket called out, "Okay, you're all set. The system's running. Thermostat's up front here."

Trevor was the disillusioned kid in the movie who no longer believed in Santa but then got the Christmas miracle. I drank in the overflow of wonder coming off him. No one had ever done anything like this for him before.

We discovered the other changes as the last of the workers cleared out. Wrought-iron stairs—so steep they were almost a ladder—now extended to a small loft above the coatroom. I hadn't known there was anything up there. I climbed up to explore.

A twin-sized bed nearly filled the tiny loft. The wrought-iron canopied frame formed a protective cage around it. Dr. Williamson had thought of everything. Clean blankets and pillows sat neatly in the center of the mattress. A second new mattress waited against one wall of the sanctuary, still wrapped in plastic.

We were home.

I started to laugh—Trevor was reality-testing.

I'm pretty sure we're not dreaming. I wrapped my arms around his waist.

You got all this for us?

Actually, I wanted to get a whole new building for you, but I think this'll work.

I—I don't know how to thank you.

I really didn't do anything. I leaned up to brush my lips across his. Feathers of red energy caressed us. *But if you want to thank me, take me to Aruba.*

Whenever you want.

I looked into his eyes and the rest of the world faded away. The energy between us sparked and flared, sending tingling waves through us. Our souls touched, wound together, merged, and we were truly home.

THE END

Keep reading for a sneak preview of:

ADVERSARY

THE SECOND GANZFIELD NOVEL BY

KATE
KAYNAK

Coming in August 2010 from Spencer Hill Press

CHAPTER 1

Were we too late? Sick fear twisted my gut as we ran, and the dark hall seemed to lengthen with each echoing step. I tried to type the code into the keypad by the door, but my shaking fingers wouldn't cooperate. Drew started burning around the lock. The sudden blare of an alarm jarred my frayed nerves to the shattering point. I felt telepathically behind the door for a familiar mind, but all that I could get were fractured images of nightmarish tortures. Tears streaked down my face; I felt so useless, so stupid. I hugged my arms around my waist tightly, as though I could keep myself together through shear, blunt will.

We were too late. I just knew we were too late.

Drew kicked the door open, and it disappeared into the dark. A little ball of flame rose above his hand, and a macabre scene floated out of the firelight. People I knew lay strapped to gurneys, with metal rings screwed around their heads. Their skin was grey in death; their eyes filmed white. Bloody head wounds shone slickly black.

The world tilted when I recognized the cold mask of anguish in front of me.

Trevor.

Oh God, no no no no no. My mind exploded in pain. I fell to the floor, racked with sobs. *Too late.*

"This one again?" A familiar voice came from behind me.

After a flash of confusion, light flooded back into the world as I recognized Trevor's voice. It didn't come from the unmoving body on the operating table. Trevor knelt next to me, beautifully whole and alive, wrapping his arms around me. I clung to him, a fairly useless mass of quivering relief, as he pulled me up to stand. His eyes fell on the corpse on the operating table next to us. It was his own mangled corpse.

OK, that made no sense—was this just a dream? Trevor and I must be sharing dreams again. I exhaled with a half-sob.

The sickening nightmare landscape faded away. Trevor's lucid-dreaming skills kept improving. He and I now stood in a high mountain meadow in mid-summer. A glittering river, white with little waterfalls, danced below us. The air felt like it cleansed my lungs with every breath. Wildflowers overflowed around us, gold and white and purple, rippling with a gentle push from the wind.

I met his warm, chocolate-brown eyes, feeling gratitude on many levels.

"You couldn't dream about kittens." Trevor smiled with mock exasperation. "Oh no. No cute little puppies for you."

I pulled closer to him, shut my eyes, and rested my cheek against his chest as I felt my heart unclench. "Thanks."

"Have you considered looking at pictures of bunnies before going to bed?" His hand stroked my hair. "Maybe baby chicks, all yellow and fluffy."

I laughed shakily, tilting up to meet his gaze again, warmed by the light within his eyes. "In my twisted subconscious, those baby chicks would become vicious monsters that would peck our brains out."

Trevor laughed as well. "Probably." he agreed, giving me a quick, sweet kiss. "You do have a dark side. You know what we could do—"

The sound of a gunshot cut him off. Hot agony ripped through me, and I cried out. I was suddenly, horribly awake, and back in the real world. Trevor was no longer beside me. I curled into the fetal position, overwhelmed by the excruciating, screaming pain.

Acknowledgements

A huge "Thank You!" to everyone who contributed to this book. A lesser "thank you" to those who grudgingly put up with me when the bouts of writing obsession hit.

Seriously, though, so many people helped with this book. My editor, Deborah Britt-Hay and all the people at Spencer Hill Press. Penny Sansevieri: Marketing Queen. The folks from Backspace, my online writers group, and Litopia manuscript swaps, particularly Gemma Cooper, Kourtney Heinz, David Blaikie, and Pat Dusenbury, gave amazing feedback. My early readers: Olin Jennings: King of Helpful Feedback, Jenny Turner: Typo-Catching Goddess, Beth Rosenheim, Heather Tessier, "Aunt Nancy" Schoeller, Mitch Ross, Alison Ross, Laura Jennings, Teddy Hess, and Pamela Johnson (who accidentally sacrificed her dinner as a burnt offering to an early draft). Gerry Garcia, my guru of Spanish conjugation (although that is the limit of our conjugal relationship). Kent Place School, for instilling the twitchy feeling I still get in the presence of a misused semicolon. Willo Davis Roberts, for writing *The Girl with the Silver Eyes*, the book that opened my eyes to the world of special abilities. The book trailer team: Brian Waldron and Glenridge, whose song "Angels" fit so perfectly; Katie Diamond, whose art brought the characters to life; Peter Alton: Demigod of Editing. Amy Fowler Rufo and Rosa Burtt: this book would not have been possible without their help with the rest of my life.

May the characters I've based on some of you survive through the end of the series.

And finally, a ginormous "Thank You!!!" to my husband, Osman, who made writing this possible, and to my kids, Taner, Aliya, and Logan, who made writing this necessary.

About Kate Kaynak

I was born and raised in New Jersey, but I managed to escape. My degree from Yale says I was a psych major, but I had *way* too much fun to have paid much attention in class.

After serving a five-year sentence in graduate school, I started teaching psychology around the world for the University of Maryland's Overseas Program.

While in Izmir, Turkey, I started up a conversation with a handsome stranger in an airport. I ended up marrying him. We now live in New Hampshire with our three preschool-aged kids, where I enjoy reading, writing, and fighting crime with my amazing superpowers.

Come find out more about *Minder* and the other books of the *Ganzfield* series at **www.Ganzfield.com.**